Trusting Viktor

This Large Print Book carries the Seal of Approval of N.A.V.H.

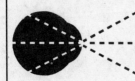

A CLEO COOPER MYSTERY

TRUSTING VIKTOR

LEE MIMS

THORNDIKE PRESS
A part of Gale, Cengage Learning

GALE
CENGAGE Learning®

Farmington Hills, Mich • San Francisco • New York • Waterville, Maine
Meriden, Conn • Mason, Ohio • Chicago

GALE
CENGAGE Learning

Map by Bob Murray.
Thorndike Press, a part of Gale, Cengage Learning.

Thorndike Press® Large Print Mystery.
The text of this Large Print edition is unabridged.
Other aspects of the book may vary from the original edition.
Set in 16 pt. Plantin.

LIBRARY OF CONGRESS CATALOGING-IN-PUBLICATION DATA

Mims, Lee, 1948–
Trusting Viktor : a Cleo Cooper mystery / by Lee Mims. — Large print edition.
pages ; cm. — (Thorndike Press large print mystery)
ISBN-13: 978-1-4104-6860-4 (hardcover)
ISBN-10: 1-4104-6860-7 (hardcover)
1. Oil industry workers—North Carolina—Fiction. 2. Murder—Investigation—Fiction. 3. Large type books. 4. North Carolina—Fiction. I. Title.
PS3613.I591995T78 2014b
813'.6—dc23 2014001180

Published in 2014 by arrangement with Midnight Ink, an imprint of Llewellyn Publications, Woodbury, MN 55125-2989 USA

Printed in the United States of America
1 2 3 4 5 6 7 18 17 16 15 14

This book is dedicated to the real Bud.

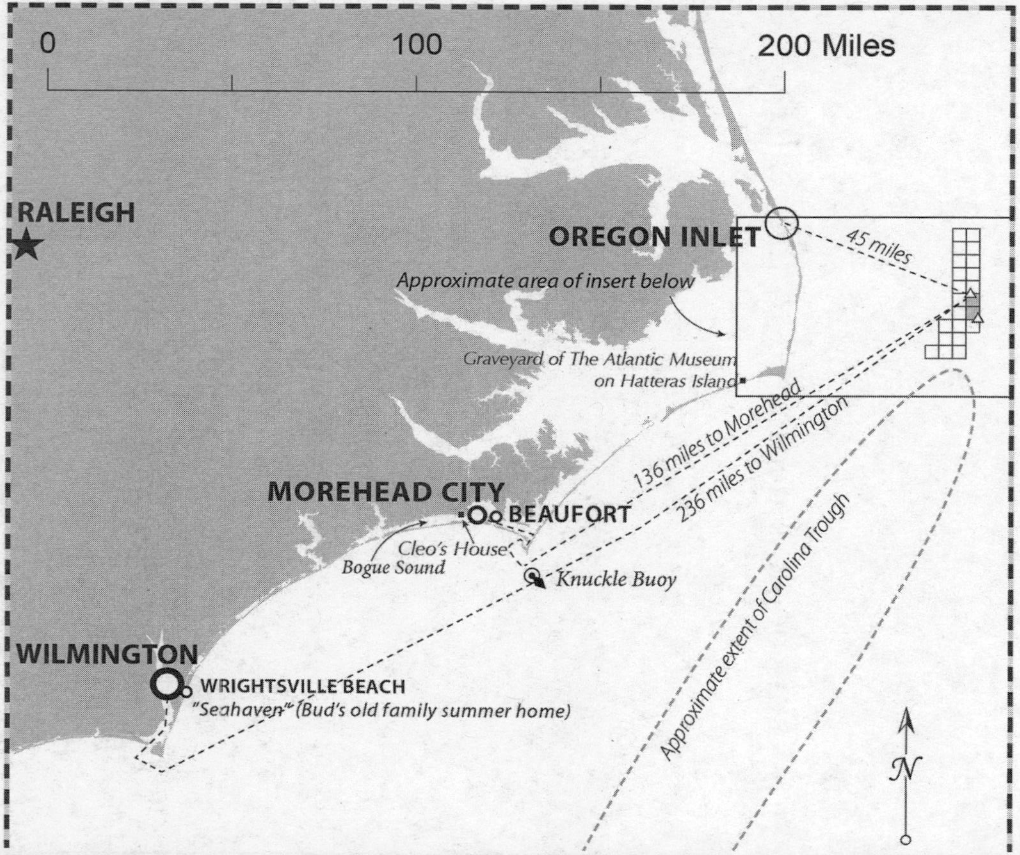
0
100
200 Miles
RALEIGH
OREGON INLET
45 miles
Approximate area of insert below
Graveyard of The Atlantic Museum
on Hatteras Island
136 miles to Morehead
236 miles to Wilmington
MOREHEAD CITY
BEAUFORT
Cleo's House
Bogue Sound
Knuckle Buoy
Approximate extent of Carolina Trough
WILMINGTON
WRIGHTSVILLE BEACH
"Seahaven" (Bud's old family summer home)
N

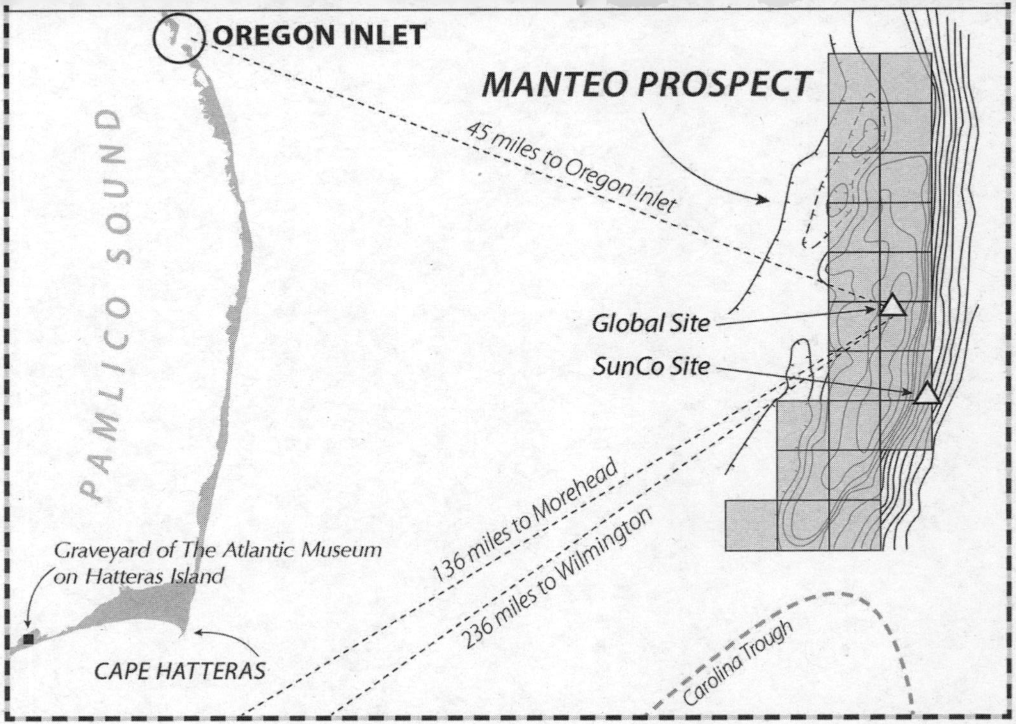

Map DATA: Meekins, Keith L. (1999) "Geology and Exploration of the Manteo Prospect off North Carolina", Marine Georesources & Geotechnology, 17: 2, 117–122. URL: http://dx.doi.org/10.1080/106411999273765

One

If I was lucky and aimed true, my shot would penetrate deep behind his left eye. If I was *really* lucky, his brain stem would be severed. The thought of struggling with a not-quite-dead brute like the one in my sights wasn't pleasant. And having to shove a knife deep in his skull cavity, then hear that grisly crunch . . . even less so.

Suddenly, my prey — a nice-sized amberjack — nosed forward in the current as a number of smaller fish darted past him. Stern-lipped and flashing bronze and silver, he finned through rays of sunlight and slipped from view behind one of the massive legs on the oil rig I was diving forty miles off the coast of Louisiana. Taking shallow breaths, my left hand and legs moving only enough to stabilize my position, I waited, my finger on the trigger. Visibility wasn't perfect and the current was growing stronger as the tide changed, but the wary fish, as if sensing danger, barely inched forward.

Mindful that I, too, could become a tasty lunch, I scanned my surroundings for predators. Behind me ancient fishing lines and snagged ropes undulated like mermaid tresses. Cautiously, I let myself drift a few inches. Then some internal all-clear signal must have chimed for the amberjack and he glided from cover.

I squeezed the trigger.

In that nanosecond between having flexed my finger and feeling it touch the back of the grip, I realized my mistake. The amberjack my spear sank into wasn't the same one I'd been aiming at. This fish was way bigger. The line snapped taunt and my body lurched forward as the fish bolted for the open water beyond the rig. A 250-horsepower Yamaha couldn't have done a better job of towing me through the water. To make matters worse, just as the monster fish shot over the first support beam, he did a quick one-eighty.

The line between my speargun and the spear lodged in the fish's side flipped over his back, and suddenly I was being dragged sideways into the leg of the rig. I slammed into the gigantic pillar, taking the brunt of the blow mid-body. Thankful I'd adhered to my rule of always wearing a full-body wet suit when diving oil rigs, I grabbed for the beam with my left hand, but my captor made like a submarine and pulled me straight down, wedging me between the beam and the leg. Having me as a human anchor was doing nothing to calm Mr. Amberjack's nerves.

Bits of coral, barnacles, and my Neoprene gloves clouded the water. The strain on my arm was unbearable. I'd already hit the line-release mechanism, but it must have jammed in the crash because nothing was happening. I had two choices: hang on and risk my arm being wrung from the socket or let go of my expensive speargun. I went with the latter.

Within seconds, both Mr. Amberjack and my gun disappeared into the cobalt blue depths of the Gulf.

I waited a few moments, hoping the sea gods would show mercy and I'd catch a glimpse of my weapon on its return trip to the surface. Once the fish either worked free of the shaft or the line was severed, the gun would float to the surface. The only trick then would be to find it before the current took it away. My position was awkward, however, so I gave up and casually made to push myself from the rig. That's when I realized I was stuck.

The situation wasn't looking good.

I looked left, right, and below me for my two diving buddies. They were nowhere to be seen. I began trying to push free, but succeeded only in sending an enormous stream of bubbles spewing to the surface.

Admittedly, I had very limited options. But then, thinking it could be a simple matter of pulling rather than pushing, I looked for a spot on the beam with relatively little sea growth where I could get some purchase. That's when I noticed how badly I'd punctured my dive glove. A little blood was seeping from one of the holes. *Great. Blood in the water. Just a little icing for my shit cake.* Banishing images of sharks in a feeding frenzy, I took a firm hold of the beam and pulled until dark spots bloomed before my eyes. I wasn't budging an iota.

A pan-sized red snapper stopped a few inches from my mask as though considering my predicament. It wasn't complicated: I was 37 feet below the surface of the Gulf of Mexico, hanging at a 45-degree angle, and quickly losing touch with rational thought. I recognized this last fact because I'd just had the brilliant idea of using my iPhone to call for help.

I glanced at my air gauge. Holy crap. All

my struggling had left me with only about ten more minutes! The few grains of logic I still possessed insisted that I couldn't have actually wedged myself so tight I couldn't get loose. Then an unpleasant thought occurred: maybe something was jamming me in place.

While I could move my right arm out and down, I couldn't move it back or up between my tank and the leg of the rig; using my left hand, I felt around behind my head near the top of my tank. Open water. Bending my arm backward, I felt along the bottom of the tank with the back of my hand, stretching my arm as far as I could. Then my heart sank.

I'd fallen prey to one of the most common hazards of rig diving: falling debris. It felt like a large piece of metal caging. Probably cut away from a long-forgotten piece of equipment by a long-forgotten welder and dropped overboard only to hang up in the rig for years, just waiting to trap me here in this moment. My fight with the amberjack had no doubt jarred it loose to pin me down like a butterfly on a corkboard.

I checked my air gauge again. Six minutes left. Only one option remained in my bag of tricks. Somehow I had to wiggle out of my tank harness. One lungful of compressed air would expand and last me until I reached the surface. But that wasn't the problem — unharnessing myself, that was the problem. The latch was now nearly unreachable, mashed as it was between my chest and the cross bar, which was encrusted with barnacles, sea squirts, and I didn't want to think of what else. I dug at the growth with my gloved fingers.

You know how it is when you're out of ideas and know what you're about to do won't work — like trying to talk your way out of a traffic ticket — but you feel compelled to try?

I began to struggle furiously.

And where were my diving buddies? Why hadn't they come back looking for me? Since we'd had no success finding the lobsters this rig is known for, they'd signaled they were going up. Not wanting to quit, I'd held up five fingers — five more minutes. They'd nodded and gone on. That's when I'd seen the amberjack and my fate had been sealed.

Tears started to sting my eyes; I thought of my family, of my sweet dog. Then my bottom timer went off. Two minutes of air left. I began to flail, trying to dislocate my right shoulder and slip free of the harness. I knew I was sucking air, but I couldn't stop myself.

Why hadn't I brought my emergency backup cylinder? Stupid!

Suddenly, I felt a calm hand on the small of my back, patting me in soothing circles, like a mother comforting a hysterical child. The hand went away and I heard clanging overhead. Rust and coral debris clouded the water. Then, in the blink of an eye, I was free! The calm hands gently pushed me away from the confines of the rig toward the open water. I didn't need any further encouragement.

Rocketing to the surface, I ripped off my face mask and sucked in a lungful of delicious air. My rescuer popped to the surface beside me. He spit out his regulator, pushed up his mask . . . and damned if I wasn't staring into the face of Ashton Kutcher. Well, at least he *looked* at lot like the actor. Probably about his age too. Several good ways to adequately thank him for saving my dumb ass immediately came to mind as I bobbed about in the choppy Gulf. Then a wave slapped me in the face. I coughed and spit. Lovely.

Ashton shot me a smile that would have baked pizzas and motioned for me to follow him. He took a few strong strokes and turned to make sure I understood. I snapped out of my daze and sprang into action, falling in the wake he churned to a nearby catamaran.

Upon reaching the swim platform of the 27-foot Glacier Bay, he propelled himself smoothly from the water like a porpoise and sat, all in one move, dangling his long legs in the water. I considered the same maneuver, but wobbly as I was after my ordeal, it wouldn't have been a pretty sight. Instead, I slipped out of my tank — so easy when you're not pinned to an oil rig — and handed it up to him followed by my fins and mask. Before boarding, however, I made a quick scan of the horizon for the boat I'd dived from.

Looking past the port engine, I saw it. It was still floating where the three of us had left it, down current off the landward leg of the rig. Both my friends were visible on the swim platform. They were still suited up and chatting.

I felt my rescuer's eyes drift over me as I climbed aboard his boat, and I tried to control my shakiness. Taking a cue from him, I dangled *my* long legs in the water.

"Thanks," I said simply.

"You are entirely welcome. I am glad I could help and that you seem all right." His expression was concerned, and his accent definitely not local. A Slav of some variety was my guess.

I looked at him curiously. "You're not from around here, are you?"

"No," he laughed. A great laugh, by the way, sincere and easy. "I should introduce myself. Afanasy Viktor Kozlov, at your service."

"And they call you?"

He seemed puzzled by this. "Afanasy Viktor Kozlov," he repeated politely.

"Okay. Umm, what does your mother call you?"

He slipped from his tank and shoved it through the open transom into the cockpit. Then he peeled off the top of his wet suit, leaned toward me and, in quite possibly the sexiest voice on the planet, said, "Maybe a little later I will tell you. When I know you better. Much better."

Now, I'm not that easy. This kid, albeit gorgeous and obviously hot as hell, was way too young for me. If I put my age at forty-six — which may or may not be correct, depending on my mood — and his in his early thirties, he'd be off limits. In my rule-book of proper dating etiquette, anyone ten or more years younger is to be thrown back, like fish under a certain size. Therefore, I gave him my best in-your-dreams smile and tried my damndest to remember how he pronounced his name. I tried picturing its spelling. “A-fan-asy . . .”

“No,” he interrupted. “Not a fantasy. I’m not a fantasy. In Russian one says Ah-fah-*nah*-seey.”

I could have argued the point but didn’t. “Sorry,” I said. “How about I just call you Viktor?”

“*Veek*tor.”

I was definitely still recovering from my close call. And I was distracted enough by my rescuer to not be thinking about my errant diving companions. At least for the moment. “*Vee*ktor,” I said, trying again.

“Perfect!” Another brilliant smile. “There is no need to introduce yourself, Mrs. Cleo Cooper.”

“That’s *Ms.* Cleo Cooper,” I corrected him, perhaps a little too quickly. “How on earth do you know my name?”

“I attended your lecture on Sequence-Stratigraphic Similarities in Subbasins, Nova Scotia to the Yucatán” — he paused, taking in the surprised look on my face, then continued — “on the last night of the conference. Very interesting. Also, I read your theory about plutonic emplacement in regard to the granite deposit you’d discovered in North Carolina farther east than previously believed. Also very interesting."

"Oh, okay. So you were in New Orleans for the USGS conference?"

"Yes, but I have a summer job here in Port Fourchon, as well, that fits in nicely with my PhD work on faulted subbasins and their chronostratigraphic relationships. On my time off, I like to dive the rigs."

"Wonderful," I was excited not only that he was a fellow geologist, but that he was interested in economic geology. Being a geologist is a calling, but being an economic geologist, someone engaged in the study of earth materials that fuel the modern world . . . well, we're a breed apart. "Where are you doing your dissertation?"

"I will be starting in the fall at Duke University," he said proudly.

"Well, you'll practically be my neighbor. I'm right down the road in Raleigh."

"I can't believe my luck at meeting you way out here. I tried to . . . intercept you . . . at the conference, but somehow, I was always a step behind. When it ended, I thought I'd missed my chance to speak with you. Then, voilà! Who do I find wiggling like a worm on a hook thirty feet down on an oil rig in the Gulf? Go figure, as you Americans say."

"I'm the lucky one," I said sincerely. "Any

particular reason you were looking for me?"

"Yes. I understand you are involved in a drilling operation off —"

Viktor was interrupted by a shout from my boat. "Hey! Cleo! We were wondering where you went," shouted Julia, my old friend from UNC who now worked for the USGS, the United States Geological Survey.

"Yeah, we were getting worried," snapped Kathy, also a pal since my old graduate school days there. She tapped her dive watch, "You shouldn't push your time so short. We were just getting ready to go back for you."

Good to know, since by my calculations I'd be knocking back rum shooters with Davy Jones by now. Still, it's the thought that counts. "No problem," I said. "It's all good."

Both women had come to New Orleans for the USGS Conference and were recreational divers like me. We'd been planning this trip all winter, studying the different rigs on the BOEMRE (Bureau of Ocean Energy, Management, Regulation, and Enforcement) website and mapping out the ones that interested us. Oil rigs, like shipwrecks, become home to large concentrations of pelagic life almost immediately upon immersion into the sea. Fortunately,

Julia had friends who kept a vacation fish camp in Port Fourchon, only two hours from the city. Even better, it was right smack on the southernmost tip of Louisiana, where all the oil rigs you could ever want to dive sat offshore. Her friends had been generous enough to offer the camp to us, along with full use of their 24-foot Grady White boat.

"We can see that!" Julia shouted. Viktor tossed them a wave, then turned back to me, at which point Julia flashed me a thumbs-up accompanied by an exaggerated wink.

I gave her a don't-get-cute scowl.

"I'll be right over," I called back to them, then turned back to Viktor. "We're going to dive a few of the South Timbalier rigs. That block is about twenty miles back toward the port. Want to come? You can tell me on the way why you've been trying to find me."

"I would be honored," Viktor said, offering his hand and pulling me to my feet. "We can take my boat, if you like."

I motioned to Julia and hollered, "He wants to go along. I'll ride with him and navigate."

Julia waved agreement, but I could see Kathy's frown.

Off we went.

Two

I leaned against the stand-up bench seat in the small helm station of the boat and watched Viktor plug in the coordinates that would take us to the oil rig in the South Timbalier block of leases. For leasing purposes, the outer continental shelf of the United States is divided into blocks, approximately 9 square miles each, and all natural resources found there are managed by BOEMRE. Periodically the federal government opens these blocks for auction to oil companies who wish to lease them.

When he finished, he turned on the autopilot and leaned back too, his arm resting lightly against mine. "I was hoping to meet you," he said, "because I read in the trade journals that you are partners with Global Oil to explore for natural gas off the coast of North Carolina."

Trying to ignore how good his arm felt against mine (and my awareness of how long it had been since I'd had time for a man), I replied, "You're sort of right. I am invested, in a *small* way, through a private equity group on that venture. Actually, my ex-husband got me involved."

"I imagine such a discovery might prove very lucrative for you both then."

He was right, even if his bluntness caught me a bit by surprise. "Sure. But that's not the whole story. Finding an economically viable deposit of gas would be life-changing for the residents of eastern North Carolina. Thousands of new jobs with the potential for millions, even billions generated in revenue. A real Cinderella story: one of the state's poorest areas could be transformed into one of the most prosperous."

"Your goals are very noble, then."

"No," I laughed. "Helping my state is just part of it. A collateral goodie, if you will. The real reason I'm involved with this venture is the same reason I became an exploration geologist: I want to know what's down there!"

"Ah, then we are of like minds." Viktor switched off automatic pilot in order to steer around a fishing boat, then he reset it. "Now that your government is . . . more friendly to exploration and production of hydrocarbons, several new offshore exploration wells are being drilled here in the Gulf. I could find work on any of them. But there is already a wealth of information on the depositional history of the reef structures here. What I really want is to be in on the opening of the new frontier of hydrocarbons on the outer continental shelf of the mid-Atlantic region . . ."

Now that we were getting to the *real* reason he was looking for me, I wrinkled my brow. "Well, that might be difficult," I said. "The only exploratory rig out there right now is owned by Global, the company I'm invested with, and I'm pretty sure they're fully staffed. However, they hold only four of the twenty-one leases in the Manteo Unit. Several other companies have leased adjoining blocks, but they aren't drilling yet. Then there's Block 220, off Virginia's coast, which is still bogged down in state permitting problems. But I heard those will soon be resolved, and the company that holds that lease is a matter of public record. You could look them up and try to get on there."

"I will explore those possibilities. Thank you for your helpfulness. I should mention that I have other options too. For now, I'll continue working with SeaTrek," Viktor said.

"SeaTrek?"

"Yes. My summer job. It's a geophysical survey company owned by a gentleman named Davy Duchamp. Oddly, he refers to himself as a 'coon's ass,' a phrase I don't understand, as he's a very fine fellow and certainly a excellent boatman."

"A coonass," I explained with a grin, "is someone who can trace their Louisiana heritage back at least three generations. But what does a Russian geologist do for a Louisiana-based geophysical surveying company?"

"The same job I've performed for a succession of Russian geophysical surveying companies since I was sixteen: whatever one they'll give me!" He smiled good-naturedly. "I need to earn money to pay for my education."

"Very commendable," I said with an admiration I truly felt, since I'd once been faced with the same obligation. "And it fits in nicely with your dissertation."

"Yes. I am also a certified ROV pilot. You are familiar with this type of equipment?"

"Yes," I smiled. "I have a little knowledge of remotely operated vehicles and you're right, it's always good to have more than one option."

"I've sent my resume to several companies

and perhaps will land a permanent job soon. I hope so. Being an ROV pilot pays well, the hours are good, and there's not too much physical labor."

As he shook his dark brown hair in the wind, I mentally chastised myself for wanting to finger-comb the soft curls and tuck them behind his ears. "It is interesting to note," he continued, "that SeaTrek did the seismic survey for Global on your mid-Atlantic prospect."

"That is interesting," I said, still trying to drag my thoughts from his curls.

"I imagine they mapped the very structure you are drilling. That makes it even more remarkable that we literally bump into each other in the middle of the Gulf!"

"It was more than that," I said. "You saved my life and you know it. I owe you big time."

He grinned and moved closer, leaning lightly against me, "Let me buy you dinner tonight. Maybe we can come up with a way for you to repay your obligation."

Normally, I'd be rolling my eyes at such a come-on, but delivered by Viktor, the effect was just plain charming. Still, since I'd already noted I was old enough to be his . . . older sister, I shook my finger, mock-scolding him. "Now, now, I think that should be the other way round. I buy *you* dinner" — as he started to protest, I continued — "but until then, tell me more about how your dissertation would be improved by finding work in the mid-Atlantic."

"By helping me back up my hypothesis that the depositional processes that occurred to form the hydrocarbons present in the mid-Atlantic are the same ones that formed the hydrocarbons off the Niger Delta and in the northern Gulf of Mexico. *And* that they occurred at the same time. This information will be helpful in finding other deep gas and oil reservoirs all over the world. My degree will be helpful to me in getting a great job in the Russian oil fields someday."

"Ah. So you want to return to Russia to start your career. That's interesting. Most people want to stay in America once they experience life here."

"Not me. In my estimation, Russia is the place to be, especially if you want to work in the oil patch. Russia today is how your West used to be. I don't mean lawless and wild; I mean, open for exploration and innovation. My country is poised for greatness!"

I felt a little twinge of jealousy. I didn't know very much about Russia, but he was right about America. It bore little resemblance now to the USA of 1901, when Spindletop — in Texas — first shot oil to the heavens, beginning the age of petroleum and laying the foundation for the modern world. Frankly, I was still amazed that we were actually being allowed to drill an exploratory well off North Carolina's coast.

Since 1981, the world's biggest oil companies had been trying to do the same thing we wanted to do in the area known as the Manteo Exploration Unit. Until now, all such attempts had failed. Most proposed plans were rejected either by the relevant state agencies or by the federal government — and those that were approved were subjected to endless suspensions of operations.

The beeper on our navigator interrupted my thoughts, informing us that we had reached our destination. I waved to my old friends following us and motioned to the rig straight ahead. To Viktor I said, "We need to come alongside so I can get my extra tank. I wish I hadn't lost my speargun. I was looking forward to carrying some grouper home to my freezer."

Viktor looked surprised. "Home? When are you leaving?"

"Tomorrow. I . . . have a friend with a private plane, so getting a cooler full of fresh fish home is no problem. Filling the cooler now that my gun is gone is a little more difficult. Neither of my friends like to spearfish, so they wouldn't have one."

"Tomorrow! That doesn't leave us much time to get acquainted, Ms. Cleo Cooper." He gave me another charming smile.

"Sad but true. Tomorrow's Monday, after all, and I've already been here a week."

"In that case, we must make the most of the time we have. If you'll allow me, I'll fill your cooler." Viktor opened a deck locker and retrieved a Hatch custom-design blue water gun. Obviously a serious spear fisherman. "That way, we have more time to get to know one another. And you can use my spare tank. I have plenty of air left in mine."

"Sounds like a plan," I said, noticing the ripple of abs tighten under his smooth skin as he wriggled back into his wetsuit. Then he hefted his tank and a spare onto the deck of the cockpit from the small cabin below. Remembering that I did owe him for saving my life, I added, "One condition though: You let me cook dinner for you."

"Yes. I agree to your condition. Now let's go have some fun!"

Late that afternoon, just as the sun was sinking in the west, we headed back to the camp, skimming the glassy water of the canals that wound through Port Fourchon. At Viktor's invitation, I rode back with him. True to his word, he'd filled his fish box and mine with beautiful grouper, snapper, amberjack, and trigger fish. We'd even filleted one of the trigger fish while at sea and cooked it on a portable gas grill. It's hard to describe the taste of fish that fresh. I'd savored the flavors of the tender white meat coupled with the twang of fresh lime and cracked black pepper and shoved it way back in my memory banks to drag out on a chilly winter day.

Viktor throttled back to accommodate the no-wake zone inside the port proper. Giant supply boats of every size and color bustled about, both coming in and heading out, serving the limitless needs of oil rigs. They ran twenty-four hours a day, seven days a week. Momentarily, the sun was blocked as we eased beside a docked 300-footer to let another even larger ship steam past us. The four-story goliath, fully loaded with supplies, slipped by on the mirror-smooth water.

I turned my face to the setting sun to feel the warmth, closed my eyes, and indulged in a moment of exhausted bliss. Today had been one to remember. Between dives, the four of us had rested in the sun, recharged with snacks and juice, and talked about our shared passion of geology. By the end of the day, I'd learned that not only was Viktor great at coming to the rescue of imperiled divers, but he was brilliantly knowledgeable about geological subjects, funny as hell, and a consummate gentleman — this last quite rare for someone his age. As the day progressed, Kathy, the eternal grump, actually had begun to warm to him, even giggling several times at his humorous asides.

Now that we were almost home, I began mentally running through the list of ingredients I'd need to prepare our dinner. It had turned out the camp where Viktor was staying was just three lots down from ours. His boss let him use it and the Glacier Bay boat in return for keeping them both well looked after. That we were bunked so close by was simply owing to the fact that they were the only vacation homes available in this remote, undeveloped southern tip of Louisiana. The nearest hotel was in Grand Isle and the only other year-round housing was for port employees.

We were greeted at the dock by the next-door neighbors of Julia's friend who'd lent us the house and boat. They'd had caught their limit of trout — twenty-five each —

and wanted us to get together with them and several other neighbors for a fish fry. We happily agreed; as far as I'm concerned, the more cooks, the merrier. Several of the men in the group were hunters as well as fisherman, which meant we wound up with a Gulf version of surf and turf. We feasted on roasted wild Louisiana boar and venison from a game reserve in Idaho along with the trout and grouper.

To say the alcohol flowed would be putting it mildly. More and more people arrived every time I turned around. At some point during the party, Viktor's boss and his twin sons dropped by. Pegging the sons to be around Viktor's age, I couldn't help but marvel at their identical features. Over the din of music and laughter, Mr. Duchamp, a bear of a man, told me in the heaviest Louisiana dialect I'd so far encountered what a smart and likable fellow Viktor was. Just like another son, he said.

Sometime after dinner, the party moved over to our camp. The more I drank, the more mature Viktor seemed — and the sexier. Several times I caught Kathy throwing me eye daggers.

When the sky grew darker, a big, round silvery moon rose above the rooftops across the channel and the no-see-ums that had kept the party on the screened porch disappeared. We all moved out onto the large deck jutting over the boat slip and dock, enthusiastically welcoming the pitchers of margaritas that now appeared. I was laughing at some incredibly witty remark Viktor made when I noticed Kathy and Julia had disappeared.

I didn't have to go far to find them. They were passed out in two lounge chairs located in a corner of the deck. Viktor came up behind me and whispered something in my ear about taking a moonlight cruise. What a wonderful idea! I looked up and tried to focus on the moon as it whirled overhead, a great silver galleon churning across the sky.

What could go wrong on such a gorgeous night?

Three

Some time later I realized two things: The bed I was sleeping in was rocking, and I had to pee really bad. Wait. The bed was rocking? The luminous hands on my dive watch barely glowed in the dim light. I looked around me. The light was coming from the open cabin door of a boat. Oh hell! It was almost six o'clock and someone, jammed against the bulkhead, was softly snoring beside me. Viktor.

Very carefully, I covered my aching eyes with my hand and pressed my splitting temples with thumb and forefinger. Good god, I'd had sex with someone at least twelve years my junior! What was I thinking? On the other hand, last night's sex . . . holy cow. I'd forgotten what sex was like when youth was on your side. A vague memory of the kid actually lifting my entire body up and down with both arms and a foot like a set of bench weights came to mind. I mean, I'm five-nine, so his feat definitely deserved respect. Replaying it in my mind, I felt my face burn. I had to get out of here.

I stared into the dim light again. We were anchored at sea, weren't we?

That I had awakened face down on the open side of the bed facilitated my stealth. Slowly, silently, I lowered my foot to the deck. Where the hell were my clothes? A quick scan of the cabin yielded nothing. The boat rocked slightly again. I slid the rest of the way out of bed and on fingers and toes, like the coyote sneaking up on the roadrunner, and moved to the open doorway. *Please, oh please, let us be anchored somewhere private. Somewhere offshore.* I looked out.

No such luck.

We were still tied snugly alongside the dock attached to the pilings supporting the same deck that had hosted last night's party. I hung my head in shame at the sight of my clothes scattered about the cockpit. The swinging door to the swim platform was open, revealing my thong dangling dangerously close to the edge.

Nothing to do now but man up. I headed quickly across the cold dewy deck and retrieved the underwear. Great. It was soaking wet. I quickly gathered the rest of my clothes, pulling them on as I came to them, then slid the wet thong into my back pocket.

I felt somewhat better once clothed. Maybe I'd get out of this with no one the wiser. Nothing was stirring but a few herons and ibises winging their way to the marshes to begin a day of feeding. Although the moon had long since set, a few stars still dotted the sky — probably hurried along by competition from my full, white moon beaming up at it. I peeped over the gunwale and saw my Top-Siders on the dock. Silently, I crept out of the boat, careful not to rock it and disturb its sleeping occupant below. Snagging my shoes on the way, I trotted to the house, wondering if Kathy and Julia were still asleep on the deck above me.

They were. Unfortunately, they were both going to have stiff necks. But, it could be worse: their self-respect could be in tatters. There'd be time to worry about that later, however. Right now, putting time and space between me, my friends, and the young Russian lothario was what was called for. Anyway, I'd already told the girls I'd be pulling out early. In under thirty minutes, I had my stuff in my rental car, my sorry ass behind the wheel, and I was on the road to Louis Armstrong International Airport.

■ ■ ■ ■

Sitting in one of the soft leather reclining chairs in the snooze room of Atlantic Aviation, one of the private aviation facilities at LBA, hardly counted as penance for my foolish behavior. During the two-hour drive from Port Fourchon, my self-assessment ran the gamut from out-of-control drunk to prowling cougar.

I'd been at the airport for two hours, alternately sitting and pacing, and still hadn't changed from last night's clothes. Worse, I'd already taken a BC powder — sure cure for Southern hangovers since 1910 — but my head was still pounding. I sipped a little of AA's complimentary coffee and tried to roust my bones enough to go avail myself of the showers in the luxury restroom and change my clothes, but my iPhone vibrated for the third time. Viktor. How had he gotten my number, anyway? The mystery was solved in seconds by a text from Julia.

WHERE R U? GAVE BOY TOY Y'RE #. OK?

Oh, for the love of Pete . . . what next? I slumped farther down in the recliner. Damnit, I was over the age of consent. Divorced, even, with two grown children and I'd paid my own way since I left my wealthy husband almost seven years ago. Didn't I deserve a weak moment or two or three or . . .

I thought back over the years since I'd left Bud, who, by the way, is wonderful, sweet, intelligent, handsome — I could go on and on. I just couldn't live with the man anymore.

People asked why not. In a nutshell, because he loved me too much and held the reins too tight. I still loved him to death, but he was just too damn protective. I was stifled, suffocating in our marriage, and I wanted out before I started hating Bud for good. Now that we're divorced, we get along much better. We actually *like* each other again — sometimes so much so that we slip up and engage in activities reserved for married folks, if you know what I mean. So why isn't that enough for me? I don't know, a flaw in my character maybe? My mother didn't think so. She used to say I was just high-spirited and hot-blooded. Most of the time, my work is enough for me, but every now and then when an opportunity presents itself . . . well, I guess last night is the kind of thing that happens then.

Still, what was the harm? You only live once and as long as I was discreet, who could get hurt? Come to think of it, I was really only distraught over my conduct because of the age thing. I had *never* wanted to have sex with a guy younger than me, no matter how hot. And I would never do it again — mind-blowing experience though it was. My hope was that I'd gotten away from Port Fourchon with no one knowing about my indiscretion.

Maybe it was the BC, maybe it was cutting myself some slack, I don't know, but I was beginning to feel human again. I pitched the empty foam cup in the trash basket and checked my watch. I still had an hour before Bud would arrive. He'd offered to fly me to New Orleans for the conference and back to the house I'd rented in Morehead City for the summer. He could easily work the flights into the comings and goings of his life as an entrepreneur and CEO of his family's business interests.

In my estimation, Bud — born Franklin Donovan Cooper IV — was by far the smartest and most-visionary member of his family since they'd first arrived in Georgia back before the American Revolution. Those original Coopers had turned a small cotton farm into an immense plantation. Subsequent generations did likewise, spreading the plantations and cotton gins from Georgia to North Carolina. It was Bud, however, who'd moved the family into the twenty-first century with diversification into other industries — everything from computer chips to parts for spaceships. The man was amazing. Controlling, but amazing.

Fortunately, I'd had the presence of mind to jam a change of clothes in my Chloe tote when I unloaded my stuff from the rental car. My bag, empty tanks — sans regulator valves — and other scuba gear were already stacked in the baggage area, so now that I felt up to freshening up, I headed for the ladies room.

Fate, however, put Bud in my path. He was balancing a coffee in one hand and a soft-sided leather briefcase in the other. "Babe! What a surprise, you're early! This is great!" He leaned forward and planted one right on my guilty, speechless lips before I could back out of the way. "Ah," he said, setting his stuff on a nearby table. "I got away with that one. Let's try another."

Before I could answer, he'd wrapped his arms around me, lifted me off my feet, and given me cause to remember just how it was that I kept backsliding with him.

Acting unimpressed, I pushed away firmly,

"Very nice," I commented. "Now put me down."

Gently complying, he gave my left bun an affectionate squeeze before pulling my damp thong from my back pocket. "What's this?"

My heart stopped briefly. Blood raced from my brain. Undaunted, I plastered on my best poker face. "Really, Bud, what does it look like?"

Usually you couldn't shut him up, but now he wasn't cooperating, so I offered a sizable hint. "Pale yellow lacy thong. Probably Victoria's Secret."

"Honestly?" he said, stepping back to look at me, a vision in yesterday's cutoff jean shorts, faded T-shirt, and salt-encrusted ponytail. "I'd have said it looks more like evidence of a fun night. Actually, from the looks of you — like a cat left out overnight in a downpour — a *really* fun night. Want to tell me about it?"

"Good grief. Talk about suspicious minds. You could teach an advanced course in conclusion-leaping." I snatched the offending garment from his fingers. "Get a grip, why don't you?" I told him before stomping off to the bathroom.

He had me at a definite disadvantage. Fortunately I'd thrown most everything I'd need into my tote, including dry shampoo. Forty-five minutes later, only minutes before boarding — on purpose, to cut down on chitchat time — I sauntered back into the passengers' lounge in fresh J Brand jeans, a sleeveless white linen shirt, untucked, and killer Brian Atwood strappy snakeskin sandals. I might be a practical dresser when I'm working, but any other time, watch out. Fortunately, I had plenty of money these days to indulge my expensive tastes in clothes, the only place my taste are expensive. In fact, I still live in the same house and own the same car I'd had before I made a small fortune — regrettably not a huge one — when I found a granite deposit in eastern North Carolina and turned it into a tidy little income for life.

Bud was quiet as we waited for the attendant to load my bags and equipment into his King Air 350 Turboprop and for the pilot to make his final inspections. I knew he was angry — really angry — about the underwear in my pocket and that I wouldn't confide in him, but I wasn't worried. Never in our entire married career had he ever shouted, screamed, ranted, or raged. As a result, we could boast that as long as we'd been married, we'd never had a real knockdown, drag-out fight. We were divorced, but still, we'd never really fought. Great record, huh?

I climbed into one of the window passenger seats. Bud ducked into the flight deck, took the copilot's seat, and adjusted his headset while the pilot went through his checklist. About ten minutes into our flight to Wilmington International Airport, I felt sure I'd dodged the bullet.

Then my ex-husband flopped down in the seat beside me.

I gave him a sweet smile and batted my eyelashes. During our twenty years of marriage, this was the signal that meant "case closed." Bud grinned back, sucking his front teeth. The standard interpretation for this was "okay for now, but I'll get to the bottom of it later." It was a familiar Mexican standoff, lasting until he asked, "Want something to drink?"

"Maybe a Coke."

Just as he rose from his seat, my iPhone vibrated. It was another text from Julia:

GIVE HOTTIE Y'R BEACH ADDRESS?

I shut my eyes for a second as my headache returned to pound in my ears. I thumb-slammed a return message — NO WAY! — and shoved it back in my pocket just as Bud returned with the Coke. "You didn't even ask how Manteo One is coming along," he pointed out reproachfully.

"Don't be melodramatic. If you recall, I didn't have a chance to say anything before you went all vice squad on me." Then I softened my tone. "You're still feeling positive about things out there, aren't you?"

My text tune sounded. I discreetly slipped my phone out again.

2 LATE. LOL.

Suppressing a grimace, I turned off the phone and tossed it in my tote.

"I don't know about geologically, but as far as Global is concerned . . . well, they just laid off another thousand employees. I've had several emergency meetings with the company executives, who insist those cost-cutting measures will stabilize things." He sipped his Coke and added optimistically, "And, honestly, they're probably better off than they were back in '84."

"That was when Global was part of SunCo?" I asked knowing he'd recount the whole sorry affair of how SunCo — after losing a pantload when the State of North Carolina closed them down before they could drill their first exploratory well — ditched the upstream end of the company (the exploration and production part) in favor of the downstream end of refining and marketing. Reclining in my seat, I tilted my head in his direction, feigning attention while dimly recalling his indignation at SunCo. Some of the fired executives had been close friends of his, and I wondered at the time if he would charge in and save them. He didn't. As it turned out, those executives formed a new company, Global.

Bud droned on, the cabin was cozy, and I fell into what I used to call in my graduate school days, my "key-word state." While thus engaged, I looked wide awake, but my mind was a million miles away, maybe resting in some pleasant daydream. It wasn't that I wasn't interested in my first venture in the land of big-boy investments. I was. But I was also exhausted. Anyway, all it takes is a key word and I'm right back to reality.

The overhead air vents hissed pleasantly as I thought about getting home and back to work when I heard Bud say, ". . . leased those four blocks, remember, Cleo?"

"Right. Sure," I replied nonchalantly, adjusting my position, "How could I forget? I was twenty-one, just finishing up my geology degree . . ."

"And marrying me, don't forget that."

"Yes, I remember," I said, turning to look out at the fluffy clouds below us. "We were just babies."

"I thought we were pretty grown up. After all, as a result of our merger we got two of the greatest dividends ever paid out."

He was referring to our two children, Henri and Will. Sensing where this conversation was headed, I returned to safer ground. "Getting back to the Manteo Prospect, I especially remember how exciting the idea of discovering a vast deposit of gas right off the outer continental shelf of North Carolina seemed to me. I couldn't *believe* it when the North Carolina Coastal Management Act found SunCo's plan inadequate and stopped them in their tracks."

"But they did. And yet it's all the better for us because now, twenty-seven years later, we can be part of it."

"And a lot's changed in the meantime. SunCo is back in the exploration business and what a behemoth they are. Has anyone seen any sign of them out at *their* four leased blocks in the mid-Atlantic yet?"

"I talked to our site manager yesterday and the answer's still no. But don't worry, babe, I have faith in you and the part you played in picking the blocks Global leased."

"Whoa!" I said. "Don't get carried away giving credit. Global made the decision to stay with the four blocks SunCo originally leased back in '84. I think they were just taking advantage of having me as an investor, figuring I might want to add my professional opinion, being as I have money riding on the well."

"You do still feel okay about it, don't you?"

"Of course. The geology's sound. Your analysis of the financial end of things has left me a bit queasy, though. What's the bottom line on their actual debt?" I asked, even though I wasn't sure if I really wanted to know.

"About one-point-five billion."

My gut tightened as I considered this. It sounds crazy, I know, but he'd never mentioned actual figures when he let me come in. Honestly, I never asked. I'd always trusted Bud Cooper to know a good thing when he saw one. "You were aware of all those things you've just been talking about — low inventories, high unresolved debt — and yet you still put this venture together?" I wasn't being disingenuous, just legitimately curious. After the fact, as it were.

He looked at me squarely. "Consider this. Manteo One is Global's chance for redemption, a way to pull themselves out of debt and prove to their investors that they're a solid, competitive company, a true independent that creates its own opportunities even in less than shiny times. They've stripped the company to its bare bones and totally reconfigured management. If they feel confident enough to throw another hundred million at this venture, then, yes, I feel good about it too."

Slugging down the last of his Coke, he absently crunched the can. No matter what Bud said, I sensed he was nervous about this deal. There was little he could hide from me. "Having said that," he continued, "I'll feel a lot better knowing you're on the job."

"What do you mean, 'on the job'? I'm just an investor."

"Things changed with this last big purge. Global's trying so hard to calm investor fears, they've agreed to let you and me, as leaders of our private equity group, go out to the exploration ship for a tour. They know you're a successful, published geologist with a well-respected client base — their words, not mine — and they want you on the team in a more active role."

"Uh. More active role?"

"Maybe I didn't make myself clear. When Global let all those employees go in this last round of layoffs, it included most of mid-level management and many of the higher level — and higher paid — geologists and geophysicists."

Sweat was starting to break out on my upper lip at the thought of how precarious my investment was becoming, minute by minute. "Good lord, Bud, that's horrible."

"I know. But they just couldn't meet the payroll if they didn't. I've talked with the top scientists on their U.S. offshore development team, in particular, their senior geophysicist — Phil's his name. He said he was so pleased with your input on which blocks to lease, he's come up with a plan. He'd like me to run it by you."

I waited. There was nothing to do but listen.

"He said that, traditionally, the wellsite geologist is a highly-skilled person hired from outside the company for their objective opinion. Normally, this person would answer to Phil back in Houston and to the company executive on the ship —"

"I am familiar with the role of a wellsite geologist, Bud," I interrupted.

"Right. Anyway, Phil said that due to budget cutbacks, Global went with a lesser-known consulting firm and hired a kid still pretty wet behind the ears. He doesn't feel all that confident with him, so he suggests you supervise him."

"Me?"

"Yes. But the kid would be responsible for

being there twenty-four/seven, filing daily reports and everything else that falls under his job description —"

"The job description for a wellsite geologist is *huge,*" I cut him off again. "And they hired someone wet behind the ears? What are they thinking?" It was a hell of a lot for me to take in. As far as I was concerned, this all had come out of nowhere.

"They're doing the best they can, is what I think. You can't imagine how demoralized and shell-shocked these people are, not to mention overworked. You'd be out there only as often as you deem necessary, but we'll get a better feel for that after our tour."

"Tour? What tour?"

"The one I just told you about. You know, out to the drillship, of course."

"When?"

"Tomorrow."

"Bud! Good grief! I have to make a living now that all my funds are sunk into this investment. I've been gone eight days. I've got a ton of work to catch up on. Started out, I was just an investor in this venture, now I hear I'm going to have to babysit too. My schedule will have to be juggled —"

"Babe, this is a big deal for me. I know you understand that. A lot of people are counting on me, and not just investors.

Think of the people who'll lose everything if Global goes under — their jobs, stock options, 401(k) plans . . . everything."

I looked out the window at the tiny world below, then back at Bud. As long as I'd known him, he'd never asked me to use my job skills to help him. The truth was, it felt kind of good. Plus, I had my own investment to consider too.

"So? What do you say?" Bud asked anxiously, jolting me from my thoughts.

"Yeah, yeah, okay. What time?"

"I'll pick you up at your house around eight tomorrow morning. We're catching a helicopter in Beaufort. That's as close as they could get to Morehead City, Global's base of operations for this venture."

Great. I get to ride in a rock with a fan on top. As many copters as I'd been in, my feelings about them never changed. "Okay," I said, trying to keep the fatigue out of my voice. My eyelids were getting so heavy I could hardly hold them up. "Do you know my summer address?" I was having my house in Raleigh repainted inside and out, along with a little remodeling in the bathrooms and kitchen. I'd decided my dog, Tulip, and I needed a change of scenery for the summer, thus the need for the rental.

"Of course I do. I've *been* there."

I gave him a questioning look, trying to kick my sleep-deprived brain into gear and remember when he'd been to my new digs. I'd only moved in at the start of May, and it was only the first week in June.

"While you were gone. To see the children."

Oh. That at least made sense.

One of my eyes started to droop without the other. I gave up. Reclining my seat and turning to the window, I closed them both and said, "Wake me when we get to Wilmington."

Once we'd landed, my beloved Jeep was waiting right where I left it in the short-term lot. I felt about it like I did about myself: hard-used, but still with plenty of get-up-and-go. And fairly attractive when cleaned up, occasionally even shiny.

Bud insisted on helping me stow my gear. "I hope your nap refreshed you enough so that you don't drive off the road on your way home." He fiddled with my tanks, positioning them so they didn't clang together. "You've done that before, you know."

I opened the driver's side door, put my tote bag on the seat, first burrowing in it for my emergency stash of BC. My headache was coming back with a vengeance. I tossed back the bitter powder, washing it down quickly with some stale, hot water from a half-empty bottle in the console.

"Hangover?" Bud asked solicitously. Didn't he have something better to do?

"The *only* time I've ever run off the road was owing to a rattlesnake crawling out from under my seat, and you know it. I appreciate your concern even though it's not necessary."

"If you say so. You just looked so pitiful earlier this morning, I wasn't sure you'd recover."

"Oh, like you haven't looked just as bad after an all-nighter with one of your own young things," I snapped.

"You were out all night with a *young* thing?"

Seething at myself for letting my mouth pop out of neutral, I shut the door in Bud's face, started the engine, and proceeded to back out of the parking space.

He was still standing, palms out, innocent as a lamb, as I exited the lot.

Four

The drive from Wilmington to Morehead gave me time to calm my ragged nerves and recover from letting Bud get one over on me. Finding an hour of Chopin on the radio helped. I felt much soothed by the time I was closing in on Bogue Sound, and the glimpses of water completed the cure. Since it was early afternoon, it was the perfect time for a quick boat ride.

For all the years I was married to Bud, my summers had been spent at his oceanside family home in ritzy Wrightsville Beach. This house, facing Evans Street with Bogue Sound at its back door, was a whole different world. I guess that's why I'd chosen it.

The town itself was attractively old, offering quiet streets lined with century oaks, magnolias, and azaleas. On the property I'd rented, an expansive green lawn led to a dock with a boatlift. Across the Sound, marshes and sand bars were feeding grounds for a variety of shorebirds and crustaceans. There was an energy level quite different from that of an ocean property, and I was enjoying it for this very reason.

Tulip, a wonderful deer hound who'd adopted me while I was prospecting in the woods of eastern North Carolina nearly two years ago, adored it too. So did my children. In fact, upon seeing it, they'd instantly decided I needed company for the summer and had already spent more time here than I had.

"Mom's back!" Henri shouted from a second-story window. I heard the back porch screen door slam and knew Tulip had nosed it open. I braced for impact as she bounded toward me whimpering with delight. My beautiful twenty-five-year-old daughter Henri gave me a big hug and started helping me unload my gear, asking a thousand questions. "Did you have fun? Did you see any sharks? How was the conference? Did you eat at any great restaurants? Did you meet anyone interesting?"

"Um," I took her questions and answered them consecutively. "Yes, yes, interesting and informative, yes, and no."

"Mom!" Will, my firstborn, two years older than his sister, called to me from where he stood in Henri's Jones Brothers skiff tied at the dock. "Look what I caught for you to cook us!" He bent down and straightened, carefully holding a huge, angry blue crab by its back.

Nice to know I'm good for something. "Great!" I said sincerely. "You clean 'em, I'll cook 'em."

By the time we'd finished our dinner of crab, coleslaw, baked beans, and hush puppies — okay, the frozen kind baked in the oven, but still good — we were all caught up on my trip and what they'd been up to in my absence. I even found out that Tulip had a boyfriend, a black lab two doors down who couldn't get enough of her. No problem, she was spayed. Henri, of course, had also met someone new. But that was a frequent occurrence.

Will, on the other hand was . . . well, I couldn't quite put my finger on it. He'd always been a very serious young man. He'd even started his own business right out of college, a search engine optimization and marketing company that had prospered despite being launched during the great recession. As I was wiping down the kitchen, I was trying to decide whether his usually quiet demeanor had been more pronounced throughout our meal or if it was just my imagination. I wasn't certain, but mothers usually pick up on these things. I decided to observe him more closely on our sunset cruise.

We all clambered aboard the skiff, Tulip first. Will ran back for the cooler of iced Blue Moons and orange slices he'd packed earlier, and then we were ready to head east for the Morehead City waterfront and Sugarloaf Island beyond. I looked back in our wake, watching the ribbons of white foam that swirled and spread in the silky, still water that was now starting to take on a golden glow. Overhead, a flock of white ibises headed to a roost known only to them. Except for the discreet drone of the four-stroke outboard engine, all was splendidly tranquil. So why did I have an ominous feeling?

The next morning, a Tuesday, I woke before the alarm on the bedside table had a chance to go off. It was five minutes to six. Refreshed by a full night's sleep, I hopped from my bed and headed for the bathroom. Tulip raised her head inquisitively from her side of the king-sized bed, ascertained to her satisfaction that she wasn't missing anything, and snuggled back into the chenille throw she'd claimed as her own. Thankfully the bathrooms in this century-old house had been newly renovated, and — even better — the owner had spared no expense.

The walk-in shower in the master featured a rain-forest showerhead as big as a garbage can lid and walls of block glass. There was even a glass-block window on one end of the shower, high up on the east-facing side of the house. But when a faint red glow from that window greeted me as I stepped into the shower, I understood the reason for last night's anxiety.

I nearly ran to the window in the bedroom that faced in the same direction, opened the plantation shutters, and saw a sight that didn't make me one bit happy. Far out over the ocean were wispy clouds tinged with red and gold: a spectacular sunrise one might argue, but not for me. The old sailor's adage, "red sky at night, sailor's delight, red sky in the morning, sailors take warning" was, in my estimation, counsel to pay strict heed to.

I showered and dressed quickly in designer skinny jeans, short-sleeved T-shirt, and field boots — my uniform when I'm working — then called Bud, but only got his voicemail.

By eight o'clock, when he picked me up, the stillness of the morning had evaporated. Though it was still sunny, a slight breeze was starting to kick up. He had on an Hawaiian print shirt featuring saucer-sized, neon-bright orange hibiscus flowers.

"Nice shirt," I said. "Does it come with protective sunglasses for your companions?"

"For your information, this is my lucky shirt." He demonstrated by rubbing the front of it as if it was a rabbit's foot.

"And that has to do with our visit to an offshore drillship how?" I asked, plugging numbers into my iPhone.

"Well, I don't know about you, but since it's our first visit to the actual hole we're both dropping so much money down, I want to take every opportunity to make it a success."

"I don't remember the mystic powers of this particular shirt. Or any others for that matter. Since when do you believe in luck?"

"Don't you think luck plays a role in our everyday lives?"

"What I prefer to believe in can be found between the pages of science books. Speaking of which, I've got Weather Underground pulled up here, and the forecast calls for sunny but windy conditions with seas three to four feet," I said. I switched the screen off and turned my attention to a bright yellow helicopter landing in front of us as softly as a dragonfly on a lake.

"Yeah? Good thing we're not taking a boat, then," he said.

"Still," I said, "maybe it's too breezy for such a small helicopter."

"Maybe all the Chinooks were taken," Bud replied with a grin. "Man oh man, if I'd known investing in a wildcat would be so much fun, I would have done it way before now!" Then, realizing I wasn't amused, he added, "Babe, it's a Bell 206. Just looks small from here, wait until you get in it. It'll be great, you'll see. Besides, these oil rig pilots are the best in the world. They're usually ex-military, so their training is second to none."

"Okay," I said reluctantly.

Bud gave me a reassuring pat on the back. "You worry too much. Look, here comes our pilot now."

If a person's gait was any indication, I'd say the tall, lean man marching briskly toward us was indeed ex-military. Wiry as a winter deer, the guy was as business-minded as the flat top he sported.

"Ma'am, sir," he said like a drill sergeant addressing raw recruits, "you'll find your headsets and inflatable vests in your seat. Put them on and buckle in tight, as we have brisk conditions today. If you need to ask me something during the flight, you may do so at any time, just speak through the mike in your headset. Any questions?"

Brisk conditions? I glanced at Bud, who ignored me. No sooner had I pulled my seatbelt tight than the tail of the helicopter rose steeply to a 45-degree angle and we took off in a blur. I resisted the urge to scream but promised myself payback for Bud at a later date. Possibly killing him in his sleep.

The truth was, though, this wasn't my first helicopter flight to an oil rig. I'd spent time mudlogging for one of the major exploration companies in the Gulf during college breaks. The flights out and back every two weeks were one thing I didn't miss when I switched to land-based work. The landscape zoomed by under our feet like vacation images fast forwarded on a PC: Beaufort, Cape Lookout Lighthouse, Core Sound, Core Banks, and then a nauseating swoop to the northeast followed by an endless stretch of the Atlantic Ocean. Good thing I didn't have any questions because my two pals hadn't shut up since we lifted off.

After what seemed like an eternity — in real time only about forty minutes — our destination came into view.

From the helicopter, the exploration drillship *Deep Sea Magellan* looked like a CGI

Transformer, his head and shoulders just breaking the surface of the deep ocean as he prepared to stride ashore and wreak havoc on the tiny humans. I knew that Global, like most of the major oil companies in the world, didn't own it's own fleet of drillships. It had leased this state-of-the-art drillship from another company, Trans-World Exploration, which possessed one of the world's largest and most sophisticated fleet of exploration vessels.

Beside the time I'd put in as a mudlogger on a jackup — a drill rig used in water up to 500 feet deep — I'd also done contract work on several semi-submersibles, which were floating rigs mostly used for ultra-deep exploration in water more than 2,000 feet. But this would be my very first drillship. Even more than I wanted to stop flouting the laws of physics and exit this helicopter, I wanted to explore the technical marvel that lay so massively below us.

Five

The TransWorld Exploration logo on the helipad grew larger and larger until we hovered, buffeted in the stiff wind, right above it. I was prepared for a jolting, hot-dog landing, but our pilot settled us onto the pad like a brooding hen on a clutch of eggs. Our reception committee for the tour consisted of two men: Global's top executive onboard, Braxton Roberts, and TransWorld's top executive, Duncan Powell, who was also captain of the ship.

I pegged Powell to be about Bud's age, fifty. His hawk nose, square jaw, and green eyes gave him a harsh appearance until he smiled. Then his tan face softened and he looked more approachable. Braxton Roberts, on the other hand, was elegant, even a bit haughty. Though he was gym-fit and his unkempt mop of salt-and-pepper hair gave him a boyish air, he didn't seem to be the outdoorsy type like the captain did.

Bud and I exchanged our life vests and headsets for hard hats, shook hands, shouted greetings over the wind and the revving of the helicopter as it readied for departure, then proceeded to the head of a series of stairs. There we were greeted by a few of Global's executives visiting from Houston — in particular, Hiram Hightower. He was the last word on every aspect of this well.

Hightower was a Texan, and he looked like my image of one. Tall and barrel-chested with a ruddy complexion, he had permanent laugh lines. His presence today was due only to the historic nature of a wildcat well drilled in a part of the ocean heretofore unexplored. He would not visit the ship again. Hightower ran things from a room at Global's headquarters building in Houston called the WDEC — Well Design and Execution Center. At eight o'clock each morning, he'd meet with the well executives aboard the *Magellan* via satellite, along with a group of petroleum engineers, geologists, earth scientists, and geophysicists.

I felt a quick flash of anxiety, hearing the muffled thumping of my ride home as it left me behind. This pang was quickly replaced by awe of the vessel I was now standing on. Stretching 875 feet long and 130 feet wide, the *Magellan* was so immense that an actual tour would occupy several days. We would only get the highlights.

Every inch of deck space was crammed with machinery and supplies so that it was impossible to amble across the space as one would on a pleasure yacht.

I soon discovered that the interior of the ship was no different. After leading us through a snakelike maze of narrow corridors, Powell directed us through a door into a large room not too far from the helm station. Once we stepped through the doors, however, Braxton Roberts took over. In the parlance of those in the exploration business, he was "the company man." As Global's top drilling engineer aboard *Magellan,* he'd be there until the project was completed. I knew from past experience that every word he uttered would be run by Hightower, who (contrary to his typically Texan appearance) was quiet, soft-spoken, and liked to stay out of the limelight.

About a dozen men were seated around a laminated table, some Global officials and others representatives from different investment groups like Bud's. They rose as we entered. After Roberts had introduced them, Bud and I were offered chairs at the table. On the wall facing us were three flat-screen monitors displaying various dimensional maps of the seafloor and geologic formations below us. Most of them were two dimensional, except one that represented the target area. For it, funky 3D viewing glasses were in a basket on the table.

Phil Gregson, the senior geophysicist and apparent spokesman for Global's U.S. offshore development team, stood beside of one of the monitors that showed a basic cross section of our target area.

"Good afternoon gentlemen . . . and madam," said Phil, a fortyish fair-skinned fellow with glasses, freckles, and a band of thinning red hair above his ears. "This is our target area. It lies within the buried reef structure known as the Manteo Prospect, twenty-two hundred feet of water and fourteen thousand feet of various layers of rock below us. I'm just going to go over a few quick points about it. In the interest of time, I'll answer any questions you may have one on one later."

His bald head shone in the florescent light as he pointed to several bright spots, or areas of high amplitude where sounds waves moved farther apart as they passed through rock layers thereby revealing the possibility of oil or natural gas. "After months of poring over our seismic surveys, our team feels the best plan of action would be to drill one exploration well at the highest point of the reef structure and penetrate the reservoir rock at about eleven thousand three hundred feet."

He proceeded to the third monitor, where he pointed to several red dots on an aerial map of the coast of North Carolina extending out over the outer continental shelf. "Taking into account logs from exploratory wells drilled back in the mid-eighties, we believe the top of the reservoir to be at that level and bottom out somewhere around twelve thousand seven hundred feet. This fourteen-hundred-foot-thick reservoir — comprised of boundstones and grainstones — is estimated to be approximately thirty miles long and three to five miles wide. Porosity should be good, having been enhanced during times of subaerial weathering, when sea levels were low during the early Cretaceous. The reservoir cap was formed during the Cretaceous and Recent periods, when the reef was buried again by a thick wedge of fine-grained sediments eroded from the continent and deposited across the continental shelf."

From the corner of my eye, I saw Bud check his watch.

Phil continued: "There are several faults in the structure that could be migration pathways for hydrocarbons. Moreover, this area, the core of the reef, will have the most mature facies."

"Facies?" Bud whispered in my ear.

"Rock type."

"Mature?"

"Not now, Bud." I shook my head in warning. I could explain later.

Just then a large weather-beaten man — thirtyish, with hard-worn hands the size of baseball mitts — rose from the table and introduced himself.

"I'm David Grant," he said, "head driller for this project." He stood in a classic at-ease stance, hands clasped behind his back. His accent was slightly British. "I work under the guidance of Mr. Powell," he explained. "He, Mr. Hightower, and Mr. Roberts collaborated on the design of this well and it's my job to see that it is drilled to their specifications. My drillers and I want you to know that even though this is our first experience in the mid-Atlantic region, this well was designed with every contingency in mind and all safety precautions in place."

Grant paused to sip from a water bottle. He seemed confident and relaxed as he continued. "To add a bit of information about myself, I've drilled holes all over the world, starting in the North Sea and most recently in Africa and the Gulf of Mexico. We are not expecting Manteo One to present any challenges we haven't already faced many times over in the Gulf." He paused, seeming to invite questions, and, when there were none, continued.

"Regarding temperature and pressure at a vertical depth of thirteen thousand feet or better, the bottom hole conditions will be two hundred degrees Fahrenheit and seven thousand psi. *Magellan* is used to twenty-five thousand feet and bottom temperatures of four hundred twenty-five degrees, twelve thousand psi. So, no worries there." He went on to explain the current conditions of the well — that it had been spudded (the well head and support casing had been placed into the seafloor), that the critical cementing process had been completed successfully, and that they were now preparing to set the blowout preventer, or BOP, in place.

I sensed Bud stifling a yawn. Hours of detailed information to bring me up to speed followed the more general presentation. Bud and the other company officials and investors slipped out, leaving me with geophysicist Phil Gregson. Just as we were finishing inspecting some of the cuttings brought up during the casing process, Powell stuck his head in the door and in a heavy Cajun accent I hadn't noticed before said, "Would you two care to join us for lunch?"

Phil Gregson looked at his watch. "Good grief," he said. "I didn't realize it had gotten so late, Ms. Cooper. I hope I haven't starved you." I looked at my watch. Three o'clock. Time flies when you're having fun.

"Not at all," I said as we followed Powell. "But, tell me, how's it going with the wellsite geologist? What do you think of him?"

"I'm glad you asked. Poor young fellow is going to need you to lean on, what with this being his first offshore rig."

"When did he get here?"

"He was here pre-spud, to get the logging lab settled in. As to what I think of him . . . he's such a nervous type, it's hard to say. Doesn't seem to have much confidence, which could be a problem since he's in charge of the mudloggers. I'm afraid they're going to take advantage of him. It's a good thing you'll be backing things up. We'll go meet him right after we grab a bite."

Still following Powell, we made our way to the end of another maze of interior hallways, each one exactly like the other, all with gleaming white walls, florescent lights, rounded brushed aluminum handrails, and spanking clean linoleum floors smelling of pine disinfectant.

As he opened a heavy sea door to a third-story catwalk, Powell said, "Weather's kicked up a little since we started our meeting."

Barely catching my hard hat before it lifted off my head in the stiff wind, I squinted into the stinging rain. Phil stepped out after me and we did our best to keep up with Powell, grabbing the bright yellow handrail from time to time to keep from being blasted backward. Finally we ducked down more sets of metal stairs, clanging our way to another long and narrow hallway that opened into a brightly lit galley, its aromas a mingled array of rib-sticking he-man food.

After making our choices, we joined Bud and the other men already seated. I could only pick at my chef's salad — the only thing I could find that wasn't fried or drowning in gravy — worried as I was about being tossed about like a leaf in the wind on our flight home.

Meanwhile Phil was entertaining the table with hair-raising tales of exploration off the coast of Africa. As I listened, a loud speaker overhead hummed, sputtered, and then requested Mr. Powell's presence in the radio room. He slid his napkin under his plate. "If you'll excuse me," he said, departing hurriedly.

About five minutes later, he was back at our table. "Attention, everyone," he said, clinking his glass. "I'm afraid I have some bad news. The Sikorsky SK 76 that was scheduled to return company officials and investors to Wilmington International" — he paused and dropped his gaze to Bud and me — "and drop you two in Beaufort, has suspended operations until the wind gusts drop below thirty knots."

There was dead silence at the table, then Phil said, "I thought a Sikorsky could fly in any weather."

"They can and often do with no problems," Powell replied. "We're simply following the TransWorld safety rules that dictate takeoffs and landings on this ship."

"Not to worry," said Phil, addressing me. "That'll just give us more time with Elton, the wellsite geologist."

"Right," I said. "I'm ready when you are."

"If it's okay with you," Powell said. "I'd like to introduce you to the chief steward first. He'll show you and Mr. Cooper where you'll bunk for the night."

Bud and I exchanged glances as I blurted

out, "You do have separate accommodations, don't you?"

I dropped my trusty tote on the bottom bunk in dormitory-style crew quarters about the size of my walk-in closet. Bunks and a small bedside chest of drawers on the right, bath and two lockers on the left. No windows. "You need to imagine an invisible divider cutting the room in half, top to bottom," I said to Bud who was sitting on the top bunk, swinging his legs, grinning like a jackass.

"Okay, I'm imagining it."

"Your side is the top half and mine's the bottom. Got it?"

"Got it. Might make taking a leak a little . . . challenging, but it could be worse. We could be sharing a suite with the egghead."

I narrowed my eyes. "Are you referring to Phil? The scientist with PhDs in both geophysics *and* theoretical physics?"

"I wasn't referring to his abundance of education. Didn't you notice the shape of his head?"

I sighed and headed for the tiny bathroom, agog at how easy it had been to make him accept my ground rules for room sharing.

When I came out, Bud was gone. I

grabbed my hard hat and went to catch up with Phil so he could introduce me to the wellsite geologist, Elton Patterson.

We met in Elton's small office, which was located next to Braxton Roberts's one deck above the drilling floor. It gave an unobscured view of the drilling floor below. Phil stayed only long enough to make introductions. I shook Elton's damp, limp hand.

"Ma'am," he said shyly, then hooked his thumbs in the back pocket of his starched khaki jumpsuit.

Closing the door, I unfolded a metal chair, sat, and said, "Tell me what you've done on the ship so far, Elton."

Elton's eyes widened behind his Coke-bottle glasses, making for a comical effect that fought with the rest of his no-nonsense appearance. His skin was dark and luminous, his black features handsome. Neat cornrows marched across his scalp to end in tight little balls at his hairline. Phil was right, he *was* a kid. He looked to be around twenty-five. He paced about the room as he gave me a quick rundown of the actions he'd taken since arriving on the *Magellan* and finished by asking, "Would you like my daily reports?"

"I would," I said, motioning for him to sit. "But I'd also like to know if you've had any problems and if the mudloggers have been helpful to you."

Elton blinked like a baby owl.

Taking another tack, I said, "Did you have any trouble installing your gas sensors down in the pit room?" A negative head shake. "What about over the shale shakers?" Another negative shake. "What about the sensors for the hook load and the kelly height?"

"All the sensors are installed and working. I've checked all the electrical cables from the van and made sure they're grounded to the rig. Video feeds are connected and functioning too," he said, pronouncing each word carefully.

I looked around his office, noticing the hydrogen sulfide monitors and remote video displays of other pertinent drill data. "Sounds like you're getting things done right on schedule. As I recall, Phil said your last job was on the North Slope of Alaska."

"Yes," Elton said. "That would be correct."

"You know where your lifeboat station is?"

Elton shot out of his chair, a look of panic flashing across his face as he looked out the window, past the derrick to the far horizon. "Yes ma'am. That's the first thing I checked out, 'cause there's a whole lotta water out there," he said, slipping out of his precise diction.

"I know this is your first offshore rig, but is this your first time at sea?"

"Yes ma'am."

Uh-oh. "Have you ever seen the ocean before, ever been to the beach?"

"No ma'am."

Good grief. I leaned forward, elbows on my knees, looked him straight in the glasses, and asked softly, "You going to be all right out here, Elton?"

"Yes ma'am," he said with grim determination. "I have to be. I have a wife and a new baby girl. I have to be all right and I will."

"I believe you," I said, standing. "You can give me copies of your daily reports tomorrow, but right now I want to see the logging lab. If I remember correctly, Global hired TravelTech, right?"

"Yes ma'am."

"They're a great company, I've worked with them before. Lead the way, Elton."

Like many of the scientific personnel required to drill an exploratory well, the mudloggers are hired from outside the company. In this case, Global had hired TravelTech. Elton was hired from yet *another* private firm, the goal here being objectivity. As wellsite geologist, Elton would oversee a crew of men who likely had degrees in earth sciences. A good working relationship with them was essential. Having myself been both — mudlogger and wellsite geologist — I can say firsthand that neither is counted as very important by the operator or the rig crew. This always amazes me, since without them, no information on the well would exist.

Aside from all the other data the mudloggers accumulate, they most critically monitor gas readings that would indicate an imminent blowout like the one that took out the *Deepwater Horizon* back in April of 2010 in the Gulf. In that instance, BP was the operator or owner of the well and they'd contracted Transocean to drill it for them.

Buffeted by high winds and driving rain, Elton and I ran for TravelTech's van. As soon as a drillship arrives on site, the company hired to log the well has its own van delivered, a small travel trailer containing all its scientific equipment. This is usually done by helicopter. They're most often referred to as logging labs and are always located in an area at least one flight up from the rig floor, to avoid contamination by poisonous gases.

Upon our entrance, a skinny pressure engineer from Louisiana named Tom greeted us with a big toothy smile. He was a little confused at first about my being on board since Elton was the wellsite geologist, but after I explained my somewhat unorthodox role to him, he seemed relieved to have me there. As crew chief, he would convey it to the others.

I spent a couple of hours of inspecting the lab and looking at the most recent samples — chips of rock brought up in the drilling mud. Elton, who'd gone to take his mud inventory, then reappeared. Tom left and another mudlogger took his place as loudspeakers chimed a shift change. Like Tom and the other mudloggers, this new man wore a light blue jumpsuit. I spoke with him only briefly, as I was becoming anxious to go find Bud. The hours I'd just spent in such stressful conditions had taken their toll and I longed for the quiet snugness of the tiny soundproof room.

But Bud wasn't in our bunk when I returned. Since I preferred to eat dinner with him instead of by my lonesome, I lay back on the narrow bed to wait. Next thing I knew I heard country music softly playing and sat up so abruptly that I cracked my head on the overhead bunk. After a few off-color words, I realized I'd fallen asleep and the sound was coming from a radio, obviously set for the seven-thirty evening shift. My first coherent thought was that these living quarters must have been wired with antenna outlets, because normally radios won't play on a rig. The metal walls inhibit radio waves. My second thought: Bud still wasn't back.

Snagging my hard hat, I opened the door to my quarters, trotted down a hall and down a flight of stairs, and headed for the working deck. Regardless of the type of rig you are on, crew quarters are always placed as far away from the drilling operation as possible. They're also designed with blast walls, which cut out the noises associated with living on a giant drilling machine.

I pushed open the heavy blastproof door and lowered my shoulder to push through wind and rain. As if accompanying the storm, the air vibrated with the humming of generators, the clanging of metal on metal, and the roar of the diesels powering the drill. Men in jumpsuits of various colors to denote their job stations were in movement all around me. They shared a common goal — getting their job done in spite of the deplorable weather.

Darkness was already settling in, and the

ship's automatic lights twinkled about me. I tried to think where Bud might be. In weather like this, it would have to be somewhere inside.

I checked the galley, a small Internet room, the gym, and lastly, a lounge area for off-duty crew. There I found several people engaged in watching one of my favorite movies, *Master and Commander* with Russell Crowe, on a large plasma TV. I sat down and enjoyed the last hour with two tool pushers — one from Norway, one from Belgium — and an electronic technician from New Orleans. About nine o'clock, I went to the galley, scarfed down a burger and fries, and returned to our room.

I found a note slipped under the door that said the helicopter was scheduled to pick us up at 8:00 a.m. sharp. Cheered by this, I watched the news on the small television mounted in the corner of the room. Around eleven, I unlaced my field boots, folded my jeans and T-shirt neatly, and went to sleep.

At 4:00 a.m. on the dot, I awoke from a restless sleep. "Bud?" I called softly to the bunk above me.

No answer.

I didn't want to disturb him if he was sleeping, so I got up in the pitch darkness of the room and tentatively reached toward the center of his bunk. Still empty. I had a feeling he was off somewhere with his new BFF, Braxton Roberts, whom I knew he'd gotten friendly with during investment meetings. Still, I'd feel better if I was sure he knew what time we were supposed to meet the chopper in a few hours.

Slipping back into my clothes and boots, I went down to the deck. The level of noise and activity at 4:00 a.m. was unchanged from what it had been at 4:00 p.m. Which isn't surprising since every minute of operation on a drillship like the *Magellan* costs in excess of $400. One thing was different, though: the air was still. The storm had blown out to sea.

Basically retracing my steps of earlier this evening, I checked all the logical places without success. Considering the vessel's immense size, I knew I couldn't look everywhere for my errant ex, so I took the only option left for me and texted him:

BE AT THE HELIPAD AT 8 A.M.

Then, not feeling the least bit sleepy, I decided to take the opportunity to poke around this marvel of modern technology, sans an official company tour guide. I especially wanted to see the ROV — remotely operated vehicle — since we had made only a cursory pass by it the day before.

Making my way along the main deck, I came to several flights of metal stairs beside the brightly lit 228-foot-tall derrick. I climbed them, looking up at it as I went — *Close Encounters of the Third Kind* came to mind — then turned down a catwalk and walked to about mid-ship. This was so I could look down into the moon pool, the opening in the center of the ship through which the drilling equipment passes on its way to the seafloor 2,000 feet below. Amazing. The level of water rose and fell 10 feet or more with each passing swell, yet the ship itself hardly moved. It was held in place by six electric thrusters guided by GPS.

Each of the three engines on either end of the ship was powered by its own 5-megawatt generator, run on diesel fuel. There were over a million gallons of it on board, with the next fill-up probably in about six months.

From my perch, I could easily view the different activities on the drilling deck. Inside the DC — the driller's cabin, a large three-sided, glassed-in room raised above the drill floor — a drill tech sat back in his ergonomic chair and removed 40-foot sections of drill pipe, three at a time, from a rack inside the derrick so a team of four roughnecks out on the drilling deck could connect them and send them down the borehole. Watching all the activity and hoping the drill was chewing its way to the first of many large natural gas deposits and thinking of what that would mean for North Carolina raised goosebumps on my arms.

After indulging my imagination a few more minutes, I turned left and made my way back down the catwalk, then up another short set of stairs to a working landing from which the ROV was lowered into the sea. Behind it was the van where the crew and pilot worked the robot's controls and monitors. I had the area all to myself. As I stepped up on the landing, I breathed a sigh of admiration. They had a Voyager Maximus! And a brand-spanking-new one at that.

I walked around the bright chartreuse Mini Cooper–sized machine. *"Arrh, arrh, arrh,"* I said, doing a good imitation of Tim the Tool Man Taylor and wishing Bud was here. Where was he anyway? He loved techy toys even more than I did, and here was one of the all-time ultimates. This 9,000-pound baby could tie shoelaces in 13,000 feet of water barely above freezing *and* send you pictures of it in 3D.

I rubbed my hand over the shiny blue

metal of the TMS — the Tether Management System. Basically it was a cage that housed the underwater robot and brought it to the seafloor. What a marvelous creation it was, too, with its own cameras and lights. I stood on tiptoe and noted it had 4,000 feet of tether cable.

Turning my attention back to the ROV, I stooped to look at its dual manipulating arms and cool little propellers. That's when I noticed something caught between it and the bottom support rails of its cage. It caught my eye because unlike the shiny, new metal of the robot, it looked old and beat up. I extended my hand and touched the object. It felt like a little metal wheel, maybe 3 inches across with five spokes, like a starfish. Being the terminally curious person I am, I *had* to have it for further inspection.

As I wriggled the artifact back and forth, trying to work it loose, I realized I'd seen an object similar to this one, I just couldn't place where. Grabbing the object should have been easy, but for some reason the crusty round of metal was defying me.

At that moment, for reasons unknown to me, the entire section of lights illuminating the ROV landing and several sections on either side went out, leaving me completely in the dark. I wasn't worried. Someone had probably thrown a breaker for this small section of the third floor to correct an electrical problem. I could see that all the other areas of the ship were still ablaze. I told myself I'd just have to be careful where I stepped on my way back to the light, which I planned on doing as soon as I had my mystery prize.

I doubled down on my determination, and got on my knees so I could use both hands. Furiously I pried and pulled, trying to free the little wheel. Suddenly it popped free and shot from my fingers with an accompanying clang as the ROV settled in the track of the cage.

Damn it. I squished myself against the cage, reaching as far as I could into the darkness, but I couldn't feel where it had landed. Backing away, I sat on my heels and was feeling around the platform outside the cage when someone slammed into me with the force of a runaway mule, shoving me sideways into the railing.

Oh shit, I'm going overboard!

Flailing wildly behind me, I grabbed a handful of greasy hair and felt a heavy growth of coarse stubble and massive furred arms, which were grabbing me everywhere at once. It felt like I was being attacked by a giant ape. My head smacked into the middle bar of the handrail so hard I saw stars, then I dropped chest first onto the landing. I blearily wondered why this guy was running around ramming into people helter skelter — then a work boot to the middle of my back forced every last molecule of oxygen out of me. This was no accident.

I tried to push up, hoping to turn over and maybe grab this creep's leg, but King Kong sat hard on me, a hand as big as my whole head holding the side of my face onto the metal floor. One finger was over my eyes, another mashed my nose flat to the metal grating. Then he leaned forward and wrapped a tongue wide as a cow's practically around my neck.

Fighting the impulse to vomit, I decided to lay still, like a possum, hoping he'd think I was dead and run away. But I couldn't, my lungs burned and I was gasping for air. It was about then I felt King Kong grab the back waist of my jeans with his other hand and start to pull my pants down.

No! Hell, no! This was not going to happen as long as I had so much as a spark of life in me. Adrenalin rushed through my veins. I pushed myself upward with a strength I never knew I possessed, curled my body enough so that I could get my teeth into his knee. I bit down for all I was worth. Kong shifted his weight just enough for me to squish out from under him and let fly with a mule kick to the chest, then an elbow to his nose. Both connected, but he barely grunted, just grabbed me again with the speed of a striking snake, jerked me to my feet, and ripped my T-shirt like it was tissue paper, grabbing my breasts and squeezing so hard, I cried out.

Swinging, slapping, and scratching in the darkness, I knew I was making contact with flesh, but the more I did, the more it seemed to excite the dark, sweaty creature. With my left thigh in one hand and right underarm in the other, he shook me so violently my teeth clacked together. Never in my life had I been so physically overpowered, so totally helpless. I called on another burst of adrenalin, but terror had rendered me helpless. I was all done in.

Wishing now he *had* thrown me overboard, I considered jumping — if I could get away long enough — but it was more than 20 feet to the ocean's surface. While I'd probably survive the fall, the current was ripping like rush-hour traffic down the length of the ship. More than likely I'd be sucked under the ship and pulled into one of the thrusters.

Still, getting chewed up in the giant

propellers seemed far preferable to being some ape's plaything.

With my last ounce of strength, I kicked out in the dark with my right leg, hoping to connect with his crotch, my plan being to squirm free and jump the second he doubled over in pain.

My foot landed somewhere in the groin area, but the rotten bastard seemed to like it. Panting and whimpering, he clutched my wilting body to him, like Steinbeck's Lennie hugged his dead puppy, and jammed his paw down the front of my pants. Snaps popped, the zipper busted, and Kong groaned, gave a mighty grunt, and . . .

I fainted.

SIX

Unintelligible rap music blasted from the clock radio beside me. I bolted upright, cracked my head — again — on the top bunk, and slapped the Off button. It was seven thirty Wednesday morning. I looked around the room. Bud still wasn't back. I prayed I'd only had a bad dream . . .

Yet every muscle in my body screamed in pain. Last night's horror sprang fully formed into my mind's eye, like an automated ghoul in a carnival spook house. I darted into the bathroom and gasped at the sight of myself in the mirror.

Sadly, my face and clothes told a sad tale. I had a goose egg on the left side of my forehead at the hair line and my clothes were all but ripped off me, revealing a nasty purple-red bruise on my right shoulder that wrapped around my armpit. There was no snap on my jeans and the zipper was kaput.

I squeezed my eyes shut, but tears popped

out anyway and ran down my face. I choked back a sob and, with shaking hands, pulled down my jeans. I had to know.

There was a massive bruise on my left thigh, *but* my white cotton thong was still intact. I checked in with myself and noted that none of the soreness I felt was coming from between my legs. I still didn't know what had happened or how I'd gotten back here, but it was clear that I'd had an extremely close call.

After cleaning my face and jerkily applying fresh makeup from my purse, I blundered around and found a man's white undershirt in one of the lockers. It was clean enough and only a few sizes too large, which was a good thing since it would hide where I'd fastened the waist of my jeans with a safety pin from my tote — always be prepared, right? I tied a knot in the undershirt at my left hip as best I could considering how bad my hands were shaking. After swallowing one of my emergency BC powders, I picked up my bag, gently put on my hard hat and dark glasses, and made my way to the steps leading to the helipad.

I knew I should march in indignation up to the helm station, find the captain, and report the assault. The Cleo I *should* have been would. But while admittedly rattled, I could still assess the situation enough to know I was in a very untenable spot. On the one hand, yes, I was a victim, and my retreat left a very bad person loose on board.

On the other hand, what's done was done. Reporting a near-miss incident that happened four hours ago by an attacker I couldn't identify didn't seem the way to go. Plus, the minute I said I was wandering around on a self-guided tour in the wee hours of the night, ship officials would be ready to hang *me* from the yard arm. I'd been breaking the drillship's safety regulations by running around alone in the dark. At the very least, I'd probably be asked not to come back onboard, thus letting down Bud and our investors.

Overriding everything — and increasing minute by minute since I'd become conscious — was pure murderous rage at whoever had tried to rape me last night. I knew I needed to get somewhere and gain control of myself. In the meantime, a 5-gallon bucket of paint under the stairs leading to the helipad made for a perfect spot to wait for my ride out of sight.

Wincing at the stab of pain that shot through my left thigh as I sat, I promised myself that regardless of how I went about it, I'd have my revenge on the SOB who'd jumped me last night. I'd never been one to look to others to take care of my problems, and I wasn't about to start now. But I still had my job to think about, so I dragged my thoughts back to things I would normally do before leaving the ship. Only checking in with Elton came to mind; I could do that later via email.

Within a few minutes I heard the distant thumping of the big Sikorsky. I watched it land, the rotors spooling down. No one noticed me as they clanked up the stairs. I waited a few more minutes until exactly 8:00 a.m., then trotted up the stairs, crossed the pad, and hopped in after handing a deckhand my hard hat. There were two seats left. Fortunately they were separated by several rows so I wouldn't have to worry about Bud noticing my unkempt appearance. Selecting the one closest to the rear, I was careful not to let the headset disturb the hair pulled across my temple and hiding the growing goose egg. Phil Gregson, sitting a few seats over, smiled and nodded as the engines began to rev and the rotors spin faster.

"Wait," I called to the pilot. "Mr. Cooper isn't here yet."

Phil leaned over to me and said something.

"What?" I yelled back.

"I said he's catching a flight back after lunch. He was playing poker all night with Duncan, me, and a couple of other guys. I think a fifth of Maker's Mark . . . or two . . . might've been involved." Then he winced, rolled his eyes, and rubbed his temples.

"Okay!" I yelled and waved to the pilot. At least I'd caught a break in the nosy ex-husband department.

Later, as I lay on my own bed, I realized I couldn't remember anything, not even the smallest detail, about the helicopter flight or my drive home. I was pretty sure you'd call that being in shock. I did remember coming straight up to my room and lying down — but little more.

Tulip was with me. Sensing my distress, she scrunched up as close to me as possible and gazed at me with soulful, all-knowing eyes. I rubbed her bony head as I heard the screen door slam shut downstairs.

"Mom!" It was Henri. I checked Mickey Mouse on my wrist and saw that several hours had passed.

Painfully, I slid off the side of the bed and limped to the door. "I'm getting ready to take a shower. Be down in a little while."

Hot rain from the fancy showerhead

streamed over my battered body and I tried to come up with some sound psychological advice to counteract the deep feelings of guilt and betrayal that fought for dominance within me. It had simply never entered my mind that anyone working on a drillship could morph into a violent attacker. At the same time, I felt guilty that I'd put myself — and thus Global and Trans World — in a vulnerable situation. But, honestly, in my time spent aboard various offshore rigs, I'd been prepared for danger in the form of accidents or from the forces of nature. I had always felt extremely safe with my fellow workers.

Even though crews change every two weeks, there is a sense of camaraderie among the close-knit group, of us against the elements. Everyone looks out for everyone else. It was unheard of, at least by me, for criminal activity to take place offshore.

The confusion in my brain grew thicker, as did the steam in the bathroom. Bits and pieces of the attack flashed before me. I remembered the lights going out, thinking originally of electrical maintenance. Now I wondered if King Kong had flipped a breaker. I remembered the little metal wheel I'd been trying to retrieve. What was it? What happened to it? Did I pull it loose?

Why did the attack stop? The sound of those repellently loathsome grunts and groans echoed in my ears. My insides lurched. I dry heaved until my empty stomach was sore, then sat on the warm tile floor, cocooned in steam and warm rain and pondering the biggest question of all:

How had I gotten back to my room?

With my hair artfully arranged and clothes covering my bruises, I went down to the kitchen where Henri was making a tomato sandwich. I'd managed to arrive at a clear plan of action regarding yesterday's events: compartmentalize.

Learning the identity of my attacker had to come first, before any revenge, of course. Then came the delicious question of how to get that revenge. A lead pipe to his hog-tied, prone body topped my list, though I knew it was unlikely I'd get someone his size in such a position. A more civilized option would have to do. And lastly, I absolutely had to steady myself — witness my embarrassing episode of crying and hurling in the shower — and for that, time was the only cure.

"Want one?" asked Henri, offering her sandwich.

"None for me, thanks."

"Dad called me and said you aren't answering your cell. He says to call him."

I moved to the refrigerator, poured a Coke over crushed ice, and sipped. "Must've left my cell in the Jeep. I'll call him in a little while. Where's Will?"

"Probably off in my boat again. I swear, Mom, he uses it all the time. I can't imagine what he's doing with it. He says he's fishing, but he's not."

"How do you know?"

"Leslie and Juliet saw him the other day when they were out on their paddleboards. They said he had the Bimini top up and was just sitting at the edge of the salt marsh staring into space."

"Maybe what he wanted was to be alone . . . to think."

"About what?"

"I don't know. If he wants to tell us, he will. Right now, best to leave him alone."

"So you've noticed a difference in him too?"

"Well . . . he may seem a little moody. But, like I said, just leave him alone and let him come to us if he wants to."

Henri was still processing my nonintervention strategy as I carried my Coke up to my temporary office. There I made arrangements to move up a week a consulting job

I'd scheduled in the natural gas fields of Pennsylvania. Now I'd be leaving Thursday — tomorrow.

Three days later on Sunday afternoon, my consulting job completed and recovered from my attack (physically anyway), I was back in Morehead City.

More precisely, I was wading in the breakers on Atlantic Beach, throwing a tennis ball for Tulip and thinking of my upcoming work calendar. Except for an American Association of Petroleum Geologists convention in Houston, where I'd be presenting a paper, I'd cleared it of all but a few small jobs so I could devote more time to Manteo One. Being asked to back up Elton, the rookie wellsite geologist, would give perfect cover and plenty of extra time to discreetly root out the identity of my attacker. How hard could it be? I mean, how many apes were onboard *Magellan*?

Bud and I had finally connected while I was in Pennsylvania. He mentioned our trip to the *Magellan* only once, making fun of himself and Dunk — his new BFF name for Duncan Powell — for their all-night poker game excesses. I never spoke of my time there except to answer his questions relating to the briefings I'd had and the observations I'd made.

Elton had dutifully sent daily reports and called a few times regarding routine questions, for which I cut him some slack. One thing I noticed was he didn't seem to be calming down any. During one of our conversations, I began worrying he was about to hyperventilate and found myself giving him a pep talk. He ended our conversation that day with a let-me-back-in-there-coach attitude, which seem to indicate progress.

Tulip body-surfed in, tennis ball held high, and charged toward me flinging sand and water. She stopped mid-stride when the handsome black Lab from my street swooped down from the dunes, charged across the beach, and intercepted her. I thought Tulip would ignore him as she does all other dogs, but she immediately dropped the ball and took off with the him.

"Hey!" I called as the abandoned tennis ball rolled back into the breakers. "Come back here, Tulip! Here, girl . . ."

I was interrupted by my cell. "You back yet?" Bud wanted to know.

"Yep. Got in around lunchtime. What's up?"

"They've got that thing installed on the well and they're at about five thousand feet."

That thing? I wondered. "Uh, the blowout preventer?"

"Yeah, that," Bud said.

"Any problems?"

"Not with the drilling, and no one with the company has said anything to me, but in the last couple of days I've seen some rather curious news in the *Carteret News Times.*"

"Yeah? What?" I said, keeping an eye on Tulip and her new buddy romping in the dunes.

"Well, Thursday I read where a corpse washed up on Atlantic Beach. Since the body was fully clothed and not wearing a bathing suit, the first assumption was that it was a fisherman or boater who'd fallen overboard. Then today I read that since no boating mishaps have been reported and no one along the coast has filed a missing person's report, the police are now wondering if the man could be a worker from the drillship. The article says an investigation is ongoing."

My heart did a double-clutch. Several different scenarios flashed through my mind, but my memory of what happened after I heard Kong groan was still a complete blank.

"You there?"

"Oh, sorry. I'm just distracted. I'm on the beach with Tulip. She just got herself a boyfriend, a black Lab, and they've gone over the dunes where I can't see them. We'll talk later." I clicked off, my I'll-get-even-with-the-bastard state of mind suddenly a thing of the past. Now I felt anticlimactic. Disappointed even. If the body that washed up was that of my attacker and he'd stupidly fallen overboard in orgasmic bliss, I wouldn't get the satisfaction of carrying out some tantalizing form of revenge.

Still, if it *was* him, I'd just gotten shed of a task that could potentially have been foolhardy for me. Satisfying probably, but foolhardy nonetheless. And right now, maybe that was best. As I scaled the dunes to find Tulip and the lab, my thoughts turned back to the corpse and how to find out for sure who it was.

I didn't have to study on the problem for long.

I was in the back yard hosing sand and salt off Tulip when I heard a car pull into the drive. Since neither Henri nor Will appeared to be here and the boat was gone, I put Tulip on the porch and walked around front just in time to see two men exit their car: one buff but chunky, the other his antithesis

— lean and wiry. The way they intently checked their surroundings as they climbed from their black sedan reminded me of TV cops. Both wore khakis, knit shirts, and aviator sunglasses. Both looked to be about my age, mid-forties.

"Hi," I said, with outward nonchalance but inward trepidation. When the cops pull up in your driveway, unless they're asking for a donation for the policeman's ball, it's probably not a good thing.

"Ms. Cleo Cooper?" asked the lean one, stepping forward with outstretched hand.

"Yes," I said, shaking it.

"I'm Detective Sergeant Alex Pierce of the Atlantic Beach Police Department," he said. Then turning to his companion, he introduced, "my partner, Detective Billy Myers."

Detective Myers nodded. "Ma'am."

Somehow I didn't think these guys were here about the policeman's ball. "Gentlemen," I said, "Let's go inside, out of this hot sun."

SEVEN

Having declined my offer of iced tea, my visitors sat sedately at the kitchen table. It was lean Pierce who spoke first. "Ms. Cooper, we hate to bother you on a Sunday, but we're investigating the body of a John Doe that washed up on the beach on Thursday. We have reason to believe the man could be a crew member from a ship that's presently working off our coast" — Pierce paused to pull a small spiral notebook from his back pocket and check it, then added — "the *Magellan.* We spoke to company officials at their base of operations."

He looked at Myers, who chimed in obligingly. "We talked to the guy that's in charge of all the employees coming and going out there —"

"The site manager, Duncan Powell?" I interrupted.

Pierce checked his notes. "Right," he said. "He met us at the port."

Myers continued. "He confirmed that a crew member from one of the subcontractor firms on the ship didn't show up for work on Wednesday. They're looking into it, meaning they're making sure he didn't hop a helicopter or one of the supply boats without letting anyone know. He said that while that is highly unlikely and against the ship's rules, it's not impossible. So we're letting them cover all their bases before they release the name of this individual. Which seems a good way to avoid wild goose chases."

He paused. "However, Mr. Powell also gave us a list of six people who visited the ship the day before they discovered the missing crew member. You were on it and he mentioned you were spending the summer in Morehead. Naturally, since you're local, we thought we'd start with you, hoping you might be able to answer a few questions that would aid in our investigation."

Considering the situation and how precarious my role in it might be, answering questions for detectives was not high on my list of things I ought to do. Still, they were here now and it seemed best to at least sound forthcoming, so I said, "Of course. How can I help?"

"First, what's your specific business on board?"

"Basically, I'm consulting, but I'm also invested through a private equity group."

Now Myers pulled out his notebook as well. Both men jotted for a moment, then he asked, "How long were you there?"

"From mid-morning on Tuesday until the next morning. We had to stay over longer than anticipated due to high winds and severe thunderstorms."

Myers seemed to be comparing what I said to notes he'd taken earlier. "Did anything unusual happen while you were there?"

"Like what?"

"I'm asking you just to think back. We'll be interested in anything that caught your attention, however small. Say, for instance, any . . . unpleasantness on board among crew members?"

Now, I'm not squeamish about lying when necessary, but I have a preference for creative parsing of words. Carefully I said, "No. I didn't get any bad vibes from any crew members and I didn't see any fights." This was sailing a bit close to the wind, I realized.

"So, when you say you didn't *see* a

fight . . . what do you mean?" This, from Pierce.

Oh dear, this wasn't going well at all. "Uh, that I didn't see one."

Pierce was less a fool than I'd thought him. "So you *heard* one, maybe?

"Kinda." I was aware I was squirming. Not only could this screw up my attempt to handle things on my own, but now I was beginning to wonder if *I* could be in trouble. Maybe I needed a lawyer. The problem was, I'd seen enough episodes of *Law & Order* to know that lawyering up meant you were probably guilty of something. Which I wasn't, and I didn't want to be perceived in such a way. Therefore, I decided now might be a good time to explain what happened. I told them in short concise sentences what I remembered about the attack. I ended by emphasizing that I had no way of knowing whether the man who attacked me was the same man who washed up on Atlantic Beach.

Their response: dumbfounded gawking.

Pierce was first to break the silence. "Why didn't you report this *immediately*?"

"I told you. I fainted. I wasn't conscious *immediately*. Besides, it is not in my nature to whine and complain. What good would it do? I couldn't identify the man. It was dark, it happened quickly. I didn't see him . . ." I paused but then decided against mentioning the slew of shipboard rules I'd broken wandering about on my own in the middle of the night.

"How did you get to your room?"

"Again," I replied patiently, "I don't know."

"You don't have any impression of the assailant at all?"

"Other than he was big, hairy, and very strong, no."

"Is there anything or anyone who would help verify your story? Did you go to a doctor?" Meyers asked.

Verify my story? Now I was losing patience. "I told you. I wasn't raped. I was just bruised," I said, lifting my hair on the right side and exposing the fading yellow bruise. I pulled up my capris and stretched open the neck of my T-shirt, exposing what was left of the discoloration on my shoulder and thigh.

"Hold it there for a moment, please." Myers took out his iPhone and snapped a quick succession of pictures.

I hadn't even told them I'd almost instantly taken myself and my assorted injuries, not to mention my shock and trauma, across state lines to Pennsylvania. But that could wait.

Pierce chewed a hangnail, then said, "Where are the clothes you had on that night?"

"In the laundry room," I said. "Still at the bottom of the chute, I guess. I'll go get them." My companions jumped up to follow me.

I opened the narrow door to the chute and looked down. Except for one hand towel, there were no dirty clothes. Turning back to face the detectives who were peering so closely over my shoulder we practically butted heads, I said with relief, "I guess my daughter washed everything. It's one of my rules. You live here, you pitch in." The thought of having to hand my undergarments over to these two guys was actually very creepy.

They both shook their heads and Myers, scowling, put pen to notebook. "Describe your outfit." I did as he asked, remembering to mention that the undershirt I wore home was not mine. Since I hadn't been wearing it during the attack, however, they weren't interested in it. On the walk back to the kitchen, Pierce asked, "You said you fought back, slapping, scratching, kicking, right?"

"Yes."

"You think you inflicted any damage? Maybe a black eye, a fat lip?"

I looked down at my hands. "Reasoning tells me my knuckles don't look like I made any serious contact, plus my nails aren't broken or chipped. I don't know. I guess it's possible I could have scratched him . . ."

The detectives exchanged glances. Myers nodded as if reading Pierce's mind. Pierce said, "I hate to ask, Ms. Cooper, but would you be willing to drive over to Chapel Hill and look at the body?"

"It was in the water for several days, but nothing chewed on it," Myers reassured me. "Now that it's in the cooler, decomp's arrested. It won't be too bad."

My face must have conveyed my distaste.

"The ME won't get to him for a few days, and I'd like you to look at the scratches on his face," Pierce said. "What I'm thinking is, maybe looking at them and his overall size and appearance, it would jog your memory. You'd possibly be able to establish him as your attacker. That would aid us not only in identifying him, but also in piecing together what happened to him."

Thinking it wouldn't be wise to refuse whatever they requested, I agreed to meet them at the medical examiner's office the next morning at ten thirty.

I walked them out to their car. Pierce opened his door and put one foot inside. Myers stood at the passenger-side door directing a steady gaze at me over the roof of the car. Pierce said, "I'll be honest with you, Ms. Cooper, there are large holes in your story."

I didn't like the sound of that. But I chose to reply by saying simply, "There are large holes in my memory, Detective."

Some things never change, and Chapel Hill and the endless construction on the highways leading there and the University of North Carolina's campus streets are no exception. After making several detours around massive holes outlined with orange cones and workers leaning on rakes and shovels, I finally found, albeit a little late, the medical examiner's office just before the appointed time the next morning. Not a part of the campus I'd frequented as a student all those years ago.

You know how most detective novels have a scene at the ME's office, a.k.a. the morgue? Well, this one smelled just as the novels said it would. It took more than a few minutes of stalling at the entrance before I was able to deal with the stench of something rotten overlaid by the heavy, cloying smells of formaldehyde and disinfectant.

Pierce had told me where to meet him, so I made my way down the long tiled halls, following the overhead directional signs. He was waiting for me outside a surprisingly normal-looking office door, talking on his cell. Myers wasn't with him. He held the phone against the lapel of his lightweight navy sports jacket as I approached. "Go on in," he told me. "An assistant is waiting to show you the body. I'll be right there."

No, thanks, I'll be fine. You don't need to go with me. I mean, I look at dead bodies all the time.

Tentatively I pushed the door open and stepped inside a large room with industrial tile floors and white walls. The door swooshed closed behind me, trapping me in the stark space. I stood blinking in the blue-white florescent light, surrounded by vaults that I knew contained bodies. Jeez. Were they all occupied? Two stainless-steel autopsy tables complete with wash-down hoses, cameras, and suspended microphones stood silently on either side of the room, awaiting their next customers.

"You Miz Cleo Cooper?" asked the only other person — well, *live* person — in the room, a young Asian man wearing a stiff white lab coat. He stood across the room in front of the wall of vaults, his dark hair slicked back. His name badge read LARRY TAN.

"Yes. I'm here to make an identification —"

"Over here please, ma'am," he said impatiently, sliding out a sheet-draped body.

I took a position opposite him, the body between us. I looked down, took a deep breath, nodded, and . . . Larry Tan's iPhone rang. Incredibly, he actually answered it, holding up one finger as if that made it okay. "Yeah. Yeah, I'm here, dude, hold on," he said, flipping the sheet from the face of the corpse and retreating to the far corner of the room, where he continued his conversation.

My first thought: who knew Smurfs got to be this big? My second was that besides the blue skin, he was in remarkably good shape for a dead person who'd been floating in the Atlantic Ocean for several days. At least his face was, and Lord knows I didn't want to know if the rest of him was intact. I could tell he was a very tall, heavyset man. He had long black hair, heavy facial stubble, and thick lips.

What caught my attention the most, however, were three long scratches on his left cheek. Pulling the sheet back just slightly from under his chin with two soon-to-be-scrubbed-clean fingers, I noted that they extended to his neck. Gingerly I lifted the sheet enough to expose his arm and hand. Just as I expected: very hairy, and his hands were huge. I let the sheet drop back in place and stood quietly beside.

I had every reason to believe this was my attacker, and yet, I couldn't be sure. I had gotten no sudden insight, no flash of clarity at seeing some feature I'd blanked out.

Atop the corpse's ankles rested a large manila envelope and a clear plastic bag with a drawstring. John Doe's clothes were folded in the plastic bag, but I couldn't see what was in the envelope. I looked to Tan. He was still in the corner, his back to me, engrossed in conversation. The buddy he was talking to must have been a real comic because the guy's shoulders were shaking with laughter, "Get out, man! Twenty feet? Just a two-liter diet soda and a Mentos?"

Good grief. Not wanting to interrupt their critical professional exchange, I decided it would be all right to open the envelope, which revealed only a cheap, drugstore watch.

There was something about the watch. I lifted it from the envelope. It had a link bracelet band in some type of polished silver metal, dented and scratched. I laid it against the scratches of my arm. It could have been what made them — hard to tell — but there followed no sudden burst of clarity. Well, maybe a little twinge of it, a flashback of trying to pull loose from a vise-like grip. Then I noticed something lodged between two of the links of the band that sent chills down my spine.

"Don't touch that!" Detective Sergeant Pierce commanded, banging the door open.

I jumped like a startled rabbit. The watch slipped from my fingers and dropped back into the envelope.

"Sorry," I managed to squeak.

"That's police property." His expression was disapproving as he glared in Tan's direction, then shouted, "Hey!"

Tan spun around, slapped his phone shut, and visibly paled. "Sir?" he croaked.

"What the hell are you doing way over there? Bodies are *never* to be viewed unattended!"

"Well, the exterior preliminary is over. Samples have been taken and the body's been thoroughly photographed, so I thought —"

"You thought you'd just change the rules to fit your social life?"

Tan grimaced but wisely chose not to respond.

"I'll be filing a report on you," Pierce said, then turned to me.

I wordlessly handed him the envelope, and he pulled out the watch. "Huh. I didn't notice this when I first examined the body on the beach." He removed a pair of tweezers from the pocket of his khakis along with an evidence bag, then pulled a small scrap of bright orange fabric from the underside of the watchband. It was no bigger than half a dime, but I was pretty sure the moment I saw it that I'd seen the fabric before. The bright orange hibiscus on Bud's lucky shirt flashed before my eyes.

He held it up eye level to me. "What color did you say your T-shirt was?"

Brushing invisible lint from my blouse, I made sure my face was deadpan before inspecting the tiny scrap. "I believe the Boston Proper catalogue described it as soft blush, certainly not Halloween orange," I sniffed.

"You didn't have on anything orange?"

"No. It's not my color."

"Well, I guess we just have your word for that, huh?"

"I guess."

Pierce glanced at the body, then back up

at me, and shrugged. "So, what do you think? This the guy who attacked you?"

"I'm not trying to be a smart aleck here, Detective, but how about a wallet? Didn't he have one with some ID in it?"

"Would we be here if he did?"

Well, it *was* a dumb question, but I'd been thrown off my game by the scrap of fabric. Except for the buzz of the florescent light overhead, the room grew quiet.

Then, in a slightly kinder tone, he asked, "So, again, is this the guy who attacked you?"

"Look," I said, "I know you were hoping for some definitive answer here, but I just can't be sure. I'm sorry."

"Actually, since I last talked to you, Captain Powell has confirmed that one of the crew members who operates a remote robot on the ship is missing. The guy hasn't returned home and there is no record of him flying out of any of the local airports. So, we're pretty sure this is Mr. Nuvuk Hunter, who did not report to work Wednesday. We're having two of his coworkers flown in to give us a positive ID."

I couldn't help myself, I snorted exasperatedly. "Then you didn't need me for identification at all."

"Correct. But keep in mind, Ms. Cooper,

my job is to find out not only *who* he is, but also to ascertain what happened to him."

"Maybe he just fell overboard and drowned."

"You mean *after* he attacked you?"

"No. I agree he's a highly likely candidate for my attacker, but like I said, I can't be positive. Moreover, the medical examiner hasn't ruled on his cause of death, since they haven't even done the autopsy yet. He could have died of natural causes, a heart attack, an aneurysm — hell, I don't know."

Having ushered me across the room, Pierce nodded to Tan, who was now off his phone, and opened the door leading to the hallway for me. I walked through, expecting him to make arrangements for another meeting. He didn't. Instead he headed off in the opposite direction.

We were about twenty paces apart when Pierce, in true Columbo fashion, called out to me, "Oh, by the way, Ms. Cooper?"

I turned back to him. "Yes?"

"You aren't planning on leaving town anytime soon, are you?"

My throat suddenly felt very dry and tight. "For the most part, I'll be in Morehead all summer. I do have a few consulting jobs that will take me away for several days at a time, but they're right here in North Carolina. Should I . . . inform you if I go anywhere?"

"Yeah, that'd probably be a good idea."

Eight

My Jeep, having been parked in the full sun for a little over an hour, was two degrees above Hell inside. Cranking the air conditioner to high, I exited the parking lot, still processing the fact that my attacker was more than likely dead and I would not be extracting any revenge. Was this cosmic retribution? Maybe. Right now, however, Bud Cooper retribution seemed the more reasonable explanation. Or, at least it would be in the eyes of the law — not by me. In my eyes, Bud Cooper might be a take-no-prisoners kind of business man, but I'd never seen him so much as harm a fly. I hit speed dial for him on my iPhone.

"Babe," he answered quietly, as if I'd caught him in the midst of something important.

"Uh, am I disturbing you?"

"Actually, I'm in a meeting, but we're about to break up. It's five thirty here. Can

I get back to you?"

"Where's *here*?"

"Paris."

"Paris? What?" I was incredulous. "I just talked to you yesterday! You didn't say anything about France. Why are you in Paris?"

"Can I . . . can I call you back?" he asked with his quiet voice again.

"Never mind, it's not important. Just tell me when you're coming back."

"Wednesday."

"Okay. I'll talk to you then."

I clicked off and made a beeline straight for Wrightsville Beach and Seahaven, Bud's old family beach house.

Lifting the third conch from the left in a line of shells that marched along the back porch railing, I shook it, holding my palm to catch the key Bud always kept there. Slipping in the door, I went straight upstairs to his room and carefully went through his closets and drawers looking for the horrid Hawaiian shirt he'd worn on the day of our tour of the *Magellan*. The one with the grotesque orange hibiscus blossoms all over it. I had to know if it was a match for the small scrap of material I'd seen twisted in the watchband of the corpse.

Downstairs, I flipped through the dirty clothes pile. Towels, hand cloths, and a few dish cloths, but no lucky shirt. My ex wasn't one to leave clothes lying around — one of his better points — so there was no point going through the other rooms. Before I left, however, I did check the wastebaskets and kitchen garbage. No luck there, either. Finally, I locked the house back up, still racking my brain as to where the shirt might be. I doubted, somehow, it was with Bud in chic Paris.

I crossed the long expanse of dunes via the raised wooden walkway, then trotted down the steps to the parking area by the road. Before getting back in my Jeep, I decided to check the trash can waiting for pick-up. Its contents included a pair of old sneakers, a mildewed boat cushion, and a full bag, which I rifled through to no avail. Then I headed to Morehead City with an uneasy feeling. If I had found the orange shirt, inspected it, and discovered no tear that looked like it could be filled by the small scrap from the watch, I would have felt better. I'd have known for sure Bud had nothing to do with the death of another human being because of me.

Had he started looking for me that night, as I had been looking for him, only to find I was about to be raped by an ape man and come to my aid? Had he attacked my attacker in a rage, getting a hole ripped in his shirt in the process? If that was what had happened, wouldn't he have destroyed the evidence? Was that why I couldn't find the orange shirt?

Later that Monday afternoon, I felt Tulip stir at my feet. I'd been in the upstairs office for an hour. Vivid rays of afternoon sun poured through the plantation shutters, decorating the sisal rug with slashes of light. I'd just finished paying current bills and making up my schedule for the coming weeks, keeping in mind the warning I'd received about leaving town, when my iPhone rang. Absentmindedly, I said, "Hey," without checking the caller.

"Uh, hey. Ms. Cooper?"

Time to note the ID: Global.

"Yes?"

"Hi. This is Phil Gregson at Global."

"Yes, Phil. How are you?"

"Well enough, thank you. But I'll be better if you say you can work in a trip out to the *Magellan.*" When I made no response, he continued. "With so much riding on this wildcat, I would be more comfortable if you could go out there."

"Is there a problem with Elton?"

"Well, let's just say there are some ambiguities in the interpretation of some of the samples. They're trying to mark the top of one of the formations. Mudloggers are saying one thing, I'm thinking another."

"What's Elton saying?"

"He seems to be in agreement with the mudloggers, but it's hard to tell. He's even more nervous than before, if that's possible. Keeps obsessing about personnel descent lines and safety stations . . ."

My chest tightened at the thought of being back on the *Magellan.* Then there was the helicopter ride out . . . oh joy. Plus, I no longer had the fuel of revenge lighting a fire under me. It had been replaced by the creeping fog of the unknown — that missing time from when I fainted on the ROV platform until I woke up in my bunk on the *Magellan* — had been pushing hard at the back of my consciousness. Finding the orange scrap of fabric that might or might not be from Bud's lucky shirt had only increased my desire to fill in the blanks.

If returning to the *Magellan* would help dispel the fog and reveal what I needed to know — good or bad — then that was what I should do. Surely Detective Pierce would have no objection to me being a few miles offshore of Morehead City. Well, 136 miles, but who's counting?

"When would you like me to go?"

"Just as soon as you can work it in. All you need to do is check with our operations shorebase and they'll arrange transportation. Helicopter or boat, whichever you prefer. The office manager's name is Wanda. Call me if you have any problems."

"All right," I said, hearing the beep that indicated another call. "I'll make arrangements right now." I clicked over. "Yes?"

"Sorry it took me so long to get back to you," Bud said.

"I thought we'd agreed to talk Wednesday when you get home, so you're early. Maybe it's good you called now, though," I said, thinking aloud, "because I might not be here Wednesday — not in town, anyway, if you were thinking of dropping by before going to Seahaven."

"Actually I was. Where are you going?"

"To the *Magellan.* Phil Gregson just called. He's got some doubts about the readings coming up from the wellbore, with the larger problem being the lack of confidence in Elton. I can't go tomorrow because I need to run errands, so Wednesday it is."

"You won't stay overnight, will you?"

Did I detect a note of anxiety? "I hope

not," I said. "Why?"

"Nothing. No reason." Bud cleared his throat. "How long will you be staying?"

"Probably just a couple of hours," I said. "In fact I need to call right now and see about catching a ride out on one of the supply boats."

"Supply boat? For heaven's sake, Cleo, this is why the military invented helicopters. Learn to enjoy them."

"Actually, Da Vinci came up with the idea, and frankly, I don't think they've progressed much since his time. So, no thanks, I'll stick with the boat."

After putting in a help-is-on-the-way call to Elton and with quitting time fast approaching, I drove over to the port and Global's shorebase. While the company headquarters was in Houston, its deep water group was in New Orleans. Exploratory wells located in far-flung parts of the globe use the closest port as a temporary shorebase of operations. In the case of Manteo One, that was Morehead City.

"Can I help you?" asked a tan, fit woman. Her spiky brown hair was tastefully highlighted, her face deeply lined and weathered, yet her lips were full and her bright blue eyes sparkled. Her accent was Cajun.

"Are you Wanda?"

"Sure am, doll, and I bet I know who you are," she said, scrambling through some papers on her desk and retrieving a Post-it note. "Ms. Cleo Cooper?"

"That's me," I said.

"We don't get a lot of woman boarding, only a few, but not enough to make my guess a risky one," she laughed. "Got your TWIC card?"

I pulled out my Transportation Worker Identification Credential, a tamperproof biometric card required by the Coast Guard, the Department of Homeland Security, and the TSA for anyone boarding a commercial exploration vessel. She checked it and handed me a form. "Sign here, here, and here. Just liability release forms. Helicopters are based over in Beaufort — 'course you already know that — and supply boats run out of here. Here's your port pass, a boarding pass for the *Magellan,* and a list of all the numbers you'll need, including mine." She'd made a tidy stack of document in front of me as she spoke.

"Thanks."

"I'm going to chase you outta here now, 'cause I got a bunch of errands to run and a hot date tonight." She laughed, then said, "Oh. If you want, you can make arrangements direct with any of the captains if you catch 'em at the dock. I believe Eddie's down there now on one of the crew boats."

I said a quick goodbye and made my way across the yard, my feet crunching on a zillion tiny limestone fossils in the marl that had been hauled in to create the enormous square-shaped port. I was headed to the western seawall, where three supply boats were docked. Exploration companies like Global don't own their own, but instead contract with others maintaining a fleet of different types of boats, each designed and outfitted to meet the specific needs of the rig being serviced. In this case Global had hired a Louisiana outfit, Belou Brothers. I drew near the boats as I mused about the complicated mess of contractors and subcontractors involved in such a huge undertaking — no wonder it was costing so much money.

Three of Belou's heavy-duty steel boats were tied up at the dock. All had bright-blue hulls and white superstructure and ranged between 100 and 200 feet. Two of them were veritable beehives of activity: one was being loaded with large tanks of drilling mud, the other with pipe. Hopping aboard the third boat — a 108-foot crew boat appropriately named *Iron Responder* — I climbed metal stairs to a helm station and tapped on the thick glass window.

The captain waved me inside. A thin, mustachioed man of about fifty with dense, white hair pulled in a short mullet, he introduced himself as Eddie Cheramie. Said to call him Captain Eddie. In no time I'd arranged to make the 136-mile trip out to the *Magellan,* departure scheduled Wednesday morning at the ungodly hour of 3:30 a.m.

When the alarm went off, I jerked awake, having slept for what seemed like ten minutes, and wished not for the first time that I was a morning person. I'm not, and this was a serious morning. That my short sleep had been marred by tossing and squirming, thinking still about that scrap of orange material, didn't help me feel all bright and shiny either. I'd managed to get all my little errands done yesterday, but returning to the *Magellan* had my emotions running high.

By the time I'd parked the Jeep and taken a sip of the giant coffee I'd picked up at the Kangaroo station, I was a bit more pulled together. Part of me was resistant to what lay ahead, but I sensed that another part was actually eager. I hate mysteries, is all. I needed to know.

"Morning, Miss," Captain Eddie said. "Find a seat anywhere you like. It'll be a few more minutes before we depart, so just make yourself at home."

I dropped my pack in a seat and went to the window to watch a crane operator load boxes of food stores on the *Iron Responder*'s deck. Behind me about twenty sleepy crew members began to file aboard carrying duffel bags. Most MODUs — mobile offshore drilling units — have crews that work fourteen-day shifts.

A low rumble of engines was followed by a shudder and a slight lurch. The *Responder* was dancing in her lines like a racehorse pushing on the gate. We were about to get underway. Several dock workers tossed lines to crewmen as I took my seat. Then Captain Eddie, one deck above me, spun the bow of the boat smartly into the channel and we were off.

As we slipped past Radio Island on our port side at a sedate speed, the Civil War gun mounts at Fort Macon showed themselves on the starboard side. Once we were beyond the rolling swells of Beaufort Inlet, the captain throttled down on the engines until we planed off in the open Atlantic. From past fishing trips in this area, I knew we would keep this heading until we rounded the Knuckle Buoy, which marked the end of Cape Lookout shoals. At around twenty knots per hour, the trip would take at least four hours, so I reclined my seat a little and settled back to enjoy the beauty of the ocean before sunrise. Even though I knew what our arrival would bring, I relaxed.

But all good things, as we know, must end.

As we came alongside the *Magellan,* I picked two extremely tough-looking guys in gray jumpsuits to follow as they moved up in the line waiting for the air tugger, or personnel basket. This demonic device is used to raise passengers from the crew boat sometimes as much as 40 feet to the deck of the rig. Picture a large drawstring purse made of fish net with a round, flat bottom. Suspend it from a crane and you've got a pretty good idea what an air tugger looks like.

Worse still, crane operators often think it's funny to dunk new people in the water. That's why it's wise to ride up with guys he wouldn't want to take on. Making sure my life vest was pulled tight, I stuffed myself between my new large friends, tossed my pack in the center with their duffels, grabbed the rope netting, and hung on for dear life as the crane lifted us aboard and set us gently on the deck. At this point, everyone, including me, set off on their appointed jobs.

With only a few hours before the *Responder* was fully unloaded and ready to head back to port, I wanted to complete all my tasks, after which I hoped to have a few minutes to revisit the ROV platform. This time, in the full light of day.

Collecting my hard hat, I went first to the radio operator to have my name added to the POB — personnel on board — list and be assigned a lifeboat station. Then I went to find Captain Duncan Powell to let him know I was aboard.

I didn't have to go far. Powell was standing at the bottom of the stairs leading from the helipad, having what seemed like a tense discussion with Braxton Roberts, the company man. They stopped talking and stared at me as though drawing a blank as to who I was.

Saving them embarrassment, I put my hand out to the hawk-nosed captain and said, "Cleo Cooper, I'm —"

"Oh, right, you're Bud Cooper's wife, the wellsite geologist."

"Ex-wife," I said. "And Elton Patterson's the wellsite geologist. I'm just helping out."

"Glad to have you aboard," he said. Giving me a pat on the shoulder, he explained to Roberts, "She's basically here to calm Phil Gregson by making sure he gets the information he needs when he needs it."

"Yes, glad to have you aboard," Roberts said. Terse but polite.

"Well, speaking of that," I said, "I'd better get to work. Nice to see you both again." As soon as I walked away, headed for the logging lab, I could hear their heated discussion start up again. It seemed the relationship between the company man and the site manager was a fractious one.

One of the most important tasks of the mudlogger is to record in real time the lithology, or mineral makeup, of the rocks in the well hole. They mostly accomplish this through analysis of rock chips returned to the surface in the drilling mud and sifted out in large shaking screens. If the drill is penetrating a soft rock, it moves faster, and samples have to be collected and analyzed very quickly. Since Phil wasn't happy with the daily readouts he was receiving, my job was to identify the problem, correct it, and facilitate the flow of information.

I entered the trailer and introduced myself to a crew-cut, middle-aged mudlogger from Texas named Charlie. We looked at the newest samples to come up in the mud, and I collected several to study at home later. When I asked him how things were going with Elton, he looked a little annoyed. "Well, some of them guys in the crew think it's kinda funny to scare somebody."

Uh-oh. "What do you mean?"

"Well . . . Elton was up on the derrick — I'd say about forty feet — checking the kelly-height sensor. I don't know who was on deck holding the other end of the cable he was harnessed to. Anyway, *somehow* he . . . lifted and swung out a little. They lowered him right away, but not before he screamed like a girl. I think it might've embarrassed him a bit."

My eyes must have looked like they were about to pop from their sockets, because he hastily added, "There's no way he was ever in danger. He had on a safety harness."

That explained Elton's obsession with safety and knowing every possible way off the ship. Poor man. Curbing my impatience with such stupid guy tricks, I asked, "Did he complain about it or make a report to Mr. Powell?"

"No ma'am," he said.

"Then let's not mention it again, okay?"

"Yes ma'am."

Gathering my samples, I quickly made my

way to Elton's office, where he was working on his daily report. After we'd gone over what had occurred downhole and what type of rocks had been drilled during my absence, I took a breath and said, "I know about what happened with the crew and your trapeze act."

He stared at the floor waiting to hear what I was going to say next.

Feigning the impatience of a mother with a daredevil child, I admonished him, saying, "I know those types of antics don't scare you guys and you need a little something to fight boredom. But understand they *do* scare me, so find some other way of staying amused."

"Uh, yes ma'am."

"That said, I very much approve of your safety station checks. Mr. Gregson mentioned what a swell job you're doing there." I checked my watch. There was still an hour before the crew boat departed, leaving plenty of time for a visit to the ROV platform. "Well," I said, standing, "that's about it. I'll be in touch later tonight."

Elton stood as I left and, while I couldn't be sure, I thought I detected a whiff of cockiness that hadn't been there before.

As I climbed the stairs to the platform, I was relieved to see no one was working with the ROV. I walked around it again much as I had the night of the attack, only this time I looked to the glass control box at the top of the crane. It was unoccupied now. I walked to the edge of the platform and looked down at the water so far below. A chill crept over me remembering the night of the attack — those feelings of desperation and terror so intense I'd rather have jumped than submit, even though the consequences would probably have been fatal.

Had it just been a strange twist of fate that preserved me, or human intervention? Would I ever know? I knew confronting Bud was step number one in finding the answers I needed — but I couldn't do it. What if he *had* killed this Nuvuk Hunter? What would I do then?

And, if all that wasn't enough, I'd let the gambler in me — the same one who dwells in all prospectors — take over and run roughshod over my common sense. What I'd failed to tell Bud was that I'd gone way out on a limb on this deal. I had actually put up the future royalty income I was set to receive from my quarry deal as collateral for a loan hefty enough to allow me to play with the big boys.

While my contribution to our investment group was certainly nothing like Bud's $15 million, and a pittance when compared to our group as a whole, it was big bucks for me. Moreover, the possibility existed that everything — and I did mean *everything* — I'd saved would be gone. I'd used my $1.5 million along with $3.5 — borrowed from the same friendly banker who'd given me the money to clinch the granite deal — to reach the nice round number of $5 million. While I wouldn't be out on the street if we hit a duster, I'd definitely be back on a boloney-and-cheese diet for years and years.

No granite quarry income, no retirement account, no real savings.

Usually investor groups like ours partner with major oil companies through large investment institutions such as banks, trust funds, and hedge funds. But that means buying into the hedge fund and not necessarily buying a particular deal, thereby diluting the profit. In our case, Bud was the managing partner of our fund, and we were investing directly as working interest holders. While that meant a much higher return on our investment, it also guaranteed that hitting a dry hole would constitute a complete loss of our money.

But the worst part? Bud would know I'd been foolhardy. I couldn't have that. I'd been very proud that he hadn't questioned me about the size of my investment. That meant what he'd told me after I'd cobbled together the financing for my granite quarry — that he'd been impressed at my ability to put together such a complicated deal — had been true. I didn't want to do anything to erode the real progress we'd made toward the new post-divorce equality we seemed to be reaching.

I inhaled deeply, drinking in the beauty of the day, the far horizon, the gentle lift of ocean swells against the ship. Sea birds dove hungrily into schools of bait fish that swarmed in the turbulent currents created by the ship's giant thrusters. Just then, an air return came on below me and caught my attention. Looking down through the grating, I spotted, on top of the ventilation housing, the metal wheel I'd been trying to pry loose the night of the attack. But as I started back down the stairs, my iPhone vibrated in my pocket.

Pulling it out, I checked the screen: Detective Sergeant Pierce. I decided to return the call later when I'd be sure of uninterrupted service. At forty-five miles from shore, as the crow flies, I was at the maximum reach for cell transmission. I shoved the phone back in my pocket and went after the wheel.

That's when I heard footfalls on the catwalk above me. "Cleo!" a voice shouted.

NINE

"Stay there, I'll come to you!"

Struck speechless, I gawked as the last person in the world I would have expected to see rushed headlong down the stairs to me: the young Russian I'd met in Louisiana. Before I could stop him, Viktor Kozlov grabbed me and gave me an exuberant hug.

"Whoa," I said, politely pushing from his embrace.

"I can hardly believe this . . . the way we keep meeting," Viktor said. "And look at you. Even more beautiful than I remember."

Work duds, no makeup, and a hard hat. Yep, a regular Aphrodite. I scanned the area. Fortunately, no one was nearby. Some of the things I'd done with this kid came to mind, and I knew I was blushing. That really ticked me off. I struggled to regain my professionalism. "What on earth are you doing here?" I blurted.

His smile broadened. "I work here. Don't

you remember, I told you I had resumes out with ROV companies?"

Past conversations, in fact, were *not* what I remembered about him, but I didn't say so. Instead I said, "Yes, so you said, it's just I never expected you'd actually get a job, you being a student and all."

"Actually, being a student worked in my favor."

"How's that?" I asked skeptically.

But he ignored my question and instead, his eyes getting all dreamy, he said softly, "I have to say, I've missed the way you called me . . . Vic-*ter* that night we were together. It was so charming, so . . . what's the word . . . rural?"

"I *hope* the word you're looking for is *Southern,* as in a Southern accent," I said dryly.

"Yes," he laughed his wonderful laugh. It was almost enough to pull a smile from me, but not quite. "That's probably the word I'm looking for. But what about you? I didn't expect to find you in the employ of Global too."

"Oh, I'm not," I said. "I'm just here consulting."

An uncomfortable silence bloomed between us. He must have sensed my anxiety because he took a few steps back, leaned against the ROV's cage, and studied me. I studied him back. God, he was hot even in an orange jumpsuit and hard hat. I gave up trying to remember any past career discussions. "So who are you working for?"

Viktor stepped away from the ROV, answering with a nod in its direction.

Duh. "Oh, right, Voyager."

"Yes. They called me last Wednesday and said they needed someone who could come out here right away and would be interested in working only on a job-by-job basis. Of course this is perfect for me, as I'll be working on my dissertation during the winter months. That's what I meant when I said my being a student is an asset."

I nodded my understanding.

"So," he said, extending his arms in a here-I-am gesture. "I flew to their headquarters in Texas, went through training, and Saturday was transported out here."

"What about your other job?"

"With the geophysical surveying company? Yes, I'm glad you remember." Viktor now grinned. "Mr. Duchamp was sad to see me go, but he understood. And, after what happened to the guy I'm replacing — he fell overboard in the middle of the night, did you hear? — and because his sons make up the rest of the team, I think he wanted me here. Maybe to help watch out for them."

"His twin sons? The ones I met at the party?"

"That's right."

"They work for Voyager too?"

"Yes," Viktor said. Then, abruptly, he shifted gears. "Aren't you happy to see me? You left so very quickly . . ."

Now there's one for the books, I thought. It's not every day your last one-night stand turns up unexpectedly replacing the guy who died trying to rape you. I had to ask, "Did you know the . . . fellow who fell overboard?"

"No. I'm told he was from Alaska, where he'd been dragging seismic cable. Duchamp met him up there and offered him a full-time job if he came back to Louisiana, so he did. After several years he quit Davy and was hired by Voyager, where he learned to be a pilot. The twins said he was a good worker but" — he spoke as if remembering their exact words — "couldn't hold his booze. We don't know the details, but it's being said he got drunk and fell overboard."

The last bit was spoken as though it were a secret, but it sounded like a stupid rumor to me. "Hell, you can't even have a lighter on board, let alone alcohol." Which didn't stop Bud from tying one on with the boys over poker that night, so who knew?

Viktor just shrugged. "Sad to say, but one person's tragedy is another's opportunity. Well, enough of that. Come. The twins will want to say hello. They are in the galley — we're on a break." He put his arm around my shoulder and began to usher me to the stairs.

Slipping out from his casual embrace, I said, "I'll meet you there. First I need to go, um . . . take care of something I forgot to do . . . in the logging lab. I only have a little while before I have to catch the boat back to port."

"Then hurry, Cleo," he said, cheekily. "See you in the galley."

I made my exit into the maze of aisles created by stacks of supplies and equipment. After a few moments, I checked to make sure Viktor was out of sight before returning to retrieve the strange little metal wheel. I quickly pocketed it, then hurried to the galley.

"Cleo," Viktor said, standing and pulling out a chair for me. "You remember Tim and Dean Duchamp?"

"I certainly do," I said, shaking their hands as they stood to greet me. They were of average height and build, their brown hair parted and combed identically. "I'm sorry to hear about what happened to your co-worker," I said. "Was he a good friend?"

The young men looked at each other with obvious discomfort before Tim spoke up. "I wouldn't say that. Dad sometimes put us on jobs with him. Then, fortunately, he went to work for Voyager a couple of years ago."

"Fortunately?"

A sheepish expression crossed Tim's face. "It's just that he wasn't the brightest light in the hall and he . . . well . . . he was downright mean sometimes."

"You shouldn't speak ill of the dead." Reminding his brother of this, Dean turned to me. "He was an experienced pilot. That's why they put us with him for this job as Team One. It's the first time we've worked with him since the Voyager deal."

"Team One?" I said.

"The one in charge of the ROV during the spudding process. Voyager leaves a first team in place until routine drilling starts. By Monday, we'll have been out here for two complete rotations."

"Are you guys pilots too?" I asked.

"No," Tim said. "We both have engineering degrees. But Dean has a double major in computer sciences, so he does the programming of the unit. I specialize in welding, pipe fitting, deployment, that type of thing."

"And now that Nuvuk is gone, Viktor's our pilot," Dean said. "He's got lots of experience."

I looked at Viktor. "Yes," he said. "Back in Russia I was a pilot during the daytime, a student at night."

There was plenty I didn't know, but it also was no time for catching up on Viktor's resume. I felt my cell vibrate. Retrieving it, I checked the screen — Pierce again — and said, "What made you guys decide to become ROV techs?" I put away the phone.

"Working for our dad," Tim said, laughing. "We've done every type of job SeaTrek offers, and he didn't like the way we did *any* of them."

Dean chimed in. "We decided to get jobs somewhere else —"

"— but we didn't want to leave the ocean —" Tim continued.

"— so we decided on working in the very diverse ROV industry," Dean said, finishing the sentence.

"Oh, come on," Viktor said. "Your dad's great and you know it. He is simply . . . demanding."

"That he is," Dean agreed. "Well, break's over, and Captain Powell runs a tight ship.

It was nice to meet you, Miss Cleo." He rose from the table in unison with his twin. They pushed their chairs in and left.

"I must go as well," said Viktor. As we scooped up our hard hats and headed for the door, he added, "Not to worry, though, I have your address over on the beach. As soon as I finish my rotation, I'll come by to see you. We'll do something fun."

Figuring now was as good a time as any to set things straight, I stopped at the door. "Viktor," I said, being careful to use the proper Russian pronunciation, "about that. While I had a lovely time with you in Port Fourchon, that was then and this is now. I know you care as much about your professional life as I do, and since this ship is our workplace, you have to agree that it would be a bad idea to . . . engage in any more . . . fun things."

He totally ignored my attempt to let him down easy. "Now that the well is completely spudded and drilling is underway, the teams will go back to regular fourteen-day rotations. Ours ends Monday when a replacement crew comes in. We'll get together then."

"Didn't you hear what I just said?"

Viktor opened the galley door for me. The roar of diesel engines and generators mixed with the deafening hiss of a sand blaster, making conversation difficult. To add to the cacophony, the loudspeaker bleated three chimes, the warning to be at the crew boat in five minutes or be prepared to spend the night.

"Listen," I said, trying to raise my voice above the din, "I've got to run. That's my boat leaving. Remember, next time we see each other . . . strictly professional, right?"

Viktor donned his hard hat, lifted mine from my hands, put his lips to my ear, and said, *"Ne boysya, milaya moya."* He then planted my hat back on my head, squeezed my shoulder, and left.

"What?" I called after him, but another wave of the sand blaster blew my words to the wind.

On the way back to Morehead, I tried to return Detective Pierce's call but only reached his voicemail. I left my name and number, unable to quell the queasy feeling I got wondering why was he trying to reach me. Had the medical examiner ruled on the cause of death? I'd become convinced that the corpse I'd seen had been my attacker and was fervently hoping for a finding of accidental drowning. That would be one less complication to deal with. Maybe that pesky Pierce would even write off the scrap of material as work related and I wouldn't have to worry about Bud living out his days in the slammer because of me.

When I got home late Wednesday afternoon, the black Crown Victoria parked in my drive told me my new little friends, Detectives Pierce and Myers, were back and the day was about to get longer.

Down by the dock Tulip yelped a greeting and hopped out of Henri's boat, where she'd apparently been keeping Will company. He had the cover off of the outboard motor and was working on it. He looked up as she loped across the yard to greet me. I tossed him a wave. "What's up?" I called.

"Not much. Just setting Henri's timing!" He bent back to his task as I went inside.

A laughing Henri sat at the kitchen table, batting her eyes and flirting shamelessly with the detectives, regardless of the fact that both guys were old enough to be her father. Oh well. As far as I was concerned, softening them up before they questioned me again couldn't hurt. Both men rose courteously from their seats at my entrance.

"What's going on?" I asked

"Oh, hi, Mom," Henri said. "These very nice policemen came to see you. I told them you'd be back soon, and here you are. I've been keeping them company."

I'd had experience with cops once before when a body turned up on a piece of property where I was doing exploration work. In that instance, the sheriff and his deputies were fairly amenable. These detectives on the other hand . . . well. I slipped my poker face snugly into place.

Pierce cleared his throat and said, "We need to talk to your mom now, Henri. Thanks for your time. And for your hospitality." Both men, I noted, had Cokes in front of them.

"No problem," Henri said, then looked at me, "Mom?"

"It's okay," I said. "Go check on Will. He's working on your boat."

"What? I told him to leave that motor alone." The door slammed and she was gone.

Pierce pulled out a chair for me, and they reseated themselves.

"We just wanted to let you know the ME has done his work. The preliminary ruling is drowning" — my heart soared as Pierce paused to pull his trusty little spiral notebook from his pocket — "following trauma to the back of his skull by a blunt object."

My heart sank. "What?"

"Yeah, apparently the crack in his skull

wasn't obvious when he was first brought in because the body had been in the water."

Both men stared at me, looking, I assumed, for a reaction. When I just stared back, Pierce asked, "So does hearing about the killing, that it was a blow to the back of the head with a blunt object, jog your memory? Give you any . . . insight? Any clarity?"

"No."

Pierce looked at Myers, who said, as if on cue, "Well, the toxicology report isn't back yet. Maybe we'll know more then."

"Right," added Pierce. "We'll keep you abreast of any information in the case as we get it."

I gave him a what-the-hell-for look.

"After all," he said with feigned patience, "we're still trying to jump start your memory of that night, aren't we?"

I nodded but wondered if this indicated some manipulative police psychology. Make the suspect think they're helping with the investigation, then catch them in some kind of stupid slipup.

"For instance, we ran Mr. Hunter's name through NCIC and he popped up right away. He was charged twice in Alaska with rape, but both times the charges were dropped. The victims changed their minds."

Jeez. How could a guy like that get employed on a drillship? It didn't make sense.

"Thoughts?" Myers asked.

"Actually, I'm wondering how he got employed with a rape record."

"He was only *charged* with rape, not convicted. And the only reason I can think of why an employer probably didn't feel it necessary to do a criminal background check is because someone pulled strings for him."

"More thoughts?" Myers chimed in again.

"What now, is all." Then I shrugged.

"We have a bit of a strange situation here," Pierce said. "Our usual procedure in the case of murder is to immediately cordon off the crime scene and have CSI go over it. But, in this case, the crime scene —"

"If there is one," I interjected.

Both detectives nodded. Then Pierce continued, "The *potential* crime scene, then, is somewhat out of our jurisdiction. Add to that the fact that days went by before the body washed up miles away, during which time the scene was contaminated by the day-to-day activities there . . ."

"But we are still inclined to want to see it," Myers added. "Tomorrow, in fact."

"Good luck with getting on a working drillship without certification and a TWIC card," I said, knowing that quickly obtaining these would be nearly impossible under ordinary circumstances. "Even if you managed it, your department would still have to be willing to drop about fifteen large on a helicopter ride out there." I could tell I'd gotten their attention by the sudden look of surprise that came over their faces. "Unless you're an employee with transportation provided by the operator or the subcontracted company you work for, *or* you're a VIP guest of the operator, you're responsible for your own transportation. I don't think you guys fall under the VIP category, do you?"

"We don't have to," Pierce said, "We're good friends with the fellows out at our local Coast Guard Station at Fort Macon. They're all the permission we need, plus they're going to ride us *and* a CSI team out to the *Magellan.*"

Anger and frustration boiled up in me. "Need I remind you, you're entering my workplace and could seriously endanger my position there?"

"How so?" asked Myers innocently.

"You know damn well if it got around that I was involved in an attempted rape that ended with one of the crew dying, it would make my professional relationships there even more difficult than they already are. In case you haven't noticed, I work in a male-dominated industry, especially when it comes to offshore exploration. Right now the word on board is the guy fell overboard and drowned. Why can't you leave it at that?"

"Because the back of the victim's skull was crushed, Ms. Cooper. Because you were there. Because you conveniently can't remember anything."

"What would my motive be?"

"Self-defense comes to mind. But there's also the nagging fact that you said nothing to the captain of the ship."

"What would I say? Hell, I couldn't even identify the guy I grappled with! What would be the point?"

"How about this," Pierce said, standing. "The investigation is still ongoing, but we'll make sure your name isn't mentioned in connection with the case while we're out there."

I sighed and said nothing. Pierce hesitated at the door. I waited, unsurprised at his ploy. "We've ascertained that your husband . . . er, ex-husband, is out of the country. When's he supposed to be back?"

"I don't know." I shrugged again.

Pierce pursed his lips and nodded like he'd expected my answer, much as I'd anticipated his throwing in one last question.

My callers had hardly made it to their cars when Henri came back in, Tulip close on her heels. She opened the large oval crock pot on the counter, releasing a cloud of steam redolent of baked chicken and vegetables. Poking around in it, she asked with understandable curiosity, "Why did those detectives want to talk to you about some guy falling off that drillship? I mean, just because you and Dad are invested —"

"I guess because we were out there that night. Remember, we had to stay overnight because of the storm? Speaking of Dad, he's supposed to be back from Paris today. Have you heard from him yet?"

"Yeah. I thought you knew — he's not coming back today. In fact, Will is going over to stay with him for a while. He's leaving tomorrow."

"What?" I said, as I set the table for supper and poured the tea. "Did Will say why he's going?"

"Yeah," Henri said, slicing wedges from a head of iceberg lettuce. "Get this, he said Dad needs him to update his computer . . . Oh, and don't set him a place, he says he's already eaten and needs time to get his stuff packed."

"Why can't your father have Will work on his computer at his house in Raleigh or at Seahaven? Why does he have to go all the way to Paris?"

Henri shrugged. "Good question."

TEN

After dinner I moved up to my office. There, rotating the circular stage of my old microscope, I examined a sample of freshly washed cuttings from the well. The ticking of the clock and Tulip's soft snuffles as she chased some critter in her sleep were my only distractions.

I jotted notes in preparation for the call I'd make to Phil Gregson as soon as I'd gone through all the samples. He'd said to call him, no matter the time. I glanced up at the clock, a little disgusted that it was so late. I'd have been finished by now if I hadn't had to take time for Pierce and Myers. I removed the sample and replaced it with another. I was studying it when Henri walked in.

"You're working hard," she said.

"Sometimes that's what it takes," I said. "The thing is, this job came up in a hurry and there's pressure for a return report." I looked up and registered her expression. "Hon, do you need me for something else? What's bothering you?" Mothers can always tell, which is both a blessing and a curse.

"Well . . ."

"Spit it out. Clearly something's up."

"I just thought you should be aware of the interest in your project around town."

"How so?"

"It's pretty much everywhere — in the shops, on the beach even. The bars are full of it. Even when I was getting my hair cut the other day, that's all they were talking about. How they'd be affected if you guys make an oil discovery. A lot of people are upset."

"Gas," I said patiently. "We're expecting to find natural gas, not oil. Big difference. So do you think the overall feeling's good or bad?"

She thought for a moment. "Most people I know really hope you guys find something. They know it'll improve the economy, and they want the work. But there are others, green-minded types, who seem to despise any kind of energy unless it's a wind turbine."

"I didn't know you were so political."

"I'm not, but I listen to people. And I'm just telling you what I hear. Some of those folks aren't making any sense."

"Well, here's my advice — just steer clear of these discussions. You can't win them even when you're right. Their minds are closed; the far-flung environmentalists, I mean. I could give you the ammunition to shut them up — chapter and verse about turbines versus gas platforms and their relative pollution issues — but it wouldn't matter." I paused. "Anyway, we're about halfway done with the well, so it won't be much longer before we know what we've got."

"Wow. That's fast. How far down are you drilling now?"

"Oh, just past five thousand feet. We're in some thin layers of mid-Miocene sandstone, silt, and shale." Checking my watch, I said, "I'm sorry, but it's almost ten o'clock and I've got to make a call. We can talk more about this later if you want to, okay?"

She came over and kissed the top of my head in reply.

After I reached Phil and gave him a rundown of my findings, I was just about to pull up Elton's number when he beat me to it. "My lag time calculations are suddenly all off!" he gasped. He was practically hyperventilating. "I've checked everything and can't figure out what's goin' on."

Several complications that affect the lag

time came to mind. This is the time it takes for a sample of rock chips to move from the bit to the surface in offshore wells as opposed to a land-based wells — the only wells Elton had experience with.

"Calm down, Elton," I said. "Take a deep breath." I waited a few seconds. "Everything's been fine up to now, so give me the details. Where are you in the well right now?"

Less agitated but still not happy, Elton dutifully listed the particulars. Nothing seemed amiss. Then I had an idea. I said, "Go down to the drill floor and check with Mr. Grant. The drillers could have added another pump to the base of the riser pipe and failed to inform you."

Only the hum of cyberspace let me know we were still connected. I drew a mental picture for him. "The drill pipe feeds down through the riser pipe that runs from the ship to the seafloor, right?"

"Yeah, of course," he said impatiently.

"So, since the riser is so much larger in diameter, if the drillers increased the pressure and velocity with another pump, it'd naturally throw off your calculations."

"Oh, man! Why I didn't think of that?"

"Because you're tired. Call me back if that's not the problem. If it is, that means you need to improve communications with the drillers. Make sure they know they *have* to inform you of things like this."

"Yes ma'am."

"And, Elton — after you straighten this out, get some rest."

"Yes ma'am."

As I clicked off, a yawn big enough to engulf my head overtook me, so I decided to call myself professionally finished for the day. I went to Will's room. His door was closed. I knocked softly but got no answer. Henri was just coming back up the stairs, a bowl of ice cream in her hands.

"He's already gone to bed," she whispered. "His plane leaves at seven so he has to be at Wilmington International at five."

"Okay," I said. "See you in the morning."

I gathered my discarded clothes and was about to carry them to the chute when I felt something in the pocket of my jeans. My artifact! I'd forgotten all about it what with the shock of seeing Viktor again and being interrogated by the detectives this afternoon.

I fished out the metal piece and inspected it. Obviously it had been underwater for a long time because it was encrusted with very tiny barnacles and stained almost black. I scratched gently at the encrustation with a metal nail file and discovered the little wheel had at one time been painted bright red. Deciding it needed rinsing, I put it under the tap. Once the surface was clean, though, I was still none the wiser about its purpose — or its history. I set it on my nightstand for further contemplation.

Going to bed proved a waste of time. I wiggled and squirmed until I'd practically worried the sheets off the bed. Around midnight Tulip hopped off in a huff and curled up in a chair by the window. I dozed intermittently, but every time I woke, the same thought came to my mind: What were Pierce and Myers going to find tomorrow on the *Magellan*? Would it be something to implicate me? Had I pushed King Kong, a.k.a. Nuvuk Hunter, overboard and blocked it out? Or would they find something to implicate Bud? I wanted to talk to him in the worst kind of way. It would be easy enough. As soon as MaxRoam had become available in cell phones, he'd made sure I had it so I could reach him no matter where I was. Divorced or not, he insisted I keep it because of the children.

At 2:14 a.m., with sleep still evading me, I pulled him up on my iPhone. Since Paris was six hours ahead, he'd probably be having breakfast somewhere. There was a problem though. Without coming right out and asking, I couldn't think how to find out if he'd come to my rescue that night on the *Magellan.* After putting the phone back on my nightstand and repeatedly picking it up again, I finally decided to stop torturing myself and call him.

"Hi, babe, how's the drilling going?"

"Good." I then proceeded to catch him up on the mundane work details.

When I finished, he said, "That all sounds great. How much longer do you think it'll be before we reach the pay zone?"

"Couple of weeks, if all goes well and we don't run into any snags. When we reach our target formation, we'll do a series of test logs, then make a decision on what we have and whether we need to drill any lateral wells. Of course, if it's a dry hole, that's another story."

"That's not going to happen," he said positively. "When are you going back out?"

"Well, not tomorrow." I took a deep breath. "Remember the body you told me about, the one the police suspected might have been one of the crew from the *Magellan*?"

"Yeah. What's up with that?" I was listening carefully. Had his tone changed?

"Well, it turns out he was an employee of

one of the contractors out there — Voyager, the ROV company."

"Stands to reason. Wonder what happened to him?" I wasn't detecting any extra note of concern, but I knew Bud could be cagey.

"I don't know, but the police feel further investigation is warranted and they're going out there, assisted by the Coast Guard. Best if I stay out of the way, is how I see it."

A few seconds of silence followed. "You don't think they'll cause any delays on the well do you?" What I detected now — and it didn't take Sherlock Holmes — was genuine worry.

"At half a million dollars a day, Braxton Roberts won't allow that to happen. I'm sure it's the one time your pal Duncan Powell will be glad he's out there."

More silence. Then Bud said, "I'm really looking forward to spending some time with Will."

"I was going to ask you about that," I said.

"Later. Right now, I've really got to run, babe."

As Henri and I finished our cereal the next morning, she said, "So where are you off to today? Didn't you mention something about prospecting?"

"Yep. Somewhere west of Fayetteville but

not as far as Charlotte. I'm looking for sand and gravel." I picked up my pack by the door. Tulip was eager to be off on our expedition and was urging me on. I held the door open for her. "I'll let you know where we're overnighting when I decide. I should be able to finish up between now and the end of the weekend. Call or text if you need me."

"And you're coming back Sunday?"

"Yes, Mom," I said sarcastically. I started to follow Tulip.

"Wait. What time Sunday?"

"Why?"

"Some friends are coming down from Raleigh and we're going on one of those scuba tours of wreck sites. You want to come?"

"Oh, why didn't you say so? We haven't been diving together yet this summer. Count me in," I said.

While my trip to the Pennsylvania gas fields immediately following the horrible attack had steadied my nerves and given me some resolve, being in the woods of North Carolina, listening to the sound of woodpeckers in the deep woods, smelling pine sap baking in the June sun, was soul-soothing. By Saturday afternoon, I was feeling my old self again. A little cocky, even.

I was just heading out of a 4,000-acre pine plantation on the way to my Jeep when I got a call from Phil Gregson in Houston.

"Hi, Phil," I said. "How are you?"

"Frustrated," he replied.

"Okay. Tell me." Did I have any choice?

"Here's why: I'm a little confused because Grant, our head driller — you met him — just called. He says they had to put the junk basket down the hole to clear it for our first sidewall core . . ."

"Right. It wasn't originally called for in the drilling plan but added, I was told, so we could correlate the tops of rock formations if things go well and we need to drill more wells later."

"Well, nice everyone's feeling positive, I guess. Anyway, on the way down the junk basket got stuck — so I was wondering when you were going back out."

"Uh, I'm on another job right now. Anyway, I'm not an engineer . . ."

"I know, I know." His distress and confusion lay heavy in the air, as evident as if he were standing right next to me. "It's just that Elton's starting to sound a little unhinged, and I'd just feel better if you were there." He exhaled in relief, to prove his point.

"Phil, you're wound tight as a cheap watch right now too. I guess everyone is. But if the basket's stuck, well, that's pretty much going to shut things down until they fish it out," I said, sighing a lot less audibly. "Tell you what: I'll give Powell a call, keep up with their progress, and soon as they start drilling again, I'll go out. As a matter of fact, I'm done out here and just about to get on the road back to Morehead now, so I'll be ready to roll soon's they get back down in the hole."

That seemed to satisfy him. Poor guy. Phil Gregson might be an old hand at staking his reputation on a particular deep-water site, but he wasn't accustomed to having the very existence of his company on the line. I checked my compass again as I wound through young pines thick enough to practically block daylight, then phoned Duncan Powell.

The bad news was they hadn't even completed tripping out yet — pulling the drill pipe out of the well to attach a tool to retrieve the basket. Then they trip back in, retrieve the junk basket, then come back out again to add the coring bit, then it's back down yet again to the section of the well where a sidewall core would be taken. This long and laborious process would take a few days.

The good news was the casing wasn't damaged and the well was still intact.

Tulip loped up to the Jeep at my whistle and took her place riding shotgun, prepared to give it her all in covering the windows with slobber before we made it back to Morehead.

Scuba diving off the North Carolina coast is always fun, but some days are better than others. Good days are when visibility is more than a just few feet, and Sunday proved to be one of them. Henri and I, along with about twenty-five other divers, were on a tour of a few of the wrecks within easy reach of Morehead City. We'd already seen several, each spectacularly showcasing a vast array of sea life involved in the endless drama of eating or being eaten.

I finned along behind Henri as we explored the remains of *U-352,* a Nazi submarine. A shimmering school of small silver baitfish moved over the sandy seabed toward me, then swooped up and over the sub. *U-352* had the dubious distinction of being the first vessel sunk by the Coast Guard in World War II. It had been lying on its side in about 110 feet of water since 1942. This was the last wreck of the afternoon and so far, my favorite.

I'd read a pamphlet provided by the dive shop about the sinking of the German vessel, which also told how the wreck had been discovered by the shop owner back in the seventies. He'd kept it a secret for over a year until he was ready to make it part of their tour. I found it amazing that he'd gone to the trouble to find the surviving German mariners and bring them to Morehead City for a reunion and to return personal items he'd found in the sub's remains.

Drifting in the light current over the sub's hull, barely moving my fins, I reached the main hatch, its cover still intact. I imagined the panicked seamen. Knowing they only had minutes before the sub sank and with the exit being only big enough to accommodate one sailor at a time . . . it must have been horrific. Two magnificent feathery lionfish floated above the hatch, angels guarding the remains entombed inside. I left them to their duty and kicked off to catch up with Henri.

She was inspecting a mass grouping of starfish and sea urchins on the stern. I wanted to make another pass, so I turned slowly, enjoying the sight of an enormous tiger shark cruising about 50 feet from me, then started back up the length of the sub.

At that moment, I found myself accompanied by a trigger fish who was, frankly, getting a little too friendly. As soon as I'd move in close to peer down into one of several large oblong openings in the sub, the sneaky bastard would bite the side of my face mask with his beak-like teeth.

I was poking my head as far as I dared into one of the holes to see what must have been the engine room — lots of dials and gauges and an object that looked sort of familiar — when, *crack*! The trigger fish crunched down noisily on my mask. I shooed it away and looked again into the dim recesses of the sub. No doubt about it, what I saw looked just like the little gizmo I'd left on my nightstand. Actually, there were rows of the little wheels. Seeing them in context, I knew what they were: control valves, to raise and lower pressure, for example. So how did a submarine control valve get stuck between the bottom rail of the ROV onboard *Magellan* and its cage?

Interesting.

As we drove along the waterfront on our way home, Henri and I were chattering like two parakeets, describing all the thrills we'd been unable to share owing to the fact that it's hard to talk underwater. Since she was behind the wheel, I was gazing idly out the window. But I wasn't really paying attention until I saw a man cross the street in front of us. I knew I'd seen him before, but I just couldn't remember where.

"What's up?" Henri asked, realizing my attention had strayed.

"Huh? Oh, sorry, sweetie. I just saw someone . . . I'm sure I know him. I just can't place him."

"Is he cute? You want me to go around the block?"

"What? No! That's not why I'm interested in him. It's just that he's . . . out of place. I think I've seen him somewhere in my travels of late."

"Your conference in New Orleans?"

"Yes! No. Maybe," I said.

"Which one?"

"I'm thinking . . . I met him on my trip, but not at the conference. He's not a geologist." Suddenly, I remembered and before I thought, blurted out, "Oh, now I remember, he used to be Viktor's boss!"

"Who's Veek-tor?" Henri asked, emphasizing my Russian pronunciation.

Oops. "Just someone I used to know," I said, giving a dismissive wave of my hand.

"Used to know? You apparently still do. Is there some reason you're keeping him a secret? Is this Veek-tor tall, dark, and handsome?" she teased. It seems a child's antennae are as good as a parent's.

"Don't be sassy," I said. Then, using my time-tested, surefire diversion when it comes to my children, I added, "Let's go someplace special for dinner. My treat."

ELEVEN

As I arrived at the port parking lot just before 3:00 a.m. Monday morning, wondering whether it was time to give up my stubborn determination to stay off helicopters, I was surprised to see three protesters leaning against the chain-link fence in front of the office. Frankly, I considered their presence at such an hour insane. The only reason *I* was here was because I'd gotten a call from the site manager, Duncan Powell, just as Henri and I finished eating dinner at one of our favorite restaurants, Windandsea. He'd phoned to let me know drilling had resumed. I flashed my pass to the guard and drove through the gate.

I'd been dreading going aboard the *Magellan* for fear the detectives hadn't kept their word and instead told the crew I'd been attacked onboard by the same fellow who'd mysteriously fallen overboard.

I felt transported back to high school,

when a friend would call you one night and tell you someone was spreading a lie about you and the next day, whenever you approached a group in the hallway, you knew right off who'd heard the rumor just by the look on their face. I was afraid going aboard the *Magellan* on the heels of the CSI show, starring Pierce and Myers, would be like that, only way worse.

First, of course, they'd have had to present themselves to Captain Powell. All the employees aboard the *Magellan,* regardless of which of the myriad contractors actually signed their paycheck, had to answer to him. Powell wasn't in his office off the helm station, but his assistant was. He told me the captain was on the drilling deck, four stories below.

The roar of the drill was deafening, but the din was muted inside the DC, the driller's cabin, where I knew I'd find Powell. He stood behind the chair of the head driller, David Grant. Both men were staring at the wall of monitors, gauges, and dials. Grant lightly moved the lever controlling the drill bit as it spun clockwise, grinding away at ancient layers of rock thousands of feet below us.

Neither man acknowledged me until I asked, "Are we about to have a gumbo attack?" This was the term used in the Gulf when a drill got stuck in a sticky layer of shale.

Grant looked up at me, gave a friendly nod, then returned his gaze to the monitors. He pulled the control lever back slightly, saying with a slight British accent, "Maybe I can keep from getting hung up, but you're right, miss, this shale's sticky as a good bowl of gumbo."

Powell looked me square in the eye and warmly shook my hand. "Glad to have you aboard today, Ms. Cooper." If he thought he was staring into the eyes of a possible murderess, his face didn't show it.

"Glad to be here," I said as we all directed our attention back to the pressure gages. Five minutes — and $2,000 in costs later — the numbers began to decline, indicating lessening torque on the bit.

"Whacha think?" Powell asked Grant. "Time to return to the bottom?"

Grant moved the lever back and forth a few times, watching the monitor of the pipe on the seafloor. Finally he said, "I believe we're good to go . . . for a few more feet anyway." I checked the indicator: 7,583 feet.

"I'm not worried, Grant," Powell now said, "you've got magic feelers in your fingers."

His head driller gave a little grunt at the praise. "I tell you, these rapid shifts from one bed to another, from shale to sandstone and back to shale, can cause some wild pressure differences. About the time things start going smooth, like we're zipping through a nice squishy sandstone, then we hit a real hard shale layer and zip, the drill skids off course. It's not like drilling in the Gulf, where we have lots of experience and know what to expect."

Grant stopped the drill again. I looked through the three-sided glass window to the ship's drill floor below. I could see Braxton Roberts, the company man, standing unobtrusively to one side, watching the roughnecks maneuvering the massive equipment. The top section of drill pipe paused a few feet above the drill floor, and an enormous machine called an iron roughneck — basically, a giant wrench — disconnected the pipe from the overhead drive.

Then another machine, the pipe racker, grabbed a new section of pipe and slung it into place so the human roughnecks could position it before mechanically tightening it down. It was just at that moment that Roberts stepped forward and yelled something to the roughnecks. This caused Powell to shoot out of the cabin like a racehorse out of the gate. He made it the drill floor literally in seconds.

"Oh, crap," said Grant, only with his British accent, it sounded more like, "Oh, crop."

I knew better than to say anything. I just watched as neck veins bulged and spittle flew. The roughnecks backed away. Grant held everything in place with his levers until, a minute later, Roberts backed up under the shade of an overhanging catwalk. Powell returned to the DC muttering something that sounded like, "micromanaging nincompoop," and resumed his place behind the head driller's chair. Grant once again began operating the levers to repeat the process that would happen hundreds of times before this well was completed.

I was getting ready to leave when Powell, as though the last few minutes hadn't happened, turned to me and said in a cheery voice, "This reminds me, I've been meaning to thank you for holding Phil's hand during the junk basket episode. It was very helpful to have you between us."

"No problem," I said.

"I'd be jumpy, too, if I worked for a company that had fired as many people as Global has lately," Grant chimed in.

"Global's got a long history of taking the big risks and doing what it takes to follow through. They're convinced Manteo One's gonna make the Independence Hub in the Gulf look like a bean burrito fart, and we're here to make sure that *if* it is, we put them right in it." Powell sounded confident, which, given my personal financial interest, was welcome. Definitely.

"For my part, I'm starting to wonder about this well being jinxed, what with that ROV operator falling overboard, those police detectives nosing around here Thursday freaking everyone out, then the junk basket getting stuck . . . it's enough to make a guy nervous."

Naturally, I didn't like Grant's take as much. I waited anxiously for the captain's response.

"Nonsense," Powell asserted. "There's no such thing as being jinxed and you, the leader of your drill team, need to make sure a bunch of horseshit like that doesn't get spread around on this ship. I won't tolerate it. Some say that's the way the crew of the *Deepwater Horizon* felt about the Macondo Prospect. You see what happened there. I'm telling you, it can cause a lack of concentration."

"Yes sir," Grant said. All along he'd been keeping his attention primarily on the drill monitors.

"Did you accompany the police while they conducted the investigation?" I asked Powell.

"I offered, but they told me they wanted everyone to stay clear of the area until they were finished. Since we didn't need the ROV at the time, that was fine with me. They weren't here very long. Coast Guard brought them and waited until they were done, then flew them back."

I nodded.

Powell said, "We're just getting ready to do an examination of the seafloor equipment with the ROV. Want to watch?"

"Sure," I said. What I didn't say was that exchanging the tension here for that of being around Viktor wasn't much of an improvement.

Powell and I stepped into the ROV van, where three strange faces looked up at me. Then I remembered that Viktor had said he'd be rotating out on Monday. Relieved, I shook hands with Team Two, the trio of ROV drivers, as Powell introduced them. They'd already lowered the robot over the side. It had reached the seafloor without incident and been deployed from its cage. The lights and camera on the cage were focused on the ROV, which now looked small in comparison to the four-story blowout preventer it was inspecting with its own cameras and lights.

"Great visibility," Powell said as we all watched in fascination. The robot motored slowly upward, casting a bright light in the eerie blackness of the alien environment over 2,000 feet below us. Falling plankton swept by in the rush of the current. It looked the way heavy snowfall does in car headlights on a black night.

When the ROV reached the top of the giant pressure valve, Powell turned to the pilot, a guy named Ray who looked to be older than the other two techs, and said, "I want to double-check every one of those connections, especially those on the riser, and I want photos." The pilot and his two assistants began doing his bidding.

As I watched, a mackerel swam into the eerie blue light cast by the ROV.

"Good grief," said the tech whose name tag on his orange jumpsuit read RICKY. "That dumb fish is back again."

"How do you know it's the same fish?" Powell asked.

"Because his tail's scratched up where Ray had to use the pinchers to pull him out of the BOP yesterday."

Just then a ghostly image passed at the

edges of the light. "What was that?" I asked.

"Probably a big ray," Ricky said.

"Okay, I'm out of here. I'll be in my office on the bridge if you need me, Cleo," Powell said.

"We'll send those photos right up, sir," Ray said as the captain exited.

I stayed for a while longer, watching the monitor over the pilot's shoulder as he maneuvered the ROV around the connection to the marine riser, hoping to see the giant ray again. Most folks don't think there is much sea life on the deep sea floor, but they'd be surprised. Ricky, in the chair next to the pilot, was going over some log sheets. "Hey, Ray," he said. "These don't quite jibe."

"How so?" Ray asked, a joystick in one hand, a sensor glove on the other, and his eyes glued to the monitor in front of him.

"Well, those boys on the other team logged one hell of a lot of time during their two rotations, but I can't see why. I mean, I realize they were here from the start, spudding the well, installing the BOP, and all that, but still . . ." Ricky scratched his head. "I don't know, man, just seems like a lot of hours even for all they did. Did you hear of any problems they might've encountered that would explain all this time?"

"No," Ray said distractedly. "No one said anything to me. Let them worry about that; you just make sure our team's log sheets for the *Magellan* match up with Scooter's internal log."

"Scooter?" I said.

"Okay," Ricky said to Ray, though he didn't sound happy. Then to me he explained, "Scooter's our name for the robot."

"Dammit to hell! Oh, sorry, ma'am," Ray looked at me contritely. "This current is a bitch."

"Well, don't get so close to stuff," said the third team member, Barry, who had been quiet so far.

"Well, duh!" snapped the pilot. "Damned if I don't think you're dumb as that stupid Eskimo who fell overboard."

"Nobody's that dumb," Barry quipped.

"So you guys knew him?" I asked.

"I don't think anyone really knew him," Ray said. "He worked for Voyager for a couple of years, but he was kind of a loner."

"He stunk, man," Barry said. Then looked guilty and added, "I'm just sayin'."

"You would too if you didn't bathe," Ray said. "That's what his roommate reports about him anyway. Plus, he had a mean streak in him a mile wide."

"The man's dead, guys. We shouldn't talk

junk about him no matter how much we thought he sucked at everything he did," Ricky reminded them.

"Yeah, you're right," Ray said. "But we all know he'd never have gotten his job if it wasn't for Davy."

"Well, no matter who got it for him, he's made a for-sure mess of these," Ricky said, shuffling through the log sheets.

Silence descended as the team resumed paying attention to their respective jobs. Mentally I was adding their unflattering appraisals of Nuvuk Hunter to a seemingly never-ending list. Jeez, did anyone like the guy?

"Well," I said. "This isn't getting my work done. Thanks for letting me watch, guys. I'm off to the logging lab."

"Anytime," said Ricky.

The afternoon wore away as I sat at the small desk space built into the back corner of the mudlogger's van. I was studying a sample of the first sidewall core and going over their last log while one of the loggers from Texas had his hands full retrieving samples from the shale shaker two decks below, keeping a constant vigil on the viscosity of the synthetic mud being pumped down the well, and — most importantly — watching out for an increase in the gas pressure in the well and aboard ship.

"Penetration rate has increased so much I can barely analyze the number of samples per foot the contract calls for," the logger commented. "This sandstone we're in is soft, drill's cutting through it like a hot knife through butter."

"I'll call in another logger," I said just as Elton came in and offered to help. As I continued to study the samples, I listened to their conversation. The death of Voyager's previous pilot remained a topic of interest; again, I was relieved they displayed no discomfort at discussing it in front of me.

During a coffee run to the galley, I heard more idle conversation about the accident and noticed two things. One, which I'd already registered subliminally, was that there were a lot of Cajuns aboard — not surprising, since TransWorld was headquartered in Louisiana. Two, most everyone was impressed at how fast Voyager had replaced the pilot. Frankly, I was too. In fact, the speed with which Viktor had come aboard was . . . unsettling. I couldn't put my finger on it, but it gave me something to think about.

Around one thirty, I caught the crew boat back to Morehead. On the way, I had an idea that might help shed light on questions

I had regarding the dead man, how he'd gotten his job, and how he'd been replaced by Viktor so fast. What I needed to do, I realized, was find out more about Davy Duchamp, the man in charge of hiring both the dead man and Viktor. In order to do that, though, I'd have to risk seeming too nosy, which would be unprofessional. But off the *Magellan* there was a possible source of information to hand: Wanda. Unfortunately, it was past five thirty when we reached the dock and she'd left.

No problem. She'd given me her number on my list of contacts.

Staring into the depths of one of the channels cutting through the salt marsh on the far side of the channel behind my house, I was mesmerized by a massive school of menhaden as they moved in lazy patterns below me. Watching them from her position on the front of my Hobie paddleboard, Tulip started to get excited. "Hey, dummy," I said, getting her attention. "No shifting positions. Remember last time? We both went overboard."

Tulip made a noise that sounded a lot like Scooby-Doo and craned her neck to keep the fish in sight without moving her feet. I dutifully followed the school for a while until she lost interest. We were enjoying the last of the afternoon together, but I needed to get back. Wanda and I were meeting for a glass of wine around nine.

Since Tulip takes off when the fun's over, Henri, being the good child she is, came to help me drag the big Hobie into the yard. Leaning the paddle against the back porch railing, she said in a matter-of-fact manner, "By the way, your friend, Viktor — the one you *used* to know — came by to see you today."

I tried to keep my expression neutral to mask my surprise. Apparently I didn't succeed because Henri pursed her lips and said, "He's a little young for you, don't you think?"

That did it! My face screwed up in a tight scowl and those little blood vessels that cause you to turn beet red went into overdrive. At least I didn't sputter when I slowly said, "No, I don't think he's too young. He's not too old either. His age is irrelevant since I barely know him." Well, the last part was sort of true. I'd only spent one day with him . . . and one night. But we were passed out part of that time.

Then I remembered I'd had already had this conversation with myself. I didn't owe anyone an explanation. I lifted my chin, turned on my heel, and beat a dignified retreat to my room.

Twelve

Wanda and I arrived at the same time at the Channel Marker Restaurant and Bar just over the bridge to Atlantic Beach. Amazingly, we found seats outside on the deck overlooking the entrance to the Sea Water Marina. At this time on a summer evening, the younger crowd is just starting to make its way to favorite haunts on the beach, and this was one of them. The last light of the glorious summer day was fading from the horizon as a big round moon, only a few days from being full, began its nightly trek. Our waiter, an eager-to-please college student, poured us a very nice Pinot.

As we sipped our wine, an elegant 80-foot sport fisherman rumbled past only a few feet from us. Its dual diesel exhaust pipes, each as wide as a man's body, sputtered out cooling seawater, leaving a thin veil of fumes in its wake. Wanda and I breathed in, looked at each other, and smiled. "Smells like payday to me," she said softly and chuckled.

"My sentiments, exactly," I said. Then, raising my wineglass, I added, "To the oil patch."

"To the oil patch," she responded with a click of hers, and just like that, we were bonded.

Besides the years we'd both spent working in the oil industry — affectionately known as the oil patch by those who work in it — it turned out the two of us had similarities in our private lives too. She was also divorced with two grown children. Best of all, she was a wealth of information. She'd been with Global for twenty-five years, survived two major employee purges and a near bankruptcy when the government stopped their first attempt to drill an exploratory well in the Manteo Prospect.

"With so many layoffs and all that debt, don't you worry you'll be next?" I asked.

A mysterious little smile crossed Wanda's lips. "Not at all. They can't do without me, girl. I know where all the bodies are buried."

I laughed, but I had a feeling she said it only partly in jest. Instinct told me my new friend was one worth having.

After we swapped stories for a while, I felt comfortable enough to ask if she'd heard anything about the unfortunate Voyager pilot who had fallen overboard. She said no and I believed her, so I moved on to my next topic of inquiry: Did she know anything about Davy Duchamp?

"Good lord, yes," she said. "He and I grew up in Golden Meadow, Louisiana . . . you know that's just a stone's throw from Port Fourchon, right?"

I nodded that I knew where it was.

"We went to school together until he went away to college to study physics. He had to if he was going to understand the business his granddaddy started, SeaTrek, the geophysical surveying company."

Wanda smiled reminiscently. "We were real close for most of our high school days, even sweethearts for a while. And I still have to laugh when I think of how his daddy almost had a conniption fit when Davy announced he wanted to change his major to history. To this day, he's still a huge history buff, especially World War II — Hitler, Stalin, all that depressing stuff. Anyway, he used to mope to me about it, and I told him the truth: he should get his head on straight and finish that degree in geophysics. He did, and the rest is history. His daddy ought to have thanked me."

"I notice there are quite a few folks on the *Magellan* who sound like they hail from southern Louisiana," I said. "Duncan Powell, for instance."

"You're right there, doll. Duncan grew up not far from Davy and me in a little town called Larose. Our football teams played each other. After college at the Merchant Marines Academy, he moved to Morgan City and went to work with TransWorld. He's been there, gosh, I guess over twenty-five years. He knows Davy. Heck, everybody in the oil business in southern Louisiana knows everybody else and they're a tight-knit family."

"I bet," I said. I was just about to ask her if she knew why Davy Duchamp would be visiting in Morehead since all the seismic surveying necessary for exploration had long since been completed when her cell hummed like an angry bee on the table. She checked the screen before slipping it in her purse discreetly. "Would you look at the time," she said. "It's ten thirty, and tomorrow's a work day. Let's do this again real soon."

"Definitely," I said. We both needed change for the tip, so after paying our bill on the way out, I volunteered to go back and leave it. By the time I made it to the parking lot, Wanda was long gone. I had the feeling she wasn't going home, but that was none of my business. I'd ask her about Duchamp being in town next time I saw her.

I crossed the lot still thinking about Duchamp. It didn't seem logical he'd be in town to see his boys, as it would be practically two weeks before they rotated back on duty. At that moment, Viktor Kozlov got out of a car a few spaces away and walked toward me.

"Finally," he said, wrapping his arm around my waist and giving me a nuzzle behind the ear. "I thought you two ladies would never stop talking."

I pushed him away and said indignantly, "Have you been stalking me?"

"Stalking? Of course not. Stalking means the other person is not interested. That is not the case with you and me."

"But I'm *not* interested. Don't you remember I said I'm only interested in a professional relationship with you?"

"Don't you remember my reply?"

I thought for a second, looking up at a moon so bright it was casting deep shadows in the lot, and said, "I remember you said *something,* but since I don't speak Russian, I have no earthly idea what it meant."

"Let me refresh your memory. *Ne boysya, milaya moya.*"

"And that means?"

Viktor leaned in close to me and whispered in my ear, "It means trust me, my sweet, don't be afraid." Then he slipped his arm around me again and pulled me to his chest. I knew I shouldn't have just stood there and let him hold me, but, seriously, he looked good and smelled good and felt good. Then several thoughts surfaced through the fog of lust clouding my mind: he was still twelve years my junior, we still shared the same workplace, and I had no idea what Henri's plans for tonight were.

She could be out with her friends right now. She might even drive by this very spot and see me. I stepped from his embrace and said, "You have it backwards, my dear. You'll have to trust me in this matter, because I'm older and wiser than you. Now, go home. Tomorrow's a work day."

"Don't you think I know how to protect your privacy? I do and I want to be with you so badly," he said, reaching for me again. "I have a special place where we can spend hours alone and no one will ever know."

I took another step back, images of the previous hours we spent alone sending a jolt through my system like I'd straddled an electric fence. I simply had to get away from Viktor before I did something I would probably — no, definitely — regret.

"Good night, Viktor," I said and leaned in to give him a buss on the cheek. Big mistake. He was fast with the old head fake and caught me in a lip lock that I didn't want to wrestle out of. Jeez, he tasted good too.

Only seconds passed before prudence prevailed and I scooted free, hopped in my Jeep, and left.

Ever actually tried the cold-shower cure for a case of hormone overload? Don't bother, it doesn't work. I even tried to concentrate on what I'd learned from Wanda: that Davy Duchamp was a history buff who knew Duncan Powell and virtually everyone in the industry. Which, of course, wasn't surprising, when you thought about it. My brain, however, was so addled from my encounter with Viktor that I couldn't think straight. What this information had to do with the death of the Alaskan ROV pilot, I couldn't see clearly, but it did. I was sure of it.

Giving it all up for the moment, I stepped from the shower and was toweling off when I caught my reflection in the corner of my eye. I turned, sat the towel on the counter, and gazed at myself. Sucking in a deep breath, I tipped my chin up and posed, my hands at my waist. Then I turned sideways, taking in my belly and my breasts. Not bad, but how would I, at forty-six, stack up against a thirty-four-year-old woman, one Viktor's age?

"Yes. You're still very beautiful," Bud said from the open doorway between the bathroom and bedroom.

I spun around. "How the hell did you get in here?"

"Here as in the bathroom, or here as in the house?" Bud asked. "Doesn't matter. In both cases, I used a door."

"Where's Henri?"

"Off with Will at some bar on the beach. They have a lot of catching up to do."

I snatched up my towel and wrapped it around me. "I didn't realize you two were coming back today. Nobody ever tells me anything." Bud looked as good as I'd ever seen him. Had he done something to his hair? It was subtle, but I noticed the cut was more youthful, the style more tousled, a little spiky even.

But it was the Nat Nast buff yellow shirt à la Charlie Sheen in *Two and a Half Men* that was the real kicker. Bud had never worn luxury sportswear in all the years we'd been together. Maybe it was the shirt, maybe it was just my hormones, but I was giving some thought to letting the towel slip enticingly when Bud said, "We do too. Have a lot of catching up to do, that is. Meet me in the kitchen. I'll make us some late-night pancakes."

Pancakes?

After careful deliberation, I put on a pair of ivory satin pajamas and pulled my hair up in a loose bun. When I sauntered into the kitchen, Bud was already pouring the batter. "You look nice and relaxed," he said.

Just then I noticed Will's duffel bag, computer case, and a few other personal items still stacked by the door. "What's Will's stuff doing down here?"

"That's one of the things we need to catch up on. He wants to come and stay at Seahaven with me for a while."

"Oh," I said. This was disappointing and bewildering. I was looking forward to Will's coming home so I could get to the root of what was bothering him. If he was with Bud, whom he worshiped and wanted to be just like, he'd be less likely to unburden himself. And expecting Bud to notice a faint emotional change was really leaning on a weak reed. Still, it wouldn't hurt to ask.

Bud set a plate of hotcakes in front of me.

"Thanks," I said and picked up one, tore off a piece, and popped it in my mouth. Bud sat his plate down and proceeded to drown his in butter and syrup. How he kept his fabulous physique was a mystery to me. He'd never been big on exercise. "Bud," I said. "Did Will seem a little moody to you while you were in Paris?"

"Are you kidding? No. How could anyone be moody in Paris?"

He had a point there, but he'd also confirmed my original assessment of his ability to sense things — it didn't exist.

"Catch me up on all things geological out at Manteo One."

We talked until Will and Henri came in around 1:30 a.m.

"Hi, Mom!" Will said, giving me a hug and a peck on the cheek. The minute I saw him, I could tell he was still stressed. He was hiding it well, but it was there right under the surface of his sunny expression. After telling me a little about Paris and how much he'd enjoyed any time spent learning the family business, he and Bud were out the door, headed for Wrightsville.

Henri and I went to bed. Yes, I was worried about Will, but at least I wasn't horny anymore. I slept like a corpse until the alarm went off a little over an hour later. I must have hit the snooze because next thing I knew Tulip was licking my face. I jumped up, ran downstairs to let her out, then threw on some clothes, pulled my hair into a ponytail, and jumped in the Jeep.

Something was holding up the early-morning traffic, forcing me to pull into a parking place at Dockside Marina. My plan was to park there only long enough to jog up the street and see what the problem was.

I hadn't walked 10 feet when a group of young people ran past me holding signs. Protesters again! Didn't they ever sleep? But now there were a lot more of them. Why was today different from yesterday? I started to shove my way through the throng to the guard at the entrance but luckily remembered a small side gate behind one of the warehouses.

By backtracking a block and cutting through the pool area of a private condo, I was able to reach it. Unfortunately, several demonstrators and the press members had also found this lesser-known access. Making the executive decision to leave my car where it was for the rest of the day and hope it didn't get towed, I pushed past them and showed the guard my pass. He let me squeeze through the gate. Rude shouts of disapproval followed me. Halfway across the port yard, I saw the reason for the furor.

SunCo had arrived, and in full glory:

seven different vessels bearing its logo were tied up, both at the port dock and across the New Port River on Radio Island.

SunCo was the largest oil company on the planet. They were giants not only in exploration and production, but in the downstream industries of refining and marketing as well. In every single corner of the globe, SunCo had rigs probing the depths of Earth for energy.

Since I didn't see any anchor vessels — ships that transport the enormous suction anchors that hold semi-submersibles in place — I figured they were using one of their fleet of drillships to drill their first exploration well in the Manteo Prospect.

Obviously it was the presence of the SunCo flotilla that had caused the protest organizations to ramp up their outcry against the evils of capitalism, big oil, fossil fuels, and anything else that fueled the modern industrialized nations of the world. Feeling a small twinge of anxiety about Henri alone at the house, I gave her a heads-up text on my iPhone and then headed back across the yard for the *Iron Responder*.

Spotting me from the bridge, Captain Eddie slid open the window in the wheel house door. “Come on, girl. There’s big doings in the gas patch and we’re burning daylight!”

Thirteen

Mild weather conditions made for gentle swells, and in a little under four hours, I was back aboard the *Magellan.* As was now my custom, after a visit to the radio room on the bridge, I went straight to the helm to inform Captain Powell I was aboard.

He and some of his crew were standing at the windows, each with a pair of binoculars trained on SunCo's giant drillship about six miles from us.

"We've got company," Powell said.

"I noticed. You should see the mob in town."

"What mob?"

"Demonstrators. Several hundred, I'd say. Although it's hard to be sure since they're scattered through the streets leading to the port. Most of them were jammed up by the gates."

"Shut up! No way!" said a wide-eyed young crew member from Powell's staff.

"Way!" I said, laughing.

"Glad we get to dodge all that crap," Powell said. "You might think about staying out here until it dies down. It'd probably be safer."

"Thanks. That's nice to know, but I'll be fine," I said. "Mind if I take a look?"

He handed me the binoculars.

I scanned the massive hull for the vessel's name and watched as thrusters on each end of ship kicked in, swinging the bow away from us. As the ship came broadside, I saw it: *Able Leader,* emblazoned in shiny red letters under the bow rail. Noticing the behemoth literally sparkled in the sun, I wondered if it was new.

As though reading my mind, Powell said, "She just came off the rails, one of SunCo's new generation of ultra-deepwater drillships. They have a wholly owned subsidiary, SunCo America, that builds them to their exact specifications. Notice anything different about that ship that this one doesn't have?"

I studied its structure. "Uh-oh," I said. "Would those be dual drills in one derrick?"

"Yep, sure would," Powell said. "Instead of doing each operation involved in drilling a well sequentially, they have a main advancing station *and* an auxiliary advancing station. Both stations can assemble strings of pipe and have them ready to drill or rack them back as they come up. Lower cost, less time."

"Impressive. I've read about them, just haven't seen one yet, though they've been in use for several years now."

"Well, we've got a good head start. But in the end, it doesn't matter who gets to their target first, right?"

I set down the nocks. All eyes on the bridge trained on me. "That's right," I said confidently. "In the end, it all comes down to who chose the *right* target. Who cares if your team is the first if you hit a duster?"

"But that won't happen to us, will it?" a trim young man in a blue jumpsuit, part of the bridge crew, asked.

"Of course not," I said.

"Well," he said, "I heard that twenty years ago Global and SunCo both owned this spot."

As employees of TransWorld, Powell and his crew were engaged in the business of operating the drillship and all the drilling equipment efficiently. Geologic decisions made by the operator who contracted them — in this case, Global — were out of their purview.

"Yes," I said. "That was right about the

time the two companies split and Global bought the lease on this block. Keep in mind, seismic surveys weren't as advanced twenty years ago as they are today. Technology has marched on and now we can see what's happening below ground in 3D. And more than that, with 4D we can get a feel for what's happened over time. Plus both companies have drilled countless wells since then and each one has its own lessons to teach."

I lifted the binocs for another quick peek at the magnificent ship. "I can't say for certain, but I believe that based on what happened to SunCo on a certain well in the eastern Gulf, their geologic exploration team won't necessarily try to drill the thickest part of a reef anymore."

"But isn't that our plan, to drill into the thickest part?" Powell asked me.

"Well, it's a little more complicated than simply drilling the thickest part. I'm just saying that, based on that experience and newer seismic surveys, they've chosen to go a different route. But here's the thing, you can make all the projections you want, slice and dice your 3D diagrams all you want, in the end, it's impossible to know until you drill a hole."

Captain Powell and his bridge crew looked

a little dubious. "Don't worry," I said. "When it comes to the geologic part of this operation, Phil and I have lots of rabbits up our sleeve. Right now, I need to get down to the shaker shack and check in with the guys to see where we are in the hole."

As I headed off, I remembered I'd felt my iPhone vibrate several times while I was on the bridge. The last two missed calls were from Detective Pierce. His probing blue-gray eyes and gaunt face came to mind. I'd call him back when I got to a quieter place, maybe on my return ride on the *Responder.* Before I did so, however, there was something more I needed to learn. From Duncan Powell.

I stayed in the logging lab until lunchtime. Elton was in and out but remembered to bring me his daily reports. I put them in my pack to go over later. After I'd looked at dozens of chips of sandstone, shale, and boundstones, I was satisfied that we were very close to penetrating the reservoir rock. Hopefully, our targeted bright spot, located within the 1,400-foot thickness of the ancient carbonate reef, would prove to be dry natural gas. Grabbing my hard hat, I left the lab and went to the galley to find something to eat . . . and Captain Powell. In the short time I'd known him, I'd come to think of him as a creature of habit, at least as far as his meal times were concerned.

Confirming my belief, Powell was just entering the galley at one thirty and, as luck would have it, he was alone. I waved a greeting.

"Care to join me?" he asked.

Sometimes a plan just falls into place. As I set down my tuna salad and tea on the table, he said, "I hope Bud's going to be able to keep Manteo One from suffering the same fate as the Destin Dome."

"Ah." I wasn't surprised. "So you know the whole story of SunCo and the Destin Dome."

In 1987 the Destin Dome was a proven trap for trillions of cubic feet of dry natural gas, but production there was still blocked by the state of Florida in much the same way as exploration of the Manteo Prospect had been held up by the state of North Carolina. Only in the last two years had the overall will of the country now coalesced to demand a robust energy plan after witnessing firsthand the damage done to the economy — not to mention national security — without one. With two years of frustrating experience behind him, Bud had emerged as a virtuoso at coalition-building to make the project a reality. It was a skill I'd failed to master myself when it came to the small quarry operation I'd hoped to launch.

"If history doesn't teach us, what does?" Powell observed.

I gave him a confident look and said, "Still, you must not know Bud very well."

Powell smiled. "Actually, as the rig super on the *Magellan,* I've gotten to know him pretty well over this last year. He did the coordinating for our team at TransWorld with the operators at Global and the state and federal people to get our permits. Everyone had to be on the same page regarding the drilling plan for Manteo One, the chemicals we planned to use in our drilling mud, our recycling process . . . and you're right, I shouldn't worry. Bud's one very determined guy."

Then he stopped eating, gave me a penetrating stare, and said, "I learned something else about him when you guys got stranded out here the night those heavy-duty thunderstorms rolled over us."

My chest tightened a little. "What was that?"

"He's very savvy at poker! He cleaned out me and Phil and a couple of tool pushers." Powell laughed as he speared the last of his fried shrimp and popped it in his mouth.

"Right," I said, relieved. "He told me you guys had gotten in a few hands."

"You could say that," he grinned. "But you could also say we didn't break up until about six o'clock in the morning. I was a zombie the next day. Mostly we sat right there, him making money, us losing it. Except for bathroom breaks, we didn't move."

"Sounds like honor demands a rematch," I said, finishing my salad. "But, I should get back to work. The boat's scheduled to go back at two thirty and I'll be on it."

Once aboard the *Responder*, I settled back in one of the comfortable reclining passenger chairs in its relative quiet — quiet, that is, compared to a drillship — and prepared to make my long overdue call to Detective Pierce. I wondered if he'd spoken to Bud yet. Now that I knew Bud had a solid alibi, I felt marginally better and more at ease about talking to the cops. Why only marginally? Well, there was the matter of those bathroom breaks . . .

With two approaches to the bridge of the *Magellan* (an interior stairwell and exterior stairs with a landing off the bridge), it was still possible that Bud had walked out on the landing for a breath of fresh air after going to the bathroom. Even though the ROV area was cloaked in darkness, he would have been close enough to hear the scuffle. While I couldn't remember if I'd screamed, there had to have been other distress noises. Say he arrived just as I fainted, with King Kong/Nuvuk Hunter overstimulated and unaware . . . Bud could have easily pushed him overboard.

Detective Pierce's phone rang several times, then went to voicemail. "Detective Pierce, Cleo Cooper returning your call," I said crisply, then clicked off. I settled deeper in the recliner, planning to use the quite ride back to go over Elton's daily report. But Captain Eddie opened the cabin door, spotted me, and came over.

"Have a seat," I said, putting away my report.

"Thanks," he said, standing above me, "but I only have a sec. I turned the com over to the first mate. Don't want to push my luck, but I did want to ask you about the well. How's it going? We're going to beat SunCo to the punch, aren't we?"

It's funny how there seems to be a collective conscious that connects all parties involved in a wildcat well, no matter how removed they are from the actual drilling.

When the fat lady is about to sing, everyone knows it and the excitement and tension levels ratchet up.

"I don't know about SunCo, but our well's coming along nicely. Minus any hiccups, we should be getting some show very soon." He gave me a thumbs up and went back to the bridge.

Maybe Captain Eddie was just starting to get into the spirit, but I'd been feeling the excitement all along. To think I was involved with the first well drilled on what promised to be a new frontier of energy for America! This was what it must have been like in the Gulf in the early days. Well, the tools used today were well advanced of those back then, and we were starting in over 2,000 feet of water, whereas back in the late thirties and early forties in the Gulf, they started in shallow water. Actually the first wells were drilled right on land in the town of Golden Meadow, Louisiana. The story goes that there was so much oil right under the ground that local residents were confronted with an excess seeping out of the ground, ruining the hems of women's dresses. Imagine!

I hadn't really slept so, after a bit of daydreaming about a wildcat strike, I nodded off for the rest of the return trip. Back at the port, colorful boats full of vacationers wove in an out among the support vessels. Jet skiers were clearly ecstatic about having SunCo's 200-footers around because of the enormous wakes they created. With engines whining, they swarmed behind the ships like pilot fish follow sharks, jumping the wakes in the most creative ways. Sometimes they were successful and sometimes they weren't, getting dunked in the waterway in the latter case. Thank goodness for kill switches.

I heard a throaty rumble beside me and knew it would be one of those go-fast boats, the kind often painted in garish colors and sporting bikini-clad babes on the bow. I turned to watch it go by. I was right about the garish colors; however, the only babe on the boat was behind the wheel.

It was Viktor Kozlov.

Fourteen

Viktor waved from the open cockpit of a 42-foot Fountain, definitely an eye-catcher. So was Viktor, with his dark brown curls, flashing smile, and ripped body. I was just reminding myself of his tender age and managing to drag my eyes from the twin clefts on either side of his flat belly when I noticed he was signaling something. He'd point inshore, then back and forth between us. *Meet me at the port?*

I was still trying to decipher his meaning when he gave me another merry wave and pushed the throttle forward. Engines bellowed. The boat leaped forward, practically becoming airborne, and Viktor was gone, spewing a 50-foot rooster tail behind him.

Ten minutes later, with me still at the bow rail, the *Iron Responder* bumped gently into her slip. Only a blind man could have missed the Fountain tied up at the commercial marina next door. I slipped back through the cabin, gathered my things, and hopped off. Viktor was waiting for me on the dock.

"I told you I had a special place for us to be alone," he said, pointing at the Fountain, bursting with pride.

"Whose is that?" I asked. Such a big-boy toy wasn't something a doctoral candidate, even one attending Duke, would likely be able to afford.

"It belongs to Davy, my old boss. He came up here to buy it so he could tour the factory and meet the designers and engineers. The factory is in a little town not far from here called Washington. In a few days, he and the twins are going to take the boat back to Louisiana. They have a lot to do in preparation, and so until they leave, I'm free to use it."

So that's why Duchamp was in town the other day. "That was nice of them. But back up just a sec here. Did you tell them about us?"

"Never! I'd never do that. Remember, I told you that you can trust me with your privacy. That's why this boat is so perfect for us . . ."

"Oh yeah, it just fades right into the scenery. No one would ever notice it."

Viktor thought a moment chewing on his

bottom lip. "I see your point, and I will fix this problem immediately. But, for now, *mya morkovka,*" he said, pulling me close. "Hop in. Let me take you home by water. The crowds outside the port get rougher as the evening approaches."

Mya morkovka? "Thank you," I said, stepping politely from his embrace. "That's very kind of you, but my Jeep is parked down the street. I don't want to leave it. Like you said, things could get nastier with the protestors once it's dark." Hitching my pack a little higher on my shoulder, I started to leave, but he was so crestfallen, I couldn't just walk off.

I said, "Seriously, Viktor, thank you for your concern. You're very sweet." I started to give him a little peck on the check, then remembered the last time I tried that and refrained.

I made it back to the house without incident. I was looking forward to a little downtime with Tulip and Henri — at least, I hoped Henri was home. She owned her own photography business and though it wasn't limited to brides, they made up the bulk of her client base. She'd told me earlier she had an upcoming photo shoot and needed to scout out some interesting locations.

I wished Will were there too. My heart squeezed at the thought of him, wondering what was bothering him and if he'd talked to Bud about it. I was headed for the back porch when I heard Tulip bark from the sea wall where she was patrolling for wharf fiddlers.

Apparently she'd cornered one because she hesitated, looking back and forth between me and the small, black spider-like crab. Love conquers all and I won out over the crunchy crustacean and she bounded across the yard. Whimpering, she leaned into my legs and stuck her head between my knees. I gave her sides a vigorous rub and noticed something odd about her collar.

Upon further inspection, I realized something was taped to it. I easily broke the paper, revealing a note inside a plastic sandwich baggie. I unfolded it. Scrawled in red crayon were the words YOUR DOG WON'T LIKE GAS EITHER. Mid-page was a childish drawing of a dog in a big barrel — presumably filled with gasoline — a lighted match pointed at it. At the bottom of the page, the word KABOOM! with shock waves darting from it.

My mouth went dry. Where was Henri?

I ran into the house, calling her name.

"Yo!" She bounded into the room.

Relief rushed over me, but you wouldn't have known it. "What's Tulip doing outside unattended?" I snapped.

"I just put her out a minute ago. What's wrong? You look like you just ran into Freddy Krueger."

"What does 'just put her out' mean? I'm serious. How long?"

"Minutes, I don't know, maybe five or less . . ."

Dropping the note on the table, I said, "Read it — but don't touch it!"

As quickly as my two feet would carry me, I was back in the Jeep retrieving my Beretta .380, a baby nine, still in its nylon field holster. Buckling it on, I ran to the seawall and scanned up and down its length. It was low tide, but no one was hiding down there and no footprints were evident in the muddy sand, either.

A thick hedgerow of ancient azaleas served as a divider between my yard and my neighbor's. The inevitable grapevine and greenbriers grew thickly among them, making a tangle that could easily hide an intruder. Bending to see under them, I traveled their length, looking for someone crouched there. I found no one, so I moved to the back of the house.

When I reached the front yard, I found another calling card of sorts: a clear 40-ounce beer bottle, half filled with kerosene, if my sense of smell served me right, and finished off with wick made from a scrap of T-shirt. This Molotov cocktail sat unlit right in the middle of the porch. Henri had been watching me from the windows. Now she opened the door and looked at it. "God, Mom, what are you going to do?"

"Well, for starters, I'm calling the cops. Next, you're packing up and moving to Dad's. Now."

"But what about you? Are you crazy? You can't stay here by yourself with some maniac running around leaving bombs!"

"*And* you're taking Tulip with you," I said, ignoring her. "Now hurry!"

"But —"

"No buts, Henri. Besides, I won't be here. I'll go stay on the drillship until we finish Manteo One. You can tell Dad that so he won't worry." I closed and locked the front door behind us and started for the kitchen, pulling out my phone and dialing Detective Pierce. Henri gave me one last pleading look just as he answered. I gave her my sternest scowl and pointed up the stairs, then relayed my recent troubles to him.

"Don't touch anything! We'll be right

over," he said.

I jogged out to my Jeep and deposited the Beretta back in the console just as Henri came out with her overnight bag and Tulip.

"I've decided to go to my house in Raleigh," she said. "I postponed my photo shoot. The girl is okay with it . . . for now, but you know how these brides can be. I hope this gets straightened out before too long or we'll have something more dangerous than a bomb-toting activist to worry about; we'll have a bridezilla!" She opened the door to her Chevy Tahoe so Tulip could get in. Tulip looked at me.

"Go on," I said. "It's all right."

"I need to check on a few things at my place anyway," she said. "I'll go by your house too, make sure everything's copacetic there, maybe have lunch with some of the girls. *Then* I'll go to Dad's." Tears welled up in her eyes.

I gave her a hug. "Don't worry. All this craziness will be over as soon as the well comes in and the world doesn't come to a fiery, polluted end, but gets better instead. You'll see. Go on now, scoot!"

She pulled out of the driveway about two minutes before my favorite detectives pulled in, followed by two Morehead City patrol cars, a CSI van, and a SWAT team. In less than fifteen minutes, the SWAT team — all eight of them in full body armor, carrying assault weapons, and wearing helmets with blast shields pulled down over their faces — had swarmed over the house and yard, reloaded into their armored van, and left. I stood nearly motionless that entire time, not wanting to disrupt the bizarre goings-on at my temporary home.

After collecting the note and the Molotov cocktail and dusting for prints, the CSI team left too. Apparently domestic terrorism didn't fall within the scope of Pierce's and Myers's talents, so they stood to the side while I went over the details of what I'd found with the police officers. After about an hour, they gave me their assurances that they would put extra patrols on my house and left to canvass the neighborhood. Meanwhile, the wiry Pierce and not-so-wiry Myers had taken their now-usual seats at my kitchen table.

"My goodness, Ms. Cooper," Pierce said. "When you come to town, things certainly get lively."

"Are you suggesting I somehow caused this crap?" I said, incredulously, then added, "And a SWAT team? Don't you think that was a little over the top?"

"Not at all," Pierce said. "Puts the fear of

God in the bad guys. Trust me, they were somewhere watching to see your reaction. That's partly why they did it."

"And," Myers jumped in, "it worked out real smooth, timing-wise. Morehead City SWAT was running drills, in case things get out of hand with the protestors at the port, so it was good practice for them. By the way, where's your daughter?"

"I sent her away for a few days. She took my dog with her."

"Smart move," Myers said.

"It'd be even smarter if you went too," Pierce added.

"I'll be fine. I'm not letting a bunch of domestic terrorists and political activists run me off."

Pierce cocked an eye at Myers, then said, "Let's move on to another topic, shall we? The murder of the ROV pilot seems a little less volatile."

"Sorry," I said. "Finding a bomb on your front porch might make you touchy too. By the way, I did return your call."

"I wanted to know if you'd learned when Mr. Cooper might be returning to the country. Do you know?"

"He's back. Is that all you wanted?"

"Yes, unless you'd be interested in knowing that we are very near to *actually* making a death ruling in the case of the ROV pilot and that we're still going with accidental death. Well . . . probably."

Now there was a surprise. Like a picador teasing a dangerous bull, I asked, "What about the fact that his skull was crushed?" I couldn't help it. I wanted to know.

"Impressions made of the back of his skull match perfectly with an impression taken of the railing on the ROV platform. And there were trace amounts of blood on the railing and on the platform itself that match the vic's."

"Why does that make it an accident?"

"He said *probably,*" Myers stated.

"Yes. Like women, homicide detectives are free to change their minds whenever they feel like it," Pierce said.

That's when my frustration about the entire situation boiled over. "Look, I just want to know what happened on the *Magellan* that night. I've always felt safe on an offshore rig. Safer than anywhere else, really. And now I don't anymore. What's worse, some creep is trying to frighten me away from here too. Meanwhile, you two knuckleheads are making dumb female jokes."

I felt my chin start to tremble and that made me even angrier. "You guys might try putting yourselves in my place. I was beaten up and nearly raped, and for a while there I thought I was about to be thrown overboard by someone I don't know, for some reason I don't understand. Then, somehow, I ended up back in my bunk. If you were me, wouldn't you want to know what the hell really happened? Jesus, guys."

The refrigerator hummed. The distant cries of seagulls floated on the stillness of the hot afternoon. Myers checked his loafers for scuffs. Pierce inspected a hangnail. I felt deflated now that my tirade was finished.

"You want some tea?" I asked.

"Sounds like another good idea to me," Myers said with a sigh.

I pulled open the refrigerator door, then checked Mickey on my wrist. He said it was beer-thirty. "Aren't you guys off duty now?"

"Technically, yes," said Pierce.

"Would you rather have a Blue Moon?"

"Okay by me," Myers said. "It's a pussy beer, but I like it."

"That pretty much sums you up, Myers," Pierce told his partner.

"Eff you," Myers replied good naturedly.

I set three chilled mugs and three cans of Blue Moon on the table, emptied some orange wedges from a baggie into a small saucer, and set it down too.

"Why do you think the matching impressions suggest an accident rather than a murder?" I said.

"Because you're the only person who had a reason to kill him — self-defense, of course — and you're too small to get the upper hand in a fight with someone of his size, much less slam his head into the railing and pitch him overboard."

Myers squeezed an orange wedge into his beer and said, "Couple that with the tox report — which just came back and said he'd *way* over-served himself — and an accident seems more plausible."

Pierce took a huge gulp of beer, sans orange wedge, then set the mug down. I could see the tendons in his jaw working. He was one intense guy. "Also we've talked to the other people on the tour and with the possible exception of your husband — who might have defended you if he'd known you were in trouble — there are no other suspects. Which brings us back to him and the word *probably.* We'll talk to Mr. Cooper before making a definite ruling."

Now that talk of murder and mayhem was out of the way, the three of us spent an enjoyable hour discussing the wildcat and what its coming in would mean to eastern North Carolina. But as soon as the two detectives left, I pulled out my phone to call

Bud and warn him.

But I thought better of it and put the phone away. One question would lead to another, and I'd have to tell him I'd been attacked, which I still didn't want to do. And wouldn't he get the impression that I thought he was capable of murder? I didn't want to go there either. What I wanted was for the whole mess to go away instead. So I did what I usually do and shoved it out of my mind. Then I called the helicopter service in Beaufort to see if I could catch a flight out to the relative safety of the *Magellan* tonight.

A recording at the charter service told me to call back during business hours, which sent me in search of the list of captains of support vessels. But considering how doubtful it was that any of them would be making a late-night trip unless an emergency part was needed, I detoured to the Jeep to get my gun — again. Tucking it under my T-shirt, I marched back inside, opened the refrigerator, and scooped up another Blue Moon. *Screw a bunch of activists,* I thought. *I am entitled to enjoy the evening in my own home, rented or not.*

I cracked open the beer and sauntered out to the screened-in porch sipping it. There I sat and watched the evening fall, baby nine at my side. About nine o'clock I was just finishing a chicken salad sandwich when I got a call from Duncan Powell.

"Hey," I said. "What's up?"

"Nothing good," came his exasperated reply. "Were you planning to head back out here tomorrow?"

"Actually, I'd thought about coming back out tonight after supper, but I've changed my mind."

"Oh?"

"It's a long story. But the short version is yes, I'll be coming back out tomorrow."

"You might want to rethink that plan. Right after you left, a piece of sticky shale got wedged in the well. We've having a hell of a time getting it up. We ran through the standard procedure but weren't having any luck when Braxton came up with the bright idea of increasing the weight of the mud to somehow break up the blockage and flush it out. Of course, I said a big hell no to that. Company man or not, I couldn't take the chance of busting the casing —"

"Of course not. It could potentially destroy the well. We'd have to start all over again."

"Anyway, I thought I'd let you know progress is stopped till we get the mudball out of the hole, so you'd be wasting a trip.

Of course, the offer to stay here still stands if you're uncomfortable with the protestors in town."

"No, I've decided that won't be necessary," I said, deciding to keep the whole Molotov cocktail business to myself. No sense piling more onto Powell's already stressful day. "How long do you think the delay will last?"

"Could be as much as forty-eight hours because, in trying to clear the borehole with the bit, some damage to the kelly spinner occurred. We'll need a part flown in from Louisiana, and then there's tripping time in and out of the hole."

"You told Phil yet?"

"I'm getting ready to right now. I told you first because I know he'll need some calming down. Maybe you can get him through this like you did before."

"Thanks for your confidence . . . I think," I laughed. "I'll see what I can do. Meantime, you and I will stay in touch."

"We will," Powell said, blowing out a frustrated sigh. "We were right there, right before breaking into the reservoir . . . never fails . . ."

"Even with this little snag — or mudball, to be more precise — I have faith in you. We'll bring in the well before SunCo. And what's more, it'll be one for the record books."

Fifteen

It was ten o'clock when I finished talking to Powell. What a day. A hot shower before bed sure sounded like a good idea.

Afterward, I slipped into a pair of gym shorts and a tank top — my summer sleeping attire — and decided some time spent reading the new Grisham novel might help relax muscles still bunched from the stress of the day. As I pulled open the nightstand drawer to retrieve it, the little doohickey I'd found wedged between the ROV rail and its cage caught my attention. I picked it up and studied it under the reading lamp.

I hadn't had time to inspect it thoroughly since I'd seen some wheel valves very similar to it on my scuba diving trip with Henri out on the wreck of *U-352.* The fading red paint was chipped in a few places, as though it had seen some wear, but it basically reminded me of the ones I'd seen in the torpedo room. I flipped the valve over — it definitely had a front and back side — and for the first time, I noticed letters stamped on the back.

With my previous tiredness slipping away, I carried the wheel into my study and peered at the letters with a magnifying glass. Though faint with time, they read AG WESER. Booting up my computer, I felt a twang of loneliness for Tulip and my children. I'd been so looking forward to spending the whole summer doing less work and spending time with them when they could spare it.

But now my curiosity had kicked in, and the vast informational riches of the Internet were there to be mined. I Googled *AG Weser.* What I saw made those little hairs on the back of my neck stand up. "What the hell?" I said aloud when page after page of links to articles on AG Weser, a major German shipbuilder during World War I and World War II specializing in U-boats, popped up. I clicked on the first one.

What I was learning was both fascinating and addictive. Before I knew it, it was two o'clock Wednesday morning and I was convinced that the wheel valve had come from a German U-boat. What made me so sure? I'd found another site that contained everything you'd ever want to know about

U-boats, including old photos of the interiors of the stealthy vessels that wreaked so much havoc during the early days of World War II.

The more I read about them — where each one had patrolled for freighters, warships, or any floating enemy of the Third Reich — the more I wanted to read. Still, needing to get some rest, I finally went to bed.

Five hours later, around eight o'clock Wednesday morning, I was right back in front of the screen. I found out that for the first six months of World War II, the east coast of the United States had been practically undefended. At that point, no wartime protocol existed, such as cutting off lights at night along the coast or managing ship-to-shore radio transmissions. Yet throughout this period, there were sixty-five U-boats on the prowl out there, attacking American and British boats attempting to carry supplies to the Allies fighting in Europe.

The Outer Banks of North Carolina suffered so many enemy attacks that it was nicknamed Torpedo Junction. Four U-boats are sunk off the coast there. Their positions are well known. None of them, however, were anywhere near Manteo One, forty-five miles off Cape Hatteras. Eventually, I'd investigated the possibilities of sixty-one other subs that could possibly be sunk there, but decided, for one reason or another, against every one.

My Internet wanderings, besides burning most of the day, also led me to discover a North Carolina museum I'd never known existed. It was in Hatteras and called the Graveyard of the Atlantic Museum. Spurred on by my natural curiosity, I decided a trip there was definitely in order. North Carolina, with four known U-boat locations, was the state with the most off its coast.

While Hatteras was only about 70 miles from Morehead City as the crow flies, it was, in fact, a four-hour trip — and that was only if you timed the ferries right. It would take two to get there: the Cedar Island Ferry, followed by the Ocracoke Ferry that crosses the Hatteras Inlet. Fortunately, Highway 12, which had been rendered impassible by Hurricane Irene in 2011, was now restored.

I was looking at my calendar, trying to decide how to work in the trip, when I heard Henri calling me below.

I went to the top of the stairs. "What are you doing back here?" I demanded to know.

"I was on my way to Dad's and swung by

here to pick up a few things I forgot the other day. Then I saw your Jeep and decided I'd better make sure you're okay because you said you were staying on the ship."

"Yeah, well," I said testily — having been caught in a lie. "I changed my mind when I couldn't get a flight out. But you should have called first. That's why Dr. Bell invented the telephone. You've come hours out of your way."

But even from where I stood, I could see that the anxiety on her face was more than what was called for by a death threat and a Molotov cocktail. Seating myself on the bottom step, I pulled her down beside me.

At first she didn't say anything, only stared at the floor. My body tensed for a blow; this had to be something bad. Very bad.

"What's wrong, sweetie?"

She looked at me. God, she was absolutely grief stricken. "Is it Tulip?" I prompted. "Did she get run over or something?"

"No, no. She's in the back yard."

I waited for a minute, then patted her on the knee. "Putting off telling bad news won't make it better, sweetie. Just let me know what it is, then we can deal with it."

"I know why Will's been so upset and

moody," she said. Then she clammed up again.

"You gonna tell me?" I prompted. She shook her head in confusion.

"It's Dad," she said and hiccupped back a sob.

Icy fingers clasped my heart. "What about him?" I was thinking cancer, a brain tumor, some other horrific diagnosis.

"He's got a girlfriend . . . and she's my age!" A floodgate of tears opened, and Henri collapsed into my lap.

No words would come. I just leaned against her for a few minutes, relieved it wasn't a medical catastrophe after all. Then I sat up and rubbed her back, trying to soothe her. "Oh now, precious, you're taking this way too hard. It was bound to happen. It's the way of the world. You didn't think your dad would stay single forever, did you?"

Hell, I kind of had.

Henri sat up, indignant. "Mom, she's *my* age! How creepy is that? Dad's fifty-two and she's . . . she's barely thirty. He's old enough to be her *father.* Anyway, it's wrong, all wrong. He loves *you.* Why is he doing this?"

I steepled my fingers in front of my face for a moment, then asked, "What does this have to do with Will?"

"He's known for a while and been holding it all inside. Apparently he saw them together right after he got up here from Miami. She's some hot-shot legislator he met in Raleigh, working on those permits for the offshore well. I didn't know anything about her until yesterday. I was driving through downtown and I saw Dad's car over by the legislative building. He was pulling away from the curb, so I picked up my phone to call him, see if he wanted to meet for dinner, and then I saw this blond babe with him. Their body language was pretty obvious. I called Will right away, and he spilled out his guts to me. Mom, he's really been hurting. He went to Paris and moved in with Dad to try to dissuade him."

"Where's Dad now?"

"Still in Raleigh. He told Will he had business there and wouldn't be back for a few days."

"Good thing you're going to be with Will, then," I said, pulling her to her feet. "He needs you right now. Let him know that this is fine with me, that I'm happy about it, actually. I don't want your father to live alone for the rest of his life. He needs someone to take care of him."

"*You* don't need anyone!"

"I know, but I'm a woman, dear. We can actually take care of ourselves."

"You don't have to pretend with me."

"See?" I said, pointing a finger at her. "What you just said is the reason both you and Will are so broken up about this instead of being happy for Dad: your constant belief in the fairy tale of us getting back together is the real problem."

"But —"

"And don't blame me. Lord knows, I've tried to make you understand. Just because we aren't married doesn't mean we aren't family, just a different kind of family. Families change, you know? Dad and I will always be friends."

"But now we'll have to include *her*!" Henri wailed.

"You said *her* like she's Cruella de Vil and eats puppies for breakfast. You don't even know her. If you did, you might like her. At least you've got age in common," I said, going for the easy laugh.

"That's disgusting!"

"Maybe. But it's also reality. Now, you've got to go. Tulip's waiting and the afternoon is moving on without me. I've got work to do, so scoot."

She mashed the tears from her eyes with the palms of her hand and wiped her nose with a flick of her wrist. I plucked a tissue from a nearby table and handed it to her.

"I love you," she said.

"I love you too. Call me when you get to Seahaven."

Back upstairs in my study, I gazed out the window at the Sound, sparkling in the afternoon sun like it had been sprinkled with diamonds, and tried to push back the dark mood that threatened to envelope me. I knew I needed to follow my own advice and forge ahead with my life as Bud had.

I dialed Powell out on the *Magellan* to check on the progress made unplugging the well, then I relayed everything to Phil along with reassurances regarding Powell's capabilities. With these tasks behind me, I felt free to continue planning my trip to the Graveyard of the Atlantic Museum.

I pulled up the museum's website again and checked the ferry schedules. No matter which way I calculated it, however, it was going to take over eight hours just to get 70 miles. Too bad Henri's boat was on the fritz. Will's tinkering turned out to have worsened the timing problem, causing her to haul it to the Jones Brothers shop out on 70 Highway for repairs. If I had it, I could make the trip in under two hours. I was considering renting a boat, when — who could believe it? — my plans were interrupted yet again. This time by a knock at the door.

Still wary after yesterday's events, I sat up on alert. I knew it wasn't Henri. If she'd forgotten something and come back, she'd have called out to me. I trotted to the bedroom, retrieved the baby nine, and slowly descended the stairs. Then I heard the kitchen door rattle. Crap! I'd forgotten to lock it after Henri left! Holding the gun behind my back, I stepped carefully into the kitchen.

Where I practically collided with Viktor Kozlov.

"Dammit! I just about shot you! Don't you knock?"

"I did!" he protested.

"Well . . . give a person time to get to the door. What do you want?" I sounded anything but welcoming.

If he was put off by my foul mood, he didn't show it. "I've come to show you my new boat. One less . . . conspicuous. Like you wanted," he explained.

Oh good grief.

"Viktor . . ." I was so totally exasperated with him I grasped the neck of his T-shirt, pulled his face down to mine, and said, "You don't pay attention. I didn't want you to get another boat." Then I glanced through the window to the dock, did a double-take, and burst out laughing. A 20-foot John boat painted in camo for winter duck hunting floated discreetly at the dock.

"You don't like it?" He looked disappointed.

"Viktor," I said, placing my fingers on my temples. "I just don't know what I have to do to . . ." And then it hit me: Viktor was no longer a problem, he was a solution. All I had to do was get him to switch the boats back again.

"You know what?" I said, rearranging my expression. "I like it a lot. You've done well. But there's a little problem. Can you still use the Fountain?"

"Absolutely!"

"How about tomorrow? All day?"

"How about tonight?" he said, clasping the front of *my* T-shirt and pulling my face to his. "All night?"

Dim light filtering through the plantation shutters of my bedroom along with the chirps and twitters of a dozen sparrows in the branches of a massive live oak outside my window let me know that Thursday was dawning. Soft breathing from young Viktor Kozlov told me he was catching a few winks before coming back for more. My first thought: *Why not?*

As I had told Henri, families change. That's the nature of a family, isn't it? Kids grow up and move away. At least half of all parents find new mates. Bud had. It was in the open now. Everyone moves on.

So what if Viktor was so much younger than me? One, I wasn't going to marry him, just enjoy a little diversion to help me over the hump during this change in my relationship with Bud. And two, I'd be discreet. This little romp wouldn't last long, I'd see to that, and no one would ever know.

As for my relationship with Bud, I'd always care for him and worry about him. I was worried about him now, about his interview with Detectives Pierce and Myers. As I lay listening to the world wake outside my window, I came to a conclusion. If I didn't think Bud had anything to do with the death of the Voyager pilot — and I didn't — the best thing I could do was to move faster in my search for the real killer. You know, in case the police *did* think Bud was involved.

That was assuming, of course, that there *was* a killer, and it hadn't just been an accident incurred by a drunk would-be rapist. My next move toward that end? Find out how a wheel valve from a U-boat got wedged between the rail on the ROV and its cage. Don't ask me why I thought it had anything to do with the possible murder — maybe because I'd found it at the site of my attack — I just did. The two were linked in my head. Perhaps closure about one thing would help me find closure on the other. Thinking back to what I'd been doing at the moment of the attack brought a blank. I closed my eyes, envisioned the ROV, concentrated, and then it came to me.

I'd been on my hands and knees, of course. I had to have been to reach between the ROV rail and its cage. Was there something there my attacker was trying to stop me from seeing? I had limited knowledge regarding ROVs, but that didn't seem logical. Still, it was something to ponder, and the perfect partner to help me answer this question — and plenty of others in my quest — lay right beside me. If I dared to trust him.

Viktor stirred. I slipped from the bed, tiptoed into the bathroom, and sought the refuge of the shower. I suspected some of the previous night's gyrations might have required double-joints, which, I, in fact, don't have. As the hot water soothed my body, I smiled smugly, wondering if Bud had sore abs and gluts this morning from the same kind of workout. But, of course, that was childish. Right now, I had some important decisions to make, primarily about just how much I wanted to trust Viktor.

Cascades of white lather coursed down my body as I vigorously shampooed my hair. Closing my eyes, I tilted my head back for a rinse, thinking maybe it would be better if I just played the trust thing with Viktor by ear for a while. After all, I barely knew him. Then I felt a waft of air and his body, still cool from the air-conditioned bedroom, wrapped around my hot steamy one. A fresh jolt of sexual energy shot through me. I started to protest that I wanted to get on with the day and my trip to the museum. Instead, I just rested my face against the tile wall, closed my eyes, and soaked up the pleasure.

Later, all squeaky clean but with slightly rubbery legs, I stepped out and tossed Viktor a fluffy white towel. "Tell me again why we're going to this museum today?" he asked.

"No real reason except that recently I took a scuba-diving tour of shipwrecks not far off our coast and saw my first German U-boat. I think they're fascinating, and this museum's website says they've got a display devoted to one of them."

"Do you know the way?"

"I do. While you switch boats, I'll run up the street and grab a couple of cups of coffee for now and a few subs so we can have a picnic later."

SIXTEEN

Even with the Fountain's engines at near-idle speed, Viktor and I moved swiftly out to the Intercoastal Waterway. On this dead calm day, it stretched ahead of us like silk. Slowing only for no-wake zones, we sped smoothly along, taking in the beauty of our surroundings. Herons of every size, great blues, common and great whites, little blues, and egrets left their roosts for their favorite feeding grounds. Shrimpers headed out to sea to catch dinner for vacationers, and all around us, pelicans dove headlong into the water like kamikazes, sending up little plumes of spray.

Soon I was directing Viktor to the channel markers leading us across the broad expanse of Pamlico Sound toward the town of Hatteras on Hatteras Island. At about half its maximum speed of 60 knots, the boat easily skimmed the water. About midway across, we slowed to idle again, pulled out of the channel, dropped anchor, and enjoyed an early lunch and each other . . . again.

After finding dockage within walking distance of the museum, I told Viktor I needed to make a few calls before we set off. He was patient as I checked in with Powell on the *Magellan* and Phil in Houston. When I was ready, he took my hand to steady me as I stepped from the boat. I had to admit, this chivalry was something I could probably get used to.

Somewhat resembling the bow of a ship with exposed timbers and soaring masts, the museum covered a time period from the early 1500s to the end of World War II. Shipwrecks resulting from weather, piracy, warfare, trade, and exploration made up the majority of its exhibits.

We made a quick tour of them all first, watched a few videos, and then gravitated back to the exhibit on *U-85,* the first German submarine in their Eastern Seaboard offensive of Operation Drumbeat. Viktor was fascinated with the Enigma machine, one of the famous encoders used by the Germans to send secret wartime messages, so I moved on to read the first-person accounts of residents who'd lived on the Outer Banks back then.

An elderly volunteer who'd been watching me stepped over and offered some personal insight. She said her name was Lucy and she'd been a little girl living on the banks in the town of Avon during the war. She was an eyewitness to the devastation the subs had wrought. I listened, fascinated.

"Sometimes we'd hear big explosions late in the night and next morning, the bodies of seamen would wash up on the beach. No one knows how many crew members survived a sub attack only to drown later or just drift out to sea on wreckage and die of thirst. Horrible. Bits and pieces of wreckage would wash up too, and googy black oil coated everything on the beach. One summer we couldn't even go swimming. You can still see streaks of it buried in the sand if you dig down deep enough."

"Were there ever any survivors?" I asked.

"Yes, sometimes a lifeboat would make it to shore . . ." Viktor joined us. "Oh my!" Lucy said. "Who is this handsome young man?"

Viktor grinned. "Afanasy Viktor Kozlov, at your service. I'm her —"

"Colleague," I interjected firmly.

Did I see Lucy wink? I wasn't sure. "Well, you just let me know if I can help you further." She waggled her fingers at us and moved over to a school group.

Viktor moved to my side, and it wasn't long before he slipped his arm around me. We read the exhibit's labels quietly for the next few minutes. Then his hand slid under my T-shirt.

"Stop it," I said. "This place is crawling with kids."

Viktor made a humorous gesture of disgust, looked left and right, and said, "In that case, I suggest we leave before we catch something. You didn't touch anything, did you?"

"No," I laughed.

"Anyway," he cut in, "if we leave now, we can make it back in time to . . . umm . . . rest a little before watching the sun go down. Then I'll take you out for a nice supper."

As informative and thought-provoking as the museum was, I didn't mind leaving. It lacked what I was hoping for, which was a detailed account of *all* the subs operating off the East Coast during World War II. Further online research was needed.

Before departing, we wandered over to the gift shop, where I bought a World War II documentary video. Then I stepped outside to wait for Viktor, who was still shopping. When he came out, he handed me a small felt bag. "For you," he said. "As a souvenir of today."

It was heavy for its size and opening the drawstrings, a beautiful glass paperweight slid into the palm of my hand. It was a replica of a wrecked wooden schooner laying on its side on a sand dune.

"Thank you," I said simply. And I couldn't help feeling a little guilty that I'd bought nothing to offer in return.

Later — much later — after we'd fallen asleep, a trill from my iPhone woke me. I groped for it on the nightstand. "Hello," I croaked.

"Oh, damn, Cleo," said Duncan Powell. "I forgot the rest of the world sleeps between the hours of midnight and six. I guess I woke you."

The glowing blue lighted numbers on my clock said 2:34 a.m, Friday. "Uh, that's okay. What's up?"

"The drillbit is what's up. It's hanging over the moonpool right now, and we're just about ready to send it back down. The borehole is clear, *finally,* and there was no damage to the casing. Anyway, we're just about to start drilling again. Sorry about the hour!"

"No problem. I'm on my way." I gently

replaced the phone and eased out of bed, not wanting to wake Viktor. But he wasn't asleep.

"This will work out well," he said.

"What do you mean?"

"You have to go in today, and I'll be gone all day too. Maybe tomorrow as well."

"Oh?"

"Yes. I must return the boat to Davy and the boys. They are taking it to Fort Myers on the west coast of Florida in preparation for the long run across the eastern Gulf to Port Fourchon. After that, I'm going to Durham. A friend sent me a lead on an apartment for the fall, and I need to negotiate with the owner now, before someone else rents it."

"At least you don't have to get up this minute. Go back to sleep. Just remember to lock the back door when you leave."

An hour later, I'd already slipped past the small crowd of protestors to the side gate of the port, boarded a support vessel to the *Magellan,* and was on my way. I'd intended to use the trip to jot down a few notes regarding what I'd learned about U-boats in general. My plan involved coming up with a direction beyond digging through endless data about each boat.

However, that's not what I did.

Four hours later, I jerked awake to someone shaking my shoulder. "We're here, ma'am," a round-faced crewman said.

Thinking I absolutely *had* to get over my distaste for helicopters, I rubbed the back of my hand over my mouth and hoped I hadn't been drooling.

"We'll be heading back to port sometime after lunch. Listen for the chime on the speakers."

The scene on the bridge was pretty much the same as before, with a certain amount of attention focused on the horizon. I didn't see Powell, so I checked in with his first officer. The man barely acknowledged me, so intent was he on studying the activity on the *Able Leader* with binoculars.

I asked, "Can you tell what they're doing?"

"Getting ready to drill," he said, his voice betraying his amazement.

"No way!"

"Yep. We're pretty sure they're preparing to lower the bit anytime now." Resisting the temptation to pick up a pair of nocks myself, I remembered my limited time and instead headed for the logging lab. Nevertheless, I just couldn't help stopping at the moonpool on my way for a quick look over the side.

No matter how many times I do it, I'm still awed by this extraordinary technology. The din of the drillfloor enveloped me as I gazed down into the square cutout the size of a swimming pool smack in the middle of the ship. While the Atlantic is often turbid inshore, offshore it is deep blue and clear as glass, so that when viewed in the small enclosed area of the moonpool, it looks, well, just like a swimming pool.

It simply was stunning to imagine that around two thirty this morning, the slender thread of drill pipe had again been successfully lowered through the riser pipe to the seafloor and was now grinding its way to our target in the ancient coral reef. Moreover, that all of this had been accomplished by robots, giant machines, computers, and satellites — basically untouched by human hands — seemed to me, as it would anyone, utterly amazing.

One of the loggers I'd met earlier, Tom was his name, said, "Hey, Cleo," in a friendly but distracted manner. Before I could respond, he turned to a coworker: "Go back to the pit and make sure that agitator is working. If the readings don't get any better than this, Phil's gonna have a cow."

Standing behind him, I read the chromatograph, a device that analyzes the drilling mud circulating from the ship to the bottom of the well and back. The chromatograph gives readings for its gas content, and it showed a minimal reading, just a few units above normal.

"How far down are we?" I asked.

Tom checked the chart. "Twelve thousand one hundred ninety-two feet. This limestone's very fast, they're cutting a foot every five minutes. Driller's riding the brakes, it's cutting so quick. Soon's we get some show over the background gas, we'll run a log."

"Well, there you go," I said. "It's early yet, they've barely cut into it. You're letting Phil get you all wired up."

Now the other mudlogger returned, and before Tom could ask, he blew out a frustrated sigh and said, "I told you, man, it's all working fine. Elton's down there and he's checked everything. The reason the chromatograph says there's no gas beyond the normal background is because there *isn't* any. I swear, you're starting to act like an old woman."

Hearing this, I made my next stop a check in with Elton down at the shaker. Together we satisfied ourselves that the readings were correct. I collected more samples, resolving to remain positive, then spent the next hour or so washing, drying, and studying them under the microscope and in the ultraviolet light box. I made my own notes of what I intended to discuss with Phil later.

Leaving the logging lab, I dropped by Elton's office to pick up my copy of his daily log. Since I still had time, I decided to head for the ROV area, where I hoped to borrow a computer so I could go back to the U-boat website and come up with a faster research method.

Approaching Voyager's van, I looked for the warning sign that would let me know there was no admittance to the area because the ROV was in operation. Since it wasn't there, I knocked on the door and pushed it open.

"Hey, Ms. Cooper," the tech I remembered as Barry from one of my first visits said. "You're back."

"No, Barry," Ricky said sarcastically, "she's really still over on the mainland, that's only a virtual Ms. Cooper."

"Children, children," Ray said. "Play nice in front of company. What can we do for you today, Cleo? Unfortunately we aren't filming any footage for *Sea Hunt* today."

"That's quite all right," I said. "Actually, I was wondering if you have a spare computer I might use. If not, I can run up to the internet room."

"You can use Hunter's," said Barry, pointing to the dead man's computer at the end of a long shared worktable. "He isn't going to need it anymore."

"Use mine instead," Ray said. "Hunter's won't be wiped clean until after we finish this job and the van's moved back to Texas. Besides, we don't know his password. I'll be done in maybe thirty . . . forty-five minutes. You can hang out while we're running diagnostics on Scooter."

"I'm surprised the police didn't confiscate it as part of their investigation," I said.

"Actually they cloned it," Ray explained. "Same thing. But they did take his personal computer from his room. The other crew was still here when they came. One of the twins told us that the police interviewed them individually when the company flew them over to Chapel Hill to identify his body."

"Yeah," Barry said. "They also tossed his bunk and his locker and checked out the ROV platform. They think he fell from there."

"They said he probably hit his head on the railing first, then fell over," Ricky said.

"Whatever," Ray said in his deep Texas drawl. "He was one dumb SOB. Now you boys get back to work or we'll never get done here."

I looked at the dead man's computer then said to Ray, "You mind?"

"No. Help yourself," Ray said, never looking up. "You think you can figure out his password?"

"Well," I said, "you said he was a . . . simple man. Maybe he left himself a reminder. I'll check around in his work area while I wait for you to finish what you're doing."

Finding only company-related material in his workspace — no scraps of paper with a snappy word jotted on it, nor any personal notebook — I was about to give up. Then I reminded myself that this was his company computer as opposed to his personal one; he'd naturally be less inclined to worry about his password being found. I contemplated further, then tilted the computer up and looked under it. Sure enough, right on the bottom for all the world to see was a dirty strip of masking tape on which *workingcomputer2014* was scrawled in ballpoint. Naw . . . it couldn't be. Still, I typed it in.

His desktop magically appeared. "Hot damn," I said out loud, to no one in particular. "You're right. He was a simple man."

Fortunately the computer screen faced the

wall and the small workspace allowed for some privacy. I got online, but before pursuing my original task — continuing my research into German U-boats — I found myself distracted by other thoughts.

I considered my luck. I mean, it was such a break. I actually had an opportunity to go into the mind, if you will, of the creep who'd tried to rape me. Of course, Pierce and Myers would be seriously miffed if they knew I was on the dead man's computer. But they didn't know, right? And, anyway, it wasn't like I was on his personal machine.

Deciding to forge ahead, I went straight to the history of the sites last visited. Lots of technical data on the manipulating arms of the ROV. Nothing of interest there, so I tried to get into his email but I couldn't crack that password. Next I checked the bookmarks. More technical stuff. Then I noticed a small icon blinking at the bottom of the screen. I clicked on it.

Hunter had a document in the queue waiting to be printed. Ray and Ricky got up and went to check some thingamabob on the ROV while Barry stayed behind with the controls.

I watched Barry for a minute. He seemed very absorbed in his work, so I clicked on Print. Probably just some more ROV specs or something anyway. Mechanical click-clacking across the room let me know the printer's location. Unfortunately, it was right beside Barry's chair. I hopped up and went to the machine, retrieving the first page as soon as the printer spit it out. Barry never even looked up. Good thing, as my knees almost buckled when I read the page.

At last, my suspicions were confirmed. It was a copy of an email Hunter had sent to his work computer from his personal Gmail account. It was from Davy Duchamp, instructing Hunter to a site with an article he wanted him to "read with special attention to the refit of a forward torpedo tube into a storage compartment. Study, then delete." Three more pages glided ever-so-slowly from the printer.

But after more clicking and clacking, the printer stopped and the out-of-paper light blinked politely. Damn! Just then the door to the van banged open and in its space stood an angry Ray, hands on his hips. I froze, the pages clutched in my naughty little fingers.

"Barry!" Ray snapped. "Get out here, man, I'll show you what I'm talking about."

"Fine!" Barry huffed as he spun around his desk and marched out.

Ray gave me a concerned look. "You okay?

Need some help?"

"No," I squeaked.

"Okay, then," he said, closing the door behind him. I checked out the last page to come from the printer. It was number three of three. Good thing because I was so shaken at my discovery I wouldn't have been able to reload paper into a strange printer. I ran back to Hunter's computer, shut it down, grabbed my hard hat, and made a beeline for the helm and a quiet conference room where I could read what I'd printed.

"Come back when you can stay longer," called one of the techs after me.

I threw up my hand in a nonchalant wave and swallowed hard, hoping to force my heart from my throat back to its normal resting place in my chest.

As luck would have it, all the meeting rooms around the helm station were occupied. But then I had a better idea and headed for the women's head. As far as I knew there were only three other women aboard, and they all worked on the main deck. I was pretty certain I'd be alone there.

Latching the stall door, I sat down and read the article. It was a historical account of the refitting of a very special German U-boat to accommodate certain civilian friends of the Third Reich. The article even included a blueprint of the sub's layout and a schematic of how one of the torpedo tubes was refit for the purpose of hiding things — an artifact or document box or somesuch. The writer speculated that hidden documents were top-secret military intelligence. Hunter must have been trying to print the article instead of deleting as instructed and been interrupted. Or maybe he'd had to wait for one of his teammates to finish printing something. Being dead, he never got back to it.

Reading on, the article stated the sub was one of a group of three hundred commissioned into service in the Kriegsmarine right before the end of the war. Little was know about them, and U-boats numbered 491–500 never got assigned to active duty. The writer here was suggesting — speculatively, of course — that this sub's design had included quarters for dignitaries escaping Germany. Provocatively, the author also identified the aforementioned hidden artifact as one that Hitler wanted to relocate for safekeeping. It must have been pretty special because it was being sent away with a personal guardian. Here a photo was provided.

I stared at it.

In it were three people: a smiling yet very tense-looking man in a Nazi uniform and two young men, one in a suit and tie and the other in military garb. The photo's scalloped edging suggested it had not been taken by a professional. Instead, the background and the pose of the subjects was like a snapshot. Below the photo a caption identified the young military man as Wolfgang Reckhoff, and the fellow in the suit as an art history professor at the University of Gottingen named Gerhard Coester. The Nazi officer was identified as Erich Koch.

Reckoff stood to one side as Coester was handed a cylinder about the size of a Pringles can to Koch. Besides noting his youth, I was struck by the haunted look in the professor's dark, deep-set eyes. His brown hair was slicked down, parted in the middle, and tucked behind very large ears, which poked prominently from his head. Even in the grainy photo, I got the impression of clenched teeth behind his drawn lips.

I read on. The writer believed that the cylinder the young professor could be seen taking possession of contained a map.

What? This was not *Raiders of the Lost Ark*! These people weren't actors but historical figures. I was holding my breath as I continued, stunned to learn that the map being handed over into his safekeeping would lead anyone possessing it to the Amber Room, stolen from the Catherine Palace in Russia during World War II.

Even surmising the Amber Room to be a work of art of monumental value — it must have been to have Hitler himself go to the lengths he did to hide it — I still couldn't help but wonder if this article was all speculation. I didn't know who the author was or what his credentials were. This could be a post from some ridiculous conspiracy blog. Could any of it be true? Why was Davy Duchamp instructing an ROV pilot onboard *Magellan* to read it? What did it have to do with Manteo One?

And with me?

Seventeen

On Friday afternoons in Morehead, the streets are crowded with weekend residents and vacationing renters walking toward restaurants and hot spots. I luckily made it home without wiping out one of them. I bolted the stairs two at a time to my study. Barely able to contain myself, I sat down and Googled *the Amber Room.* Thirty minutes and several articles later, I'd learned a great deal, every bit of it fascinating.

The Amber Room had been designed by a German baroque sculptor named Andreas Schluter in 1701 for Frederick I, the first king of Prussia. It was constructed from amber panels as well as gold, paintings, and jewels. In 1716, it was gifted to Peter the Great to solidify Prussian–Russian relations; the room was disassembled and rebuilt, as well as embellished upon, in Russia. By the time it was "finished," the room contained 6 tons of amber and encompassed over 55 square meters in the palace. It stayed there until World War II, when Hitler decided that since it was made by a German, the treasure ought to be his. He sent a group of men to dismantle it as soon as the Nazi Army reached Leningrad. Their plan was to store it in Konigsberg, East Prussia, until they won the war.

Little tingles of electricity rippled up my spine when I read that Hitler, upon realizing the war was lost, put the room in the care of a loyal officer — one Erich Koch. Erich Koch? I jumped up, grabbed my pack from the chair where I'd tossed it, and, with shaking fingers, pulled out the article I'd printed off Hunter's computer. Remarkably, the caption read "Erich Koch." To be sure, I looked him up on Wikipedia, where there was a photo.

It was the same man.

Koch had been one of Hitler's top henchmen and the murderer of some four hundred thousand Polish citizens. He'd fled Germany for Denmark in 1945 but later returned to Hamburg, where he was captured in 1949. The Russians had wanted him extradited, but the British gave him to Poland, where he was tried for his war crimes and sentenced to death. His sentence was commuted, however, because it was believed he knew of the whereabouts of tons of looted art, above all, the Amber Room. He lived in a Polish prison until he died in 1986 at the age of ninety, never giving up the secret.

Going back to a Google search, I realized that theories abounded as to what happened to the Amber Room, but facts were few. Only mystery prevailed.

According to some art historians, the Amber Room never survived the bombings of Konigsberg. Others believe Koch had all twenty-seven crates containing the room moved into a bunker somewhere in Germany before the bombings. Still others said he took the crates with him when he escaped to Denmark. So many people believed that Koch ordered the crates loaded aboard the luxury liner *Wilhelm Gustloff,* which was sunk in the Baltic Sea in 1945, that a team of Russian and Polish salvage divers explored the wreck in 1950. The theory was proved wrong.

"I knew it!" I said aloud. I sat back in my chair, a big smile on my face. I had a theory of my own. In fact, I was pretty sure that, incredible as it seemed, I knew the whereabouts of the map to the Amber Room. And the best thing about my theory: it supplied a possible explanation for the death of Nuvuk Hunter that had nothing whatsoever to do with Mr. Bud Cooper.

I picked up the wheel valve I'd been trying to retrieve the night I'd been attacked, turned it in my fingers, and said, "I knew you had something to do with this death, and now I'm going to prove it."

Only one person in the world would listen to my theory and not call 911 in search of the nearest mental facility, and that was Bud. I decided to call him at Seahaven so I could check on Will and Henri as well.

"Where's your dad?" I asked when Will answered.

"Uh . . . he's not here."

"Okay. Where is he? When will he be back?"

I heard Henri shout in the background. "Just tell her, Will!"

"He's with that girl."

"What girl?" I said, confused.

"The one that's a representative in the House."

"Oh . . . she's not a girl. She's a woman."

"Well, she's our age. I'd hardly call her a woman."

"Never mind. I don't want to argue. When will he be back?"

"Not tonight. He said they'd be working late. Something about that well you guys are drilling and some permit problems that might come before the Legislature."

"Okay," I said getting a slightly queasy feeling to hear there might be such issues at this late date, but more annoyed than anything. Following a quick report from Henri on Tulip, I hung up, made a light supper, and called the helicopter service to line up a ride out to the *Magellan* tomorrow morning. By the time I was ready to climb into bed, I knew sleep would be elusive.

Moonbeams scattered through the leafy branches of the live oak outside the window and found their way through the shutters to the ceiling above me. I finally fell asleep watching them dance, knowing that as I lay there, *Magellan*'s drill was chewing its way into the history books, and not far from where it dove into the seabed lay the answer to one of the world's greatest mysteries — the whereabouts of the Amber Room.

Having defied the laws of physics yet again, I climbed out of the helicopter as soon as it set down on the *Magellan* Saturday morning, ducked to avoid decapitation, and went to find Phil Gregson. He'd told me when I called him last night that he was flying in to be here when the well came in. My pilot said Phil had arrived about thirty minutes ahead of me.

Following my usual routine, I went the helm after a quick check-in at the radio room on the bridge. Duncan Powell appeared to be having a come-to-Jesus meeting with staff, so I quietly closed the door and headed for the DC, where I was pretty sure I'd find Phil.

I was right. Along with the assistant driller and several roughnecks, he was watching the monitor that displayed drilling depth.

"Hey, Cleo," he said.

"Phil," I said, shaking his hand. "Where are we?"

"Exactly twelve thousand four hundred thirty-two feet down. Progress has been pretty steady in this limestone. Cuttings show the gas is starting to bubble up — readings are over a hundred units."

"Great, I said. "We timed this just right then, we should be hitting our bright spot in the next few feet."

"Correct. Unless something happens. And anything can," Phil said worriedly. "I just got here a little while ago and met with Elton a few minutes before he bugged out to the logging lab. What do you say we go find him there?"

As we crossed under the catwalk that overlooked the moonpool on four sides, something on the opposite side caught my eye. I looked up and saw a familiar silhouette. It was Bud.

With the early morning sun breaking over his shoulder, I saw him bend to wrap his arm around the shoulders of a pretty blond woman and speak directly into her ear. I stopped in my tracks. Phil, unaware, went on. I was too far away to read their lips, and the cacophonous noise of the drill drowned out their words, but it didn't matter.

As I watched, Bud's eyes shifted down and he looked directly at me. His companion realized she'd lost his attention, followed his line of sight, and gazed at me too. For a second, I stood, frozen, then gave what I hoped looked like a cheery wave and hurried to catch up with Phil.

After only a few paces, however, I couldn't help myself — I looked back to see if I could recognize the blonde. I couldn't, but I had a pretty good idea who she was. What I didn't know was what on earth she would be doing out here with Bud. I got a hint of an answer when a scrum of reporters and government officials followed by a cameraman joined them on the catwalk.

Tom and another logger were on duty in the lab. They were hustling to wash and analyze samples Elton was bringing back from the shaker at 3-foot intervals. Cautious optimism at the new readings of "show" appearing on the chromatograph was palpable. Phil and I compared the notes I'd taken over the last two days to the ones he'd made from digital information and emails he received continuously from the loggers. Outwardly, I probably sounded like I was a hundred percent in the moment. I wasn't. Part of me was still standing under the catwalk watching my ex-husband — who was also my oldest friend — sharing his thoughts with someone new.

Phil had brought along a CD featuring various 3D views of our targeted bright spot. We carried it up to the media room off the helm station and studied it as we waited for a call from David Grant. For a while I lost myself in the early Cretaceous world of rising and falling seas, of coral reefs and tidal lagoons, of basins teeming with life and river deltas pushing their alluvial fans of organic-rich sediments far out onto the continent's shelf.

When the door opened, Duncan Powell walked in — but he didn't look like a man about to make history as being captain of the rig that brought in the first wildcat gas well in the Manteo prospect. "I see everybody's here for the big moment," he said.

"Everyone but Braxton," Phil said. "Where's he?"

"Down in the DC."

"How about SunCo and the *Able Leader,*" I asked, thinking that might be weighing on Powell's mind. "Any news on their progress?"

"They are steady at it over there," he said. "They've got both drills working. Braxton and I calculate they've shoved a little over ten thousand feet of pipe down the hole. They're in over twenty-four hundred feet of water, so that'll put them a little over seventy-five hundred feet down hole. If we come in today, we're definitely going to beat them."

"Ya-hoo!" whooped Phil and held up a palm for a high five. I smacked it back. Powell gave a weak smile in return. Then, making sure my voice dripped with nonchalance, I said, "I thought I saw Bud on the catwalk over the moon pool. Is he here for the big event too?"

"Oh, man," Powell said, shaking his head. "I hate to break the congratulatory mood here, but I have to. I've got some bad news. Bud's out here to try and stop a bad situation before it happens, manage some damage control."

"Damage control?"

"Yeah," Powell sighed. "The state is making rumblings about stopping drilling out here . . . again. Protestors are heating things up, so he got permission from Houston to bring one of the legislators and the leaders of the various government agencies out here."

At that moment, we were interrupted by the head driller requesting our presence in the DC. We practically jammed ourselves in the doorway in our excitement to get there and share in the big event.

Upon arriving, however, the news wasn't exactly what we'd been expecting. Phil and I went straight to the wall of monitors. There we saw the gas readings, instead of being higher, had dropped lower. Duncan Powell joined Braxton Roberts, and both men bent over the well plan on a small worktable.

Grant sat at the controls for the drill, the bit rotating in neutral. "What do you think's going on?" Phil inquired.

"Well," Grant replied, in his British accent crisp with tension, "Since the readings are getting weaker, we obviously have to head in a new direction. Which way is for you guys to decide."

Powell and Braxton engaged in a short

strained discussion, pausing only to look from the well design to the gas monitors. Finally they nodded at each other, and Braxton said, "We need to make a slight deviation in the azimuth angle in the bore-hole, now. Otherwise, we'll miss our target."

Just to be on the safe side, Phil and I went back to the logging lab to check the readings there. "We're close," Phil said. "Very close. We just need to head down a few more degrees. That should put us right on our target."

After a few more refining calculations, we came up with the angle adjustment to relay back to Grant and the drill team. "Of course we'll have to call a conference with the honchos in Houston." We all agreed, at which point we tromped off to the conference room. The connection was made and in minutes I was staring at Hiram Hightower himself, along with his team of some of the best, most successful earth scientists in the oil and gas industry as they studied the problem.

Fingers flew on calculators, theories were bandied about, and a few tempers flared on the screen as we on the *Magellan* quietly waited. I felt a little like God was about to speak when Hightower suddenly cleared his throat. All computing and theorizing stopped. He leaned back, looked into the camera transmitting his image to us, and said with a Texas drawl, "We need to stop wasting time and money. I believe we're all in agreement to go with the new azimuth angle."

Grant took a joystick in each hand and geosteered the bit with a surgeon's touch, using his new coordinates. In a little over an hour, the gas readings went up dramatically. We'd hit our target. Now it was just a question of how thick the gas-bearing formation was and how high the pressure was, what the flow rate of the gas would be. At five minutes per foot to drill the reservoir rock, it would likely be a couple of days before we knew that answer.

I was contemplating how large the reservoir would need to be to satisfy Global's enormous financial demands when I saw Bud and a cameraman directing the woman he'd brought with him in various poses beside the massive drill. Through the three-sided window overlooking the drilling floor, I watched Bud point toward the aft end of the ship. The woman and the cameraman set off in that direction. Seizing the opportunity of slightly less noise due to the temporary pause in drilling, I placed both pinkies between my lips and let out a Tulip field whistle. Bud turned, smiled, and trotted to me.

"Hey, babe," he said. "I've been looking for you."

"Really?" I said. "I imagine if I'd been in your friend's ear, you might have found me."

He gave a little uncomfortable laugh. "Whatever. I've been wanting to give you a heads-up on what's going on, but our schedule has been so crazy. We've got a photo session out here, then back to Raleigh for an emergency meeting with other legislators, and I've had to be on the phone with Global. Constantly."

"Duncan said there might be some problems with permitting. But I sure hope not, because we just cut into our target and there's *definitely* gas there."

Bud's face lit up. "Babe! We did it!" He grabbed me in a big bear hug.

"Bud, please," I shook my head laughing. "Put me down. Those reporters might see, and we aren't ready to make any disclosures just now. Not until we know exactly how big our discovery is. It'll take a couple of days."

"Okay, okay," he sighed happily. "It's only that I just know it's going to be a huge discovery, and I can't wait for the world to hear!"

"What would be a *real* shame is to have finally found it and then have the state shut us down," I reminded him.

"Well, that's not going to happen. Don't you worry. That's why we're here. Coastal Management may try to stop us on the basis of discrepancies in our discharge plan — that's how they halted the first exploration out here, by finding an inconsistency between the discharge permit and exploration plan and the state's regulations — but we've gone to great pains this time to make sure that doesn't happen. We brought heads of all the agencies involved to show them in person."

"Who's *we*?"

"Oh sorry. You haven't met Amanda yet. She chairs the Legislative Research Commission Advisory Subcommittee on Offshore Energy. She's been the tip of the spear in the battle to allow exploration and production of hydrocarbons on the twenty-one leases of the Manteo Prospect."

"Impressive."

"Yes, she is," Bud said. His tone was admiring. "And believe me when I say right now, without her, our chances of getting at least a Suspension of Operations or Memorandum of Understanding slapped on us would be very high. A company like SunCo might withstand the years of delay that would entail. Global couldn't. It would be the end of them — and of our investment."

The awkward silence that fell between us was cut short when Amanda appeared out of nowhere, grabbed Bud's arm possessively, and drawled, "Do hurry, dear. Everyone's waitin' on you. Oh sorry. Did ah interrupt somethin'?"

Before Bud could respond, Amanda thrust her hand at me and, continuing her Scarlett O'Hara impression, said, "Ah don't believe we've met. Amanda Whitfield. And you are?"

I hated her instantly, but consummate professional — and very good liar — that I am, I gave her hand a firm shake and responded, "Cleo Cooper. So nice to meet you and thank you in person for all your hard work during this difficult permitting process."

Amanda, whose dewy complexion said she couldn't have been much over thirty, turned to Bud, flashed a perfect Southern beauty queen smile, and said, "Now, Bud, have you been braggin' on me again?"

Bud flushed but didn't respond. I hesitated, waiting for her to add, "Well, ah do declare." When she didn't, I continued, "And for your continued help in the fight apparently to come."

"Now don't you worry," she said, removing her hard hat and smoothing her immaculate French twist. "I'm a tough Southern lawyer from a long line of tough Southern lawyers, and this type of thing is pure Pablum for me. Besides, what could be better than helping Bud and the people of my district at the same time?" She replaced her hard hat and turned to him, "It's never wise to keep reporters waitin', I always say."

Before they left earshot, however, I heard Amanda say, "Don't forget, dahlin', we've got dinner with the speaker tonight and then . . ." This she followed with a lilting laugh, holding the rim of her hard hat coquettishly with one hand while giving him a pat on the butt with the other.

I said aloud, "Well, shut my mouth." Then the ship's loudspeaker announced the arrival of the copter that I imagined was their ride back, and I got a sinking feeling. The jubilance I'd felt only moments earlier over the well coming in dimmed. Moreover, I definitely wouldn't be discussing my U-boat theory with Bud. Not today — and maybe not ever.

"There you are," Powell said, coming up behind me. "I'm headed back to the helm.

You going back today or staying out here?"

"Going back, definitely," I said. "I'm optimistic, though, that it'll take a couple of days to reach the bottom of the reservoir. Then you'll have to trip back out, run some wire-line logs for more precise measurements of gas content, and that'll take another few days. No sense in me and Elton both just marking time out here. You guys know where to find me."

"That we do," Powell said. "I'm sure glad it's looking so good, Global could stand to catch a break."

We went over a few more details with Phil over a celebratory lunch in the galley, then I caught my own helicopter ride home.

About fifteen minutes into our flight, I realized I was actually enjoying the ride. The warmth of the sun through the window felt good on my face while the air-conditioned cabin kept me cool enough to drop off for a quick power nap. My lids drooped. Predictably, my iPhone vibrated. Damn. I checked the screen: Pierce. I hadn't spoken to him since he said he was probably going to rule Hunter's death an accident as soon as he talked to Bud.

"Detective Sergeant Alex Pierce, here, Ms. Cooper. How are you?"

"Fine, and —"

"That's good. I need to speak with you. Would tomorrow be suitable?"

"Sunday?"

"I have some catch-up work in the office. If possible, I'd like to drop by on my way there. Say about eight?"

"Uh . . . can't you just tell me on the . . . hello?"

I looked at the screen. Call ended. "Bastard," I muttered. Maybe he wasn't going to close the case after all. Maybe he wasn't satisfied with Bud's poker alibi. Maybe the bathroom breaks *were* an issue with him.

All of a sudden we passed under a large cloud. As its shadow darkened the cabin, I tried to shake off the feeling of impending danger that crept over me.

Eighteen

Sunday morning I sat across my kitchen table from Detective Sergeant Alex Pierce. His trusty sidekick, Myers, was absent from today's proceedings. I stirred my coffee waiting for him to finish doctoring his.

Finally, he took a sip, "Great coffee."

"I'm glad you like it."

He took three more swallows but said nothing.

Having already grown tired of our little party, I nudged the conversation along. "Have you made a final ruling on the death of Nuvuk Hunter yet?"

"No." Sip. Sip.

What an ass. I studied my spoon.

Finally Pierce, setting his mug down, laid his palms flat on the table as though he thought it might levitate, and asked, "Can you think of what Mr. Hunter might have been looking for out there where y'all are drilling?"

Fortunately I'm an old hand at the fine art of holding a poker face. I gazed placidly at him. "Of course. Dry natural gas. The same thing we're all looking for. It's out there somewhere under twenty-two hundred feet of water, trapped in fourteen thousand feet of sand, silt, and ancient limestone."

"No. Not that. I'm referring to a more tangible object of great value. Like uh . . . uh . . ." He paused, tying to summon just the right word to describe what he meant.

I leaned forward, an exaggerated look of expectation on my face. "Like the Fountain of Youth . . . or . . . chests of gold and silver? Blackbeard's treasure, maybe?"

"Maybe not treasure in the traditional sense of the word, but something like that," he said defensively.

"Jeez. I can't imagine what you could be referring to," I lied. "Perhaps if I had more information . . ."

Pierce inscribed little circles on the table with his index finger.

How great was this? I knew just as clearly as I knew I was sitting at my kitchen table that Pierce had finally gotten around to digging through Hunter's personal computer and found a clue on it that had led him to this conclusion. I desperately wanted to know what he had, but I had to be very careful how I phrased my next question. "Did one of his Voyager teammates say something to make you think he'd been on the trail of some pirate treasure?"

"No. But there were numerous emails on his computer seemingly from a colleague, asking about the status of 'the cylinder'."

"Cylinder?" I asked with a shrug. "Sounds more like a part to me."

"I've already talked to a guy out on the *Magellan,* who does maintenance on that underwater robot, the . . . uh . . ."

"The ROV?"

"Yeah, right. I asked him about it. He said no, there's nothing on an ROV known as a cylinder. But there are several emails, all two days before he died, that tell him, in what seems to me to be a desperate tone, to" — Pierce put down his mug so he could use his fingers for air quotes — " 'find the cylinder' and 'find it quick before your rotation is over' and 'it has to be in there.' Oh, and 'look in the forward holds again'."

"Interesting," I said, nodding my head like Watson to Holmes. "What did the replies say?"

"Basically just variations on 'I already did'," Pierce said, making air quotes again.

To look extra serious, I chewed a hangnail. "So, these emails were sent right before he died. What about earlier? How far back did you go?"

"Everything was deleted after a few days, and with Gmail, you can't retrieve correspondence once it's deleted from the trash bin. It's not stored on a hard drive anywhere. Just gets scattered into cyberspace."

"Well, what about whoever they were from? Did you try to reply?"

"Yep. Returned as a failed message. But we've got someone working on it."

Good luck with that. "What about his favorites list or bookmarks or sites he usually visited? Maybe there'd be something there," I added helpfully.

"Nothing but porn. Lots and lots of porn."

"Gross."

"I'll say. At least there was no kiddie porn. One thing about him, though, he definitely favored women of your type."

"Excuse me?"

"Oh, sorry. I didn't mean that like it sounded," Pierce said, turning red. "What I meant was tall, blond, beautiful . . . you know?"

I looked at him like he was a worm that had just crawled out from under an outhouse. He squirmed. I took advantage of his discomfort at venturing too far into sexual-harassment land and said, "Know what I think?"

"What?"

"I think you've been reading too many Clive Cussler novels. Seriously, where would he be looking for this 'cylinder'? How big is it? Is it big around as a five-gallon bucket or a fifty-gallon barrel or a half-inch toothbrush holder? And what's in it?"

"As to how big it is . . . I don't know. What's in it? Again, I don't know; it could be anything from heroin to uncut diamonds. But where it is, that I *do* know."

I raised my eyebrows expectantly.

"On the *Magellan,* of course."

I couldn't stop myself: a little smile escaped my lips. Quickly adjusting it to more resemble a skeptical smirk, I said, "Sounds very far-fetched to me, but assuming this mysterious cylinder exists, what then? You planning to hire the army of lawyers it'd take to get permission through the courts to hire another army of people to tear the *Magellan* apart looking for it? Do you even know where the *Magellan* is registered?"

"The United States?"

"Hardly. Try Majuro."

"Majuro?"

"Part of the Marshall Islands, but that's not the point. You're talking about undertaking an impossible task."

Pierce looked deflated and blew out a heavy sigh.

I almost felt sorry for him. *Almost* being the operative word. I said, "You're single, aren't you?"

"Yeah, so what?"

"Divorced?"

"Maybe."

"Knock off early today. That's my suggestion. It's Sunday, for heaven's sakes. Go out to the beach, be around people. You've been working too hard."

Pierce nodded as though considering the suggestion, then stood and pushed back his chair. I walked him to the door. This time, before he could turn and ask me some last minute question, I said, "Oh, and Detective?" He stopped and turned to me. "Let me know when you make a ruling on Hunter's death."

"Oh that," he said and walked a few feet to his car. "I forgot to tell you. I'm sending the body home, but the case is still open. Given this new information, it's going to stay that way a while longer. Maybe he was looking for some kind of treasure. Maybe, even, you are too." Then he opened his car door and, resting one foot inside, he added, "Maybe that's why he's dead," giving me a wave; then, he was gone.

One of these days I'd get the last word with that bastard.

I navigated Henri's boat — now seaworthy again — beneath the Highway 70 bridge, dodging commercial vessels and weekend captains as I began retracing the route I'd taken only days ago to the Graveyard of the Atlantic Museum. I was on a mission, which fate had apparently decided would be a solo one for me this time. Viktor was busy preparing to return to school this fall, and judging from yesterday's performance by Bud's new girlfriend — whom I'd privately dubbed Miss Tobacco Worm, since she had to have at least one beauty queen title under her belt — he had his hands way too full to bother with me.

Granted, my mission today was based on a hunch, but all of life's greatest discoveries started with one, right?

In a nutshell, mine was based on my online research and the following assumptions: Davy Duchamp had discovered a U-boat when he was hired by Global to conduct the seismic survey for Manteo One. Being a history buff with a penchant for all things Nazi, he'd read about the secret mission of *U-498* to spirit the map to the Amber Room to a safe location.

He knew the bottom terrain better than anyone else, knew that the sub lay in a relatively flat location. Logic said it had to; flatness would be one of the first requirements for Global when looking for a spot to spud the well. This was a big break for Duchamp because that more than likely put the sub within tether-reach of an ROV.

Here's where my hunch had a hitch, however. All exploratory wells require a site survey. It's a primary part of the years-long permitting process. The site survey for an offshore well is no different and consists of many parts, depending on the location of the proposed well, the water depth, distance from shore, and what kind of drill rig is used. It is derived from the original 2D seismic survey and would include information regarding the existence of man-made features such as other wells, oil infrastructure, or shipwrecks.

I'd seen the site survey for Manteo One and read the reports. There was no mention of any shipwreck in either the written report or geohazard analysis, certainly not within tether-reach of the well. This told me three things: the original seismic survey had to have been altered before the site survey had been created, the alterer had to have been Duchamp, and I needed to have a closer look at the original seismic survey.

What I really needed, though, would be to compare it to an even older seismic survey of the same area. But, of course, that was impossible because even if one had been made by another seismic survey company, it would be proprietary, not available to the public. Anyway, I seriously doubted another had ever been conducted. This wasn't the Gulf, after all.

Yielding to a hulking oncoming barge, I maintained my speed, skimming the shallows at the edge of the channel. I was imagining Davy's initial excitement at seeing the shadow of the sub on his seismic readouts. He must have found it early and kept it a secret until the survey was complete. That would have given him almost a year to discover the monumental significance of his find — he'd stumbled onto the map to one of the world's greatest lost art treasures — and come up with a plan to retrieve it.

In order to accomplish that task, he needed to hand-pick the ROV crew Global hired. Not hard for a guy with as many contacts in the oil and gas business as he had. His twin sons and Hunter would make the perfect three-man team. He sent them to be certified, used his contacts again, and got them hired on at Voyager, the company Global always contracted with. But then his luck ran out when Hunter discovered the cylinder had been removed from the sub.

Right before reaching the river, I stopped to gas up. The inactivity of waiting for the attendant let a little anxiety seep in around the edges of my hunch. There'd been times in my life when some of my hunches proved to be, well, a bit out there. But in this case, I'd done my research, and you know how it is with a fascinating subject . . . one article leads to another, and pretty soon you're loaded up with all kinds of interesting side facts.

For instance, I read articles about World War II pilots bombing U-boats and claiming kills they were unable to prove later. Also prominent in the literature — urban legends, if you will — were tales of German submariners coming ashore at various places along the East Coast to purchase groceries. One account even had the body of a submariner found with a movie ticket stub from a theater in Southport, North Carolina, in his pocket.

The most compelling of these stories was the real-life account of the invasion of the United States in 1942 by German spies with the express mission of blowing up infrastructure critical to our war plan. The would-be saboteurs came ashore via two submarines that carried them to within rowing distance of New York and Florida. They used inflatable rubber boats to complete their journeys. In the end, they were caught, and six of the eight men were electrocuted as wartime spies. The other two were deported, but that wasn't the point. The point was that they rowed ashore.

If they could do it, why not the submariners of *U-498*?

So where did these stories fit into my mission today? Well, if Hunter hadn't found the cylinder in *U-498,* wasn't it possible that it came ashore with one or the other of the only two people onboard the sub who knew of its existence? The fact that it lay perched on the edge of the continental slope only forty-five miles from Hatteras, the most westerly reach of North Carolina into the Atlantic, told me two things: one, if there were survivors, they didn't come back for the cylinder later, as it was in over 2,100 feet of water. Two, rowing to land was possible.

Okay, so it wouldn't be exactly a fun outing, rowing that far in an inflatable, but it would be entirely doable by strapping young men such as Wolfgang Reckhoff, the captain of the sub, and Gerhard Coester, the professor. Question was, if my hunch was true, did they do it together or with a crew or did just one of them make it?

I was still pondering this question as I headed across Pamlico Sound. The stillness of the early morning had given way to a light breeze. Pushing the throttle forward, I trimmed the engine until the little boat planed off over the chop and thought about the realities I needed to consider. If Hunter and Duchamp were trying to find the cylinder with the ROV, wouldn't the twins have to know? It takes at least three people to deploy the 8,800-pound machine.

Clearly, since Viktor hadn't come aboard until after Hunter died, he wasn't involved during those first weeks when the well was being spudded, when Ricky said there was lots of time was racked up on the ROV that "didn't jibe" with the log sheets. But was Viktor involved now? And every time I thought of those log sheets, I got a tickle in my brain, like a signal to check something out . . . but what?

Windy conditions on the beach, blowing sand on bodies greasy with suntan lotion, sent tourists scurrying to find other activities to occupy the kiddies. On a Sunday past churchtime, the museum was a top attraction. Politely sidestepping family groups with whining children, I looked for Lucy and was just about to give myself a mental kick in the pants for not calling ahead when I saw her, soda in hand, exit through a door marked STAFF ONLY.

I knocked softly and peeped into the break room, calling her name.

"Come on in." I obeyed. "I remember you," Lucy exclaimed when she saw me. "You're the lucky lady with the handsome *young* boyfriend!"

Cringing, but at the same time unable to suppress a laugh, I said, "Guilty as charged."

"Pull up a seat," Lucy said. "I was just about to have a little lunch, but I'm not real hungry. Would you like to share my tuna salad? It won't last until dinner. Gets too soggy." Without waiting for my answer, she plopped half of an enormous sandwich on a napkin and pushed it across the table.

Realizing I hadn't even considered lunch and was, in fact, quite hungry, I graciously accepted, pulled up a chair, and dug in. Just like my mom used to make it: no egg, just mayo, diced home-made pickle, and canned tuna. Delicious.

Lucy, dabbing daintily at the corners of her mouth with a napkin, said, "Why do I get the feeling your return visit today is about something more than an interest in shipwrecks?"

"You're very perceptive," I told her. "I'm impressed. Actually, curiosity about all those people who either washed ashore dead or were swept out to sea during the height of the U-boat attacks around here brought me in. I was wondering if you ever heard of any German submariners who made it to shore alive?"

She trained a shrewd eye on me. "Like spies, or like survivors hanging onto wreckage?"

"Either," I shrugged, then qualified that by adding, "but not urban legends, you know, like the stories about sailors who came to watch a movie or buy groceries. I mean, more like —"

"Like German sailors who weren't Nazis, just people wanting to defect?"

I stared at her. "Well, I hadn't thought of that, but I guess . . . do you have a specific incident in mind?"

Narrowing her eyes at me, her demeanor suddenly changed. "You know damn well I do. That's why you're here. You've somehow heard about me as a child telling the authorities about some men I believed were German spies coming ashore on our beach.

You're here to dig it all up again! You're a reporter or a writer, aren't you? And you just want to make fun of me or write a spoof or something insulting . . . go ahead, admit it!"

Taken aback, I swallowed my last bite of sandwich and protested vehemently. "No! I'm not a reporter, and I'm not here to write a story. I'm just chasing a hunch."

"What kind of a hunch?"

"Trust me, I'll tell you later. Right now, though, I want to hear about what you saw. It's news to me, seriously, and I'm completely fascinated again."

She cocked her head studying me, then said, "And you're sure you're not a journalist or someone like that?"

"Yes, I'm quite sure." I could hardly believe my luck.

"Then why do you want to know?" she demanded, since my eagerness was so obvious. If I wasn't a reporter or writer, what was I?

I sought to seem reassuring. "You apparently saw something when you were very young, as you would have been in 1942 when the German wolf packs were hunting off our shores, right?"

She hesitated. "Right."

"And whatever you saw, you reported it to

the proper authorities or your parents and they didn't believe you, right?"

"It was more than that." She paused. "I got called emotionally disturbed just because I was. . . . well, I was a quiet kid. A loner, kind of, and people had always thought I was strange just because I didn't want to dress up dolls or play house like the other girls my age."

"What if I told you I might be able to vindicate you, maybe not publicly, but at least you'd know the truth about what you saw. You'd feel better then wouldn't you?"

She closed her eyes, took a deep breath, and nodded. "Tell me what you're talking about, dear."

Now it was I who hesitated. "First, you tell me: who did you report this to back then?"

"The sheriff. Naturally, times being when they were, I assumed the men I saw had come ashore from a German submarine. I told my folks first, and when they didn't believe me, I walked down to the sheriff's office and told him myself. I was only eight years old, so that alone was enough to get me in trouble. But you have to understand how things were . . . It was war! And it wasn't 1942, it was 1945, when it was almost over. At the time I saw what I saw, the sub attacks had all but stopped on our coast, which was another reason no one believed me. They said I was 'disturbed' and 'craving attention'."

"*When* in 1945?" I asked.

"March twenty-seventh. I remember distinctly because it was daddy's birthday and I was walking on the beach after cake and ice cream. It was right at twilight."

I got a chill down my spine. The time period was correct. Erich Koch had personally ordered and directed the dismantling of the Amber Room in early 1945 and fled Germany in April of that same year. It made sense that he would have moved as quickly as he could to get the map he'd had made of its hiding place out of the country before he left.

"What did you see?"

With a determined set to her jaw, Lucy recited to me the story that had gotten her in such hot water as a child. "I saw two men in dark clothes in a rubber raft. They were right outside the breakers. They got out of the raft, popped it, and stayed with it until it sank. Then they came ashore. One was holding a knapsack over his head. Once they got on land, they took off running for the dunes."

"Where were you?"

"Behind a dune, not ten feet from where they stopped."

"What did they stop for?"

"They stripped off their wet clothes down to their drawers and dressed in dry clothes from the pack. Nice civilian clothes — lace-up shoes, felt hats, light jackets. At one point, one of them looked right in my direction. It was just about dusk and I was behind a clump of sea oats and grass. I'll never forget his face, his eyes especially. They looked so sad."

I nodded my head. I'd bet my favorite pair of Pura Lopez shoes I'd seen those same sad eyes in a photo. I said, "What happened then?"

"They took off for the road and that was the last I saw of them . . . for a while."

"What do you mean?"

"I mean I got tired to trying to convince anyone to believe me! There was nothing to prove what I'd said. No raft, no clothes, they'd carried those with them. No one brought up the subject and I left it that way. Then, years later I *saw* one of them."

"Where and how many years later?"

"At the college I attended in Raleigh. I was a freshman, so it was about ten years after I'd first seen him. But there was no mistaking him. Those faces were burned in my brain."

"Good grief, did you say anything to him?"

"Not at first, no. He was my French professor."

"French? Not art history?"

"Art history?" Lucy repeated. "Why would you think he taught art history? Wouldn't German be a better guess?"

I was taken aback. I'd been so sure they were the two young Germans from *U-498,* charged with hiding the map to where the Amber Room was hidden. "I don't know, now," I answered, shaking my head. "First, tell me the rest of your story. Why'd he speak French if he'd been on a German submarine?"

She nodded. "Well, that threw me too. He didn't have the guttural accent you'd expect a German to have. He said he was French. His name was Adrien Dubois. He was a wonderful teacher. And by that time in my life, all the feelings of slight and disapproval that I'd felt so deeply as a child didn't matter. I'd made new friends and moved on. My story was just a bad memory and I didn't want to dredge it up again, which is why I never asked him any questions."

The muted laughter of tourists outside the door was the only sound in the room for a while as I contemplated the kink in my theory. It was Lucy's turn to reassure me.

She said, "I don't know how my story fits into your hunch, dear, but if it makes you feel any better, I do know this. The two men I saw in the boat that night were the two men who lived together in Raleigh in a brand-new bungalow in a newly developed section not far from the college."

"Both men? You saw *both* men later?"

"I sure did. I'd often see Professor Dubois walking to class. One time I followed him on impulse, out of curiosity. I watched him go up the drive to a yellow bungalow. At the time, I remember thinking what a charming little house it was. It had tapered columns, painted white with stone bases." She paused and blinked as though searching for its image in her memory, then continued. "There was another young man out front planting a crepe myrtle. They spoke for a while and went inside. But first, I got a good long look at him and was confident that he was the other man I'd seen come ashore in the life raft that night. It was all very weird."

"And still you never said a word to the professor?"

"No. For one thing, I just didn't want to cause a stink. He was very popular with students and faculty alike. But most of all, you have to admit it makes more sense that they weren't even German sailors after all. They were just two men who, for whatever reason, jumped ship from . . . oh, I don't know, a cruise liner or a tanker or maybe a merchant ship. Then they slipped into the country. Maybe they wanted to avoid the normal immigration channels for some reason. Later, after I graduated, I became an English teacher back in Avon, got married, and never thought of them again, until now. My husband passed in 2005, God rest his soul . . ."

There was a knock on the door. A woman's face peeked in, "Lucy, the crowds are getting bigger."

"Oh my! And here I am just chattering away with my new friend. I'll be right out." As she stood to leave, she said, "I fear my story has left you with more questions than answers. But you'll still come see me again, won't you?"

"I will," I promised.

"Oh, and dear?"

I stopped in the doorway. "Yes?"

"I'd like to ask that anything you find out about those two men . . . well, you won't involve me, will you? Not unless you really need to."

"I understand," I told her. "And I'll do my best."

Nineteen

Late that Sunday afternoon, as I bumped Henri's boat softly against the dock behind my rented house, I admired the way a soft haze had turned the mainland trees a dull pewter and the setting sun, like a giant celestial dipper, had tipped their edges in molten gold.

I'd had time on the return trip to mull over Lucy's story. My conclusion was a simple one: Germans can change their names and learn to speak French too. Being educated Europeans, they'd probably have known it already. In fact, English might have presented the greater challenge. I just felt certain that the men she'd seen and the ones in the photo I'd found were the same. So why hadn't I showed her the photo? For one thing, the story Lucy told came as a complete surprise; I didn't have it with me. For another, she'd convinced herself that the men she'd seen probably weren't even

German after all and was now content in that notion.

As soon as I started across the lawn, I saw Henri's car in the drive. A sound like a well-hit baseball signaled that Tulip had nosed the screen door open and, also like a well-hit grounder, was racing to meet me. I grabbed her before she could knock my feet out from under me, patting her sides and pulling her silky ears. She whimpered with joy. She might like spending time with Henri and Will, but she *loved* me.

Both my children sauntered up. "Hey guys," I said. "What brings you here?"

"We were worried about you. Besides, Tulip was starting to get depressed," Henri said. "We thought a visit with you would help."

"Probably a good idea except —"

"We would have called," Will cut in, "but we knew you'd tell us not to, so we just came on."

"Actually, asking really would have been the better plan. I'm going to drive back to Raleigh as soon as I throw some things in the Jeep. I need to see how the renovations are progressing. Questions have come up about the new refrigerator. The one that was delivered wasn't exactly the one they ordered, and the contractor's holding off until

I approve it."

"Bummer," Henri said.

"I'll say," Will agreed. "We were hoping for a nice evening together. How much longer do we have to stay away?"

"Not long. We've actually hit our target. It's just a matter of pulling the string, then running a logging instrument back down to take readings so we'll know for sure how big our gas deposit is."

"But how long will that take?"

"A few days. Then we'll make the big announcement. Hopefully, by that time, Dad and Miss Tobac . . . uh, Ms. Whitfield will have quashed any new attempts by the state to stop the project. Which doesn't guarantee, of course, that the demonstrators will go away. Unless my deep background's on the mark."

"Your what?" Henri asked.

"From what I've heard from my friend Wanda, Global's office manager at the port, the supposedly local protesters are all imports — mainly union workers brought in to make it look like people around here don't want the project. But really, nothing could be further from the truth. People were clamoring for work here before the big recession; now they're desperate for it," I said, reaching for one of Tulip's tennis balls in the grass. I threw it for her and she dashed off.

"The unions have wanted to get a foothold in North Carolina for a long time," I continued, "but it's a right-to-work state. Most of the jobs available in the oil and gas industry are provided by independent contractors. Once the dream of green jobs manned by unionized government employees becomes highly improbable and hiring picks up in the private sector, the demonstrators will go back where they came from."

Will shrugged. Henri dug at the thick fescue lawn grass with her toes and said, "Well, we were going to Raleigh tomorrow anyway. I need to check in with a few clients there, and Will's going to look at apartments. He said he might move back up this way."

I looked at my son expectantly. "Maybe. I'm thinking about it. I love Miami, but it'd be nice to be back in my old stomping grounds."

Tulip bounded up and dropped her ball at my feet. I picked it up and said, "Here's an idea. I'll take Tulip with me. That way she'll get a twofer: she can spend time with me *and* slobber on the windows. You two follow. We'll stop at our favorite barbeque place on the way, eat on those picnic tables out back so she can join us." They looked somewhat appeased, but not totally happy. "Don't worry," I added, "it's not that long. You guys can move back in just a few more days and we can spend the rest of the summer together. I shouldn't have to go out to the *Magellan* very much once we've locked in our location."

And so we set off. After a deliciously messy diner dinner roughly halfway between Morehead City and Raleigh, we parted company again. I kept Tulip with me, planning to drop her off at Henri's place before returning to Morehead tomorrow. Forty-five minutes later, we pulled into the drive at the house in Raleigh. Tulip was having a fit to get out, so I reached over and opened the passenger door for her. She trotted nervously around the house, checking all the strange smells in her territory. Bleeping the garage door open, I drove in.

Dodging piles of folded painting tarps — removed from the shrubbery for the weekend — paint cans, sawhorses, and a slew of other equipment necessary for remodeling work, I clomped up the steps and stuck my key in the lock to the kitchen door. As soon as I stepped inside, I could tell something more than remodeling was amiss.

The aroma of my spaghetti sauce was

unmistakable. Checking the sink, I found a single dirty plate, a fork, and a wine glass in one side and one of my individual baked spaghetti casserole dishes soaking in the other. My enormous powers of deductive reasoning told me only one person had eaten here. Had one of the contractors gotten hungry? Unprofessional maybe, but plausible. If that wasn't the case, however, I needed to be prepared.

With the stealth of a cat burglar, I lifted Will's old baseball bat from the umbrella stand by the door where it had lived since he was eight. I crept into the great room.

At first glance, nothing was out of place. Then I heard a low rumble . . . a growl? I cursed myself for not bringing Tulip in with me. I was just turning to go get her when I heard the growl again, this time accompanied by a snort.

I took a few steps farther into the room, but no one was there. Then I heard a shuffling sound on the couch, which faced away from me. Something was there and in a flash I knew just what it was. An opossum or a raccoon had wandered in an open door while the workmen were here! Holding the bat in front of me at the ready — they can carry rabies, you know — I tiptoed to the back of the couch and looked over it.

Bud gave another snort, this time a horrendous one, eliciting a blood-curdling shriek from me.

Springing to a sitting position, Bud yelped, "What? What?" and cracked his head against the bat I was still stiff-arming in front of me. He gave me an incredulous look, then flopped back among the pillows.

"Oops," I said.

No response from my victim.

"Bud?" I prodded him weakly with the bat.

He opened his eyes — I swore they were crossed — and gawked at me. "Good God, Cleo, you almost cracked my skull!" He rubbed the top of his head and checked his fingers for blood.

"Good God yourself! You're lucky I didn't. What in the hell are you doing here?"

For a second his face was blank, then his features transformed into their let-me-think-of-something-quick expression. I'd had a lot of experience with that face, so I stopped the wheels from grinding. "Bud! Why are you here?" I demanded.

"Uh, I came by to check on your renovation. You know, making sure everything is getting done just like you want it."

"Nice try," I said, "except you don't know how I want things done around here. So tell me why you're really taking a snooze on my couch instead of being at your own house. Oh wait, let me guess, your little friend is wearing you out and you had to seek refuge somewhere she wouldn't find you, right?"

Bud swung his feet to the floor, still rubbing his noggin. "I don't know what you're talking about. Anyway, what makes you think *I'm* not the one wearing my little friend out? Hmm?"

Looking straight at his crotch, I said, "I'm sure you are."

"Oh, very funny, and really mature," sputtered Bud. "That's not what I meant, and you know it. Besides, you should be extremely grateful that Amanda wants to help me wrap up this project —"

"Oh my lord!" I said, resisting the urge to raise the bat again. "Are you trying to tell me you're taking one for the team? I've heard lots of excuses for male mid-life crisis, but this takes the cake."

Bud reddened and his ears all but steamed. I was about to remind him about being in those heart attack years when Tulip came to our rescue, barking at the back door.

When I let her in, she took off for the great room, bristling back and neck hairs. As I put the bat away, I heard their rowdy reunion, with Bud cooing to her, "There's my girl! Least someone's glad to see me."

When he found me in the kitchen — cleaning up his mess, by the way — Bud had regained his composure. He crossed his arms and leaned against the counter. I filled Tulip's water bowl and gave it to her. She lapped up a drink, her tags clinking against the stainless steel.

Bud said, "Maybe we need to talk, babe."

Calmly, I walked to the back door, opened it again, and stood beside it. "Nope," I said. "I think we're done here."

Bud did whatever Bud does to make the tendons flex in his jaw, propelled himself from the counter, and left. Still calmly, but also tired — it had been a long day — I finished tidying up the remains of his uninvited drop-in.

Tulip and I spent a pleasant night in our own digs, but bright and early Monday morning, after a lengthy discussion with the contractors, I carried her back to Henri's house and dropped her off. Although I said I was headed straight back to Morehead, I drove instead to the old Raleigh neighborhood of postwar houses that I thought might be a good place to start looking for the one-time home of one of Southern Women's College's most popular French professors. Don't ask me why I wanted to find it. Maybe I just needed to see that it really existed.

Passing the campus, I drove several more blocks until I came to the neighborhood I was looking for and started a search, driving slowly up and down the streets. I was keeping my eye out for a yellow cottage with a crepe myrtle in front. The fact that Lucy had seen it more than fifty years before somehow wasn't a deterrent. Or maybe I should say it wasn't logic that was driving my curiosity.

After cruising the streets closest to the campus, I saw nothing that I thought might fit Lucy's description of Professor Dubois's cottage, so I expanded my search a few more blocks. Pulling down a quiet tree-lined street I listened to a classic rock station. Tapping my fingers idly as the Big Bopper sang "Chantilly Lace," I spotted a young man walk up the drive of a house, not yellow but with one important feature I could see from where I sat — a towering crepe myrtle tree.

The largest of many dotting yards along the street, the tree was a blaze of fuchsia. But then the object of my interest disappeared behind an overgrown hedgerow dividing his yard from the neighbors. From where I was stopped I couldn't see past it, so I slowly edged forward. What came into view then was worth the wait.

A cream-colored bungalow snuggled under the immense crepe myrtle tree. Additionally, it had tapered wooden columns with stone bases, just as Lucy had described from her memory of the house. The more I studied it, the more convinced I became I'd found the dwelling of the former German French-language professor who'd somehow escaped death during the sinking of *U-498* some 40 miles off the coast of Hatteras.

But was it just wishful thinking? I had no proof, only my hunch. Mystery novels always seemed so full of coincidences, but this was real life.

One possible solution seemed to be plugging the address into one of the many reverse locator websites. If I knew who lived in the house now, perhaps a call would yield information about the former occupants. I could also go to the college to see if they'd help me track the elusive professor. The trouble was, all that would take time, and I needed get back to the *Magellan.*

Talk about being torn. Should I follow the trail to one of the world's greatest lost art treasures or get back to what I was supposed to be doing, finding one of the world's most valuable gas deposits? Decisions, decisions. I figured, at the very least, I could check in with Phil Gregson.

"Hey, Cleo. Where are you?" The miracles of modern communication.

"I'm still in Raleigh," I said. "And since I need to attend to a few more things here, I wanted to see how we're coming with the log."

"Lithology is starting to change, indicating we're just about to the bottom of the reservoir, but I'm afraid it'll probably take a few hours longer than I predicted to get all the readings we need. That is, if we don't hit any unforeseen problems. The crew's really pouring it on, though. They're so hell bent to beat SunCo, it could go quicker than I predict. I'll keep you informed."

"Thanks, that's great."

"Just a heads up: all the big wheels back in Houston are waiting with bated breath to hear the numbers. As you know, this is make or break for Global. They're even sending some of the bean counters out here, like somehow their presence could summon up greater gas volumes. Hell, I don't know. Maybe they just want to be here to make themselves feel like they're doing all they can too. Lot of careers on the line . . ."

Since Phil had just given me a few hours

reprieve, I headed for the college. Seemed like the best place to start my search for the professor.

The administrative offices of the Southern Women's College were housed in a beautifully restored antebellum house of enormous proportions. Once the town residence of one of the kings of the cotton industry, it dripped with the grace and opulence of a by-gone era. Judging from the buildings and grounds, the cotton king had also left behind a healthy endowment. Once I'd told the receptionist, a silver-haired woman every bit as elegant as her surroundings, that I was looking for a professor who'd taught here the fifties, she directed me up an ancient stairwell. There she said, I'd find the Personnel Department, where a Mr. Devereaux would help me.

Once I saw him, I felt I was in luck. Mr. Devereaux was old as the rocks we were drilling off the coast and might actually be the perfect source. I pegged him to be in his late seventies, though he stood straight as an arrow and looked snappy in his shirt, collegiate tie, loafers, and khakis. Nonetheless, the hand he extended was delicate, even birdlike, and I wondered how he'd avoided forced retirement.

"How may I be of service to you, my dear lady?"

"I'm looking for a French professor who taught here in the fifties. His name was Adrien Dubois."

"I knew Professor Dubois very well. May I ask why you're looking for him?"

"Certainly. He was a friend of my aunt," I said, quickly adopting Lucy as kin.

"I see." He leaned forward, his watery eyes probing mine for more information.

Starting with the truth, I said, "They became friends when she was a student here." Then I veered wildly into the land of lies. "For years and years, they corresponded. She kept all the letters and now that she's failing, she wants him to have them."

"How very kind of your aunt. Unfortunately, I'm not sure Professor Dubois would remember her or, for that matter, even be able to read a letter. I'm told he has slipped into senility."

"Oh dear." I was momentarily stumped. Then, not willing to give up, I asked, "Do you know where I can find him?"

"Well, I don't see that telling you would do any harm." Mr. Devereaux gave a thin smile. "He retired from here after thirty years, so Accounting would have his exact address. However, I myself can tell you where he is if you want to go in person."

"That's very kind. I'd appreciate it. I'm sure my aunt would appreciate my seeing him in person."

"He's at Capital Oaks over off Blount," he said, his expression now revealing a definite distaste. "It's one of the only places around here that will take folks in need of . . . well, his kind of care."

Nursing homes by their very nature are depressing. Capital Oaks, however, gave a whole new meaning to the word. I pushed through the glass double-doors, crossed the reception lobby, and approached a pear-shaped young woman at what looked like a nurses' station. She squinted at me through prescription work goggles, then swallowed the wad of Krispy Kreme doughnut she was eating, like a heron choking down a big fish. "Can I help you?"

"Yes, you may," I said unable to resist the gentle reminder that grammar separates the civilized from the rabble hordes. I blinked, trying not to stare at her goggles. "I'd like to visit one of your guests, Mr. Adrien Dubois."

Her eyes crossed as she checked out her goggles from the inside. "Some of our residents might spit on you," she said. "You won't be expecting it."

"Thanks for the warning. Mr. Dubois?"

I followed her down a long, dimly lit hallway. Several corridors later, I was starting to feel queasy from the stench of urine and boiled cabbage. But just as I was about to comment on how intolerably stuffy it was, Goggles stopped at a door. Without so much as a brief tap, she opened it, proceeding into the dark room.

"Mr. Dubois? You have a guest," she said in her best institutional voice. Then, without turning on a light or even checking to see if Mr. Dubois was indeed still alive, she turned on her heel to make her way back to her doughnuts.

"Professor Dubois?" I called softly.

A rustle of sheets let me know Mr. Dubois was still in the land of the living, so I crossed the shadowy room to the outline of daylight behind two large window shades. Tentatively, I started raising one while studying the figure in the bed. When he had raised a frail, bony arm to protect his eyes, I stopped. At least my surroundings were visible now. I pulled a chair up to the bed and sat facing the wasting shell of a man who was undeniably the one I was looking for. Here was the man who had been entrusted with hiding the whereabouts of the Amber Room sixty-six years ago. How could I tell after all that time? His eyes.

Though rheumy with age, this man's eyes still had the exact same haunted look. Moreover, his hair, now snowy white, was still thick and cut in the same style it had been in the photo. Blunt, parted in the middle, and tucked behind his enormous ears.

"Mr. Dubois, I'm Cleo Cooper. Do you feel up to a little chat?"

He gave no reply.

I tried a different tack. "Professor Dubois, I'm a friend of one of your students, Lucy Watkins. Do you remember her?"

Still silence. Just then a phlegmy voice cracked from the doorway, "Is Adrien being difficult today?"

I looked up to see another frail old gentleman struggling toward me with his walker.

"Hello," I said, standing. "I'm Cleo Cooper. A friend of Professor Dubois — or, at least, my aunt is. And you are?"

"Just one of the old timers waiting for death. Same as Adrien, there."

I was trying to think of a reply suitable to a statement like that when the man stopped, took one look at the professor, gave me the once-over, then turned back to the door.

"Better come back another time," he said. " 'Cause if Adrien don't want to talk, he ain't gonna talk."

"Thanks for the advice. But when does Adrien like to talk?"

"Anytime you bring Ben and Jerry's Cherry Garcia."

Back in the parking lot, I lowered all the windows and turned the AC on full blast. Taking big gulps of fresh air, I wondered if could really be that easy. Could little old Cleo Cooper have stumbled upon the solution to a puzzle that had eluded the world's best treasure hunters for decades? I considered the confluence of events and realized the answer was a definite yes. I mean, who else but me had put together the existence of the sub, the mission of two Germans aboard it, *and,* by way of a trip down memory lane with my "aunt" Lucy, the origins of the pair she saw come ashore on Hatteras Island?

Davy Duchamp and his boys certainly knew of the existence of the sub and its exact coordinates, and had even searched it, but they didn't have Lucy's information. Detective Pierce had gotten a whiff of treasure in checking Hunter's emails, but he was headed down a blind alley in thinking it was on the *Magellan.* No one but me had all the pieces, and now it seemed incredible to think that the only stumbling block between me and unlocking one of the greatest mysteries of all time was a pint of Ben and Jerry's.

I checked the time. Good grief. Recovery of the Amber Room would have to wait on a more imminent discovery.

TWENTY

Back in Morehead, Viktor's car was in my drive. Since my house was locked tight as a vault and it was well over 90 degrees outside, I figured he must have sought the shade of the screened-in porch. Not seeing him there or in the back yard, I looked to the dock and the sound beyond. Then I saw him. Playing in the water like a giant otter, diving deep, then propelling himself up to dive again, sending sprays of water sparkling like prisms in the late afternoon sun. He made quite a sight.

I walked out on the dock to watch him. Even in a sleeveless cotton blouse and Dockers, the heat was still stifling. I pulled down the brim of my Panthers ball cap and adjusted my aviators to alleviate some of the glare off the water and continued to watch him at play until he saw me.

He threw up his hand and shouted, *"Mya morkovka!"* Heading for me, he cut the water like an Olympic swimmer. When he showed no signs of slowing down upon reaching the ladder, I started backing up. Like an out-of-control wet dog, he launched himself onto the dock. I couldn't help it: I squealed like a girl and took off. I didn't get far before he wrapped me up in salty wet kisses, his cutoffs dripping seawater down my legs and into my shoes.

Pushing back from him to catch a breath, I ran my fingers across his chest, stopping to play with his puckered nipples.

"It happens," he said, grinning as he rubbed his thumbs over mine now protruding through bra and blouse. "I've gotten you all wet. Come. Let me dry you off upstairs where it's cool."

"Okay," I said. Then, being my practical self, I added, "But I need to strip off these wet things first."

In the comparative privacy of the screened-in porch, I dropped my wet shorts and reached for the button on my blouse, but Viktor's hand pushed mine away.

Shortly after this, I had the answer to a question I've wondered about all my adult life. Is it possible to have sex in a one-person net hammock and not bounce yourselves out? The answer is no. At one point we managed to power-shoot ourselves into the wall.

I thought I might have killed myself, but Viktor, undaunted, carried me upstairs, which is where we were when I thought of another question. "Viktor, what does *mya morkovka* mean?"

"Ah," he said, raising his head and resting in the palm of his hand. "You are interested in the romance of the Russian language. That's good."

"I don't know about all that, but what *does* it mean?"

"It's just a . . . term of endearment. A name my mother called me when I was very small. It means 'my little carrot'," he said, pulling me close.

"Doesn't fit you anymore," I said, noticing he was ready for round two but not sure if I was. I didn't have time. I needed to get back out to the *Magellan.* Just at that moment my companion demonstrated a creative *gesture* of endearment, which caused me to postpone my leave taking.

Two hours later, Viktor was still napping, so I jotted him a back-late-don't-forget-to-lock-up note, adding the location of the hide-a-key just in case he should need it, and phoned the transport service in Beaufort. The helicopter pilot who answered sounded suspiciously like the maniacal aerobat who'd flown Bud and me on our first trip. I started to hang up, but I really needed to get on board, so I instead told him I'd be right out.

My worst fears were confirmed upon seeing the ex-military chopper pilot from hell bull through the glass doors as I waited on the tarmac.

Forty minutes later, limp as a wet cat, I spilled from the copter onto the deck. Saying, "Let me know when you're ready to leave," my tormentor disappeared from sight within seconds.

"Never again in this life," I muttered.

After notifying the radioman that I was aboard *Magellan,* I set off for the bridge and the conference room off the helm. Several copies of the site survey, along with other documents and maps pertinent to the well, were stored there, ready to be handed out if a situation arose that required a group think. There were also copies of different sections of the 2D seismic survey. I was looking for the area surrounding the wellhead out 4,000 feet, the length of the ROV's tether.

As I reached for the conference room door, one of Powell's assistants stepped from the helm. "Ma'am, we were just getting ready to call you. Captain Powell needs you in the DC."

"Uh, okay, thanks," I said and waited for him to return to the helm. He didn't. He just stood there watching me as if he meant to make sure I didn't ignore his directions. I turned and headed for the DC, disappointed that I'd have to put off following my hunch until later.

Upon reaching the DC, I was interrupted again when someone behind me called out, "Hey, Miss Cleo, you're back!" It was Ricky, the ROV tech.

"Hey," I said, turning to face him. "What's up?"

"Just heading back after a break and seeing you reminded me. I found copies of an article you left in the printer. I kept them for you if you want to drop by and pick them up."

I choked back panic and tried to sound confused instead, repeating, "Copies of an article?"

"Yeah. Something about Hitler refitting a submarine. I didn't have time to read it." Then, realizing my confusion, he added, "At least I thought they were yours since I found them in the print bin not long after you left that last day you visited us."

I shook my head with slow sweeps. "Not mine."

"Oh, I bet I know what happened," he said. "It's probably something that was in the queue on Hunter's computer before the printer broke. When you printed something else after it was fixed, they printed too."

I nodded — mystery solved, undoubtedly — and willed him to drop the subject. No luck.

Thinking for a few seconds, Ricky snapped his fingers and said, "Since there were two copies, he must have meant them for the twins. Can't imagine why, but I'll call them and let them know I have them." Giving me a smile and a wave, he turned and headed aft in the direction of the ROV van.

Uh oh. "Ricky, wait!" I shouted, but he didn't hear me over the ambient roar of drilling.

A chill shook me that had nothing to do with the opening of the DC door. I had to stop him from drawing the twins' attention to the article. I should have told him they were mine — that might have been the best thing — but he caught me off guard. Now I had to fix the situation: tell them they were mine after all and hope he'd forget about it. Unfortunately, before I could run after him, Phil Gregson appeared. "There you are. We were really starting to worry about you. It's about time to pull the logging device up."

"I got tied up . . . kind of," I mumbled, following him back into the DC.

"Hi there," Bud said, standing beside Duncan Powell, who was studying the monitors with David Grant.

"Bud!" I said, truly surprised. "What are you doing here?"

He nodded toward Powell and Grant. "We just came down to give David the word to pull the logging device up."

"Yeah, yeah, I heard that. What are *you* doing here?"

"I told you," Bud said, beaming with joy at being on one of the world's biggest big-boy toys. "We just came down to . . ."

"*You,* Bud. What are *you* doing here?"

"My, my, a little testy today aren't we? And somewhat bedraggled, I might add."

Unconsciously, my hand shot to my hair wadded up under my hard hat. Ticked that I'd let him elicit such a girly response from me and impatient to get out of the DC and find Ricky, I snapped sanctimoniously, "Sorry if I don't come up to your new standards, but this is what a little hard work will do for you."

David feathered the joysticks, Powell stared intently at the monitors, and Phil cleared his throat and ventured, "Er, Cleo, if you'll direct your attention to this updated drill log, you'll see how our new azimuth direction put us right in the new bright spot."

"Thanks, Phil," I said. After catching us up on where we were in the hole, Powell thought we needed to go back to the conference room and look at some detailed figures on one of the formations that was causing pressure concerns. That put a real kink in my plan to go over the site survey again. Darkness was beginning to fall, but the ship's lights hadn't switched on yet. My head was beginning to pound from the long day and the ghastly ride over. What's more, I was exhausted from my . . . workout with Viktor. But, more than anything, I desperately needed to find Ricky.

I was trying to come up with a way to accomplish this when Bud fell in beside me. "Sorry if I rattled you back there," he said. "I was just worried about you."

"You've had over six years to get used to your new job description — i.e., not worrying about me. One would think a smart fellow like you could have mastered that by now."

Stepping ahead of me to lead the way through a narrow, dimly lit space interspersed with giant iron support beams, Bud said over his shoulder, "It's just that you look really tired. You've got dark circles under your eyes."

Dark circles? I was just about to lay Bud low with a withering remark when I ran smack into one of the beams. "Oof!"

Turning back to me, Bud demanded, "Did you just run into that beam?"

"No."

"Yes, you did. You're dead on your feet. I know you."

"Shut up," was all I could think to say. Resisting the urge to shake my head and realign my eyeballs, I stepped past him, caught up with Powell, and said, "Do we know how many billions of cubic feet of gas it'll take to put Global back in the black?"

Powell shrugged. "Not really. All depends, I guess, on how deeply in dept they are."

From what Bud had told me, we'd better hope we hit the mother lode.

After an hour of discussion on variations in formation pressure, I excused myself for a bathroom break and made a beeline for the ROV van. I didn't have to go all the way to the van, though, as I saw Ricky coming out of one of the Internet rooms.

"Hold up, Ricky," I said to his back, noting he seemed in a hurry.

"Hi, Miss Cleo. What can I do for you?"

"Nothing really, I was just wondering about that article . . ."

"Oh yeah, it was only three pages, so I just scanned it, placed it in a folder, and emailed it as an attachment to the twins, then threw away the hard copies. I figured if it was something Hunter meant for them to have, they'd know about it; if not, they could just delete it."

I'm sure I paled visibly because he quickly asked, concerned, "You okay?"

"Oh sure. Just a little tired, that's all."

"Well, gotta go. I've been told by the powers that be that the end's in sight and to get ready for end-of-drilling operations."

"Right. See you later."

"Nice working with you, Miss Cleo."

Back in the conference room, we connected with Hiram Hightower and his team in Houston. It was after nine o'clock. Phil and I'd been over the logs several times and were in concurrence on the size of our gas discovery. On screen, Hightower tossed a pen down on the log sheets that spread from one end of the conference table to the other. With a heavy sigh, he crossed his arm over his barrel chest and said, "I'm confident our log analysts, even after a week of screwing with these figures, will come up with the same number we have."

Phil chewed a hangnail, then said, "On the upside, the quality of the gas is exceptional — dry, no contaminants, and the size of the reservoir is about what we expected —"

Hightower impatiently cut him off, "Yes. Yes. But what wasn't expected is that within this very high-quality, lower Cretaceous reservoir we'd encounter a payzone of only about ninety feet of natural gas."

Bud cleared his throat, "Gentlemen," he said. "I'm sensing a bit of panic here. I'm neither a geologist nor geophysicist, so correct me if I'm wrong, but didn't we just make the very first discovery of dry natural gas ever off the East Coast of the United States, and isn't it substantial?"

"Well, *substantial* is a relative term," Braxton Roberts said. "The eight hundred fifty billion cubic feet we just tapped into is a far cry from the two *trillion* cubic feet we need to save the company. Especially when we know there's at least a *major* field of one to five trillion cubic feet and, more probably, a *giant* field of five to fifty trillion cubic feet of recoverable natural gas down there . . . somewhere."

The silence in the conference room was punctuated only by the steady hum of the diesel engines and generators below us and the buzz of florescent lights above us.

"What I'm trying to point out," Bud said patiently, "is that, according to Cleo, the gas probably is there in sufficient quantity, it just leaked out due to a fracture somewhere. We just need to keep going." Bud looked at me. "Right?"

"Absolutely," I said, directing my comments to Hightower on the screen. "Phil and I can go over the 3D images until we're blue in the face, but the fact remains, we're still in the reservoir and the deeper we go, the greater the likelihood of equaling the recent finds by some of our competitors in Azerbaijan and Mozambique. If we just change —"

Roberts cut me off, booming, "I'm just not inclined to keep pouring more money down a weak hole. I say we pull out and start another well on our adjoining block. That would still keep us in the thickest part of the structure, but closer to the bright spot that we first looked at. Why don't we just admit we picked the wrong spot and start over?"

One of the chief financial officers for Global, Patrick Donovan — so well-known in the industry as a wizard at numbers that, despite being in his late sixties, he hadn't been forced into retirement — loosened his tie. "Dammit, Braxton," he said with a force that belied his diminutive size. "You spend money like it's water. You're talking about another hundred million at least. I want to hear why Ms. Cooper thinks we should continue in the hole we're in. Let her finish."

"Fine," snapped Roberts. "Go ahead, Ms. Cooper. Tell us what makes you think the bright spots below our current location aren't just water? Or salt?"

"Watch your tone," Bud warned.

"Gentlemen," Hightower interrupted. "I'd like to hear what Ms. Cooper has to say. She's our objective opinion and has written extensively on this group of formations."

"Thank you," I said. "As you all know, the bright spots might be water, or salt. We just don't know. But that's the nature of a rank wildcat like Manteo One, isn't it? It's high risk, high reward. What I'm saying is we need to remember the geologic history here. Organic-rich lagoonal shales like the Hatteras Formation lie buried at the foot of the structure, on the seaward edge. If we just change our angle down a little more, head in that direction, and target some of the deeper bright spots along the way, we're more likely to encounter the type of play we're looking for."

"What about the pressure?" Roberts said. "It ramps up very quickly in those lower formations. We'll need to change casing size to accommodate —"

"That'll leave us with a soda straw when it comes to production," Hightower said, suddenly looking decisive. "No, let's stay with our present casing and drill ahead. I choose to believe Ms. Cooper's right. In the end, there will be more than one play here. Like Mozambique or Azerbaijan, it will be our net play that counts and it will be more than enough to pull Global out of the red."

And that was it. Just like magic, the discussion quickly moved to how to accommodate Hightower's wishes. I silently reaffirmed my wish to be a man when I come back to earth in another life and slipped out of the room. After chugging a Coke and a BC powder, I slipped back into the conference room just in time to hear Powell address the Houston team.

"You've made your decision," he said, "and I can assure you, TransWorld will make every effort to see that it's carried out to the best possible outcome. Braxton and I will work together and come up with an extension to our well plan based on the new coordinates."

Roberts wearily nodded in agreement,

then added. "First we'll back up a ways, make the dogleg, then resume drilling. Our new target is at least six hundred feet farther on vertical depth — more, given the new angle to the east — but at about three hundred feet a day, it should only take us a couple of days."

Everyone headed for the helipad but me. I took off for the head again, where I waited for a few moments before slipping back to the conference room, hoping to find it empty. I was in luck. It looked like a schoolroom at 3:31 in the afternoon. I snagged a copy of the section of the 2D seismic survey for the area surrounding the wellhead, folded it, and stuffed it into my purse. Then, knowing some of Global's executives had made overnight arrangements on the mainland, I headed for the helipad to hitch a ride.

Bud caught up with me just as I topped the stairs and jogged ahead to the Sikorsky to offer me a hand climbing in. "Thanks," I said, then made my way to empty seats in the rear.

He plopped down beside me. "Long day, huh?"

"Not at all. I'm just getting warmed up," I said, determined not to sound like a person with dark circles under her eyes. "I'm thinking of catching up with some friends later for a drink."

Bud looked at me dubiously, then his cell rang. He checked the screen and shoved it back in his pocket. "I though you'd be staying out there until they hit the new target," he said. "You know, be there to actually watch your theory validated."

"I'll be back in time for that," I said, summoning a big smile. "I wouldn't miss it for the world." Thankfully the engine spooled up, ending any chance for conversation. I cinched up my seatbelt and jammed my helmet on my head, which was, in fact, still pounding from fatigue and stress.

When we landed, I woke with a start. I was leaning against Bud's shoulder. As I prepared to leave, I started to apologize for drooling on his chest, but he himself was so deep in sleep I could barely rouse him. I shook him a little harder, and his eyes popped open. "Feel better?" I asked sweetly. "I could tell you desperately needed some rest."

Once off the tarmac and in the parking lot, I watched Bud trot behind a service truck to his Carrera — the reason I hadn't seen it when I parked earlier today. Then, changing course, he came back to me and said, "I haven't had a chance to tell you how proud I was of you tonight," he said. "You did a masterful job of bringing those guys your way without —" His cell rang yet again. He ignored it.

"Gee thanks, Dad," I said, "but your pants are ringing."

Twenty-One

My big challenge during the fifteen-minute drive home was to make it back to the house before Monday became Tuesday while at the same time keeping my eyelids from closing, thus ending my day wrapped around a live oak tree. Some kindly guardian angel must have taken mercy on me, because I made it safely into my drive. The fact that Viktor's car wasn't there brought a deep feeling of relief. At last, I could get some rest. Maybe I *was* getting older.

Half asleep, I stumbled out and stepped to the rear to retrieve my tote from the cargo area. The dome light came on and just as I leaned over, everything went black. My head was covered by a sack as I was slammed face down on my tote. I screamed, but the sound was quickly muffled by someone's hand snaking under the sack to cover my mouth.

Kicking, thrashing, and grunting with all

my might, I fought like a puma to free myself. Adrenalin triggered by outrage and fear pumped through my veins, and an unearthly strength came over me as my attacker tried to drag me backward. Momentarily feeling the Jeep's bumper under one boot, I pushed off, throwing me and my abductor to the concrete in a jumble. Lots of wiggling and scrambling ensued.

As I tried to crawl away, two hands grabbed my ankles while another hand jerked each of my arms out from under me in turn. Two against one, not real sportsmanlike. Then I heard the sound of ripping duct tape. The fingers over my mouth let up briefly as my head was pulled back sharply and my throat clutched so tightly no sound could escape. The other set of hands was now endeavoring to hold my jaw closed to tape my mouth shut. They succeeded, but not before I chomped down like a vise on a finger. Someone yanked the sack, which I'd managed to dislodge a bit, back down over my face again.

"Goddammit! Be still!" growled a male voice.

"Shut up! No talking, you idiot!" hissed a second one.

Continuing to wiggle and squirm as they taped my wrists together, I managed to get my feet under me. Now, I've got leg muscles like a kangaroo thanks to years spent tramping about in the woods, so when I say I sprang up, I really did. Where I was springing to, I couldn't see, but it didn't matter. I just wanted to get shed of these two. Unfortunately, I only took two steps before I was jerked backward with a snatch of the sack over my head and my feet were kicked out from under me. What little wind was left in my lungs after this smackdown was pushed out with a knee to the sternum.

"I'll hold her —"

"— I'll get the car." You had to admire their cooperative spirit. Then, from what I figured to be the direction of the house, I heard a voice shouting hysterically in what sounded like Russian.

Viktor!

"Hey!" He shouted again, this time in English. "Get away from that woman!"

"Shit!"

"Leave her!" one of my attackers cried.

"No! If we mess this up —"

"Too late, Dad's gonna kill us. Just go!"

The fingers that had an iron grip on my shoulders released me at the sound of the screen door banging. I heard footsteps running across the street.

I'm sure I looked like a fish flopping on a

dock — a fish with a bag over its head — when Viktor reached me. He was still shouting. Pulling me to a sitting position, he snatched the bag off my head and jerked the tape from my mouth.

"Ow!"

"Oh! Sorry, sorry." An instant later, he was sprinting off.

"Come back!" I shouted.

"Why? They were attempting to kidnap you!" But he circled back around.

"My hands. Undo my hands!"

Trembling with rage, he pulled the duct tape from my wrists.

"Were their faces covered?" I asked.

"No. They wore watch caps pulled low and their faces were painted black. Fucking activists."

I sagged against him. "They weren't activists," I said, rubbing my wrists. "I know who they were."

"What? Who were they?"

"Let's go inside. We need to talk."

Viktor insisted I needed sugar after such an ordeal and so made hot sweet tea. I took a polite sip, then got a beer from the fridge and cracked it open. We sat at the kitchen table and I outlined what I knew about *U-498* and how it came to be discovered by his old boss, Davy, who'd put the pieces together and was determined to make one of the most amazing finds of the twenty-first century.

I'd expected the incredulous stare I got from Viktor, so I continued.

"There's more. I know it was the twins who attacked me," I said. "I recognized their voices, the way they ping-ponged their sentences. Not to mention, at one point, they said, 'Dad's gonna kill us.' It was them, I'm sure of it. Everything fits."

"How can that be? They are on their way to take their new boat to Port Fourchon. And besides, how would they know you know any of this . . . incredible . . . tale you just told me?"

"Well, either Davy changed his mind or he misled you on purpose so they could follow you and find me. Which reminds me, how did you get in?"

Viktor grimaced. "I forgot to lock up. Sorry."

"Where's your car?"

"Parked up the street. I wanted to surprise you."

"You did more than that, you saved me . . . again."

"Well," Viktor said, looking sheepish. "I could have saved you faster if I'd had my clothes on. I was upstairs, waiting to surprise you. When I looked out the window and saw what was happening, I had to pull on my pants before I could get to you." Viktor looked down at the table. Emotion trembled in his voice. "I was so scared they'd be gone with you when I finally made it to the door."

I reached across the table and gave his hand a pat. It was kind of sweet, really, and made me even more aware of how close I'd come to something I probably didn't want to think about. Then I felt my chin tremble a little. Clearing my throat quickly to stop any further erosion of my dignity, I said, "As to why they think I'm on to them, Davy sent Hunter an article with a schematic of *U-498* to facilitate finding the cylinder. Hunter went to print it off and left the number of copies set at three, which is where it stays most of the time with three members to a team — only he didn't know the printer was down at the time."

"So Hunter was in on it, too?"

"Yes. He had to be. For Davy, this operation started the minute he found the sub while surveying for Global. Hunter worked for him then. That's why Davy sent him to Voyager to become a pilot. TransWorld always contracts to Voyager. After a while, he sent the twins there too. That way, he could be sure to have an ROV team on board when the time came. No doubt Davy has an in at Voyager. He knows everyone."

"But then that guy, Hunter . . . died." Victor said, seemingly thinking aloud. "I wonder if his death was the reason I got a job so quick, or if his death had anything to do with this . . . wild tale?"

"I don't know," I said. "I only know that I came along later, used his computer, found the article he hadn't had time to delete. Then the printer ran out of paper after I ran a copy for myself. I didn't realize it had been set to run three. So later, when it was reloaded with paper, it made two more copies. Ricky found them in the hopper, figured out they must have been made for the twins, and sent it to them. That's how *they* know that *I* know the sub's down there."

"Stop right there," Viktor said. "You're basing all this on the fact that Davy made the seismic map and you found an article he sent to Hunter. I don't mean to sound skeptical, but how can you be sure the sub's even there?"

"Wait right here," I said and ran upstairs to retrieve the physical proof that the sub existed.

"What is it?"

"It's a wheel valve, a *German* wheel valve of the exact same type I've seen on other submerged U-boats. Note the name of the German shipbuilder stamped on the back."

"So? Where'd you get it?"

"I found it caught between the rails of the ROV and its cage."

Viktor whistled in amazement, then fell silent studying the little wheel. I got up and tossed my empty beer can in the recycling.

"This explains so much," Viktor said.

"How so?"

"During the time I worked for Davy and lived at his house, he and the twins and I were very close. Davy even took me aside right before I left for Duke to secure housing and said I'd become just like a son to him, said he needed to talk to me about something when I got back."

"I bet," I said sitting back down at the table. "They're frantic to find the cylinder before this whole thing busts wide open. It takes three people to operate the ROV. With Hunter dead, Davy desperately needs another pilot to help the twins. Your next rotation starts Monday. He's trying to bring himself to tell you, but he's not sure he can trust you."

And here's where things got really dicy for me too. Did *I* trust Viktor?

I watched Viktor as he rose from the table, went to the fridge, pulled out a beer, and offered me another. I shook my head. Still deep in concentration, he sat back down, sipped, and stared into space. I tried to imagine what was going through his head.

Stretching his long legs under the table, Viktor tapped my toe with his. "What do you think of this idea: you and I go back out to the *Magellan* and retrieve the cylinder ourselves? I *am* a pilot, you know. We have a small window of opportunity before the twins and I are supposed to rotate back on. You have a reason to be there. I could go back with you . . ." Viktor said, thinking out loud.

Then he stopped, looked for my reaction.

"Go on," I said.

"I haven't completely worked out a plan to get access without involving Ray and his team. What I'm thinking requires a bit of, well, lying on our parts. But if you help me with the distraction, which shouldn't be hard, I'll do all the lying. It may be, well . . . distasteful for you."

Ah, the innocence of youth.

Viktor stared at me for a moment, then continued. "I'm quite sure that together we can deceive them long enough for me to find the cylinder."

Now this was more like it! Lying. Deception. Distraction. A small list of my personal favorites, and proof enough for me as to whom Viktor's loyalties lay with. The trouble was, I needed help. Right now I was the only person on the planet who had all the pieces to the Amber Room puzzle, but if I could come up with them and piece them together, so could Davy and the boys. It was only a matter of time.

Most of all, there had to be a connection between Hunter's death and this enormous treasure. I just hadn't figured out what it was yet. But the only way to do that was to move forward and in the process clear Bud and myself of any hint of involvement in a murder we had *nothing* to do with. Right? Nothing whatsoever.

In for a penny, in for a pound. "Viktor," I said. "What if I told you the cylinder isn't on the sub anymore?"

Twenty-Two

Tuesday morning — as we hustled through the doors of Capital Oaks and after I'd brought Viktor up to speed on what I knew of the cylinder's whereabouts and how I knew it — he summed up the task ahead.

"So we're going to get this old Nazi, who also happens to be in the advanced stages of dementia, to tell us the location of the map to the Amber Room, right?"

"That's what the Cherry Garcia's for," I said as we passed the now-empty reception station and headed for the professor's room.

"Of course," Viktor said dryly, then added, "it makes perfect sense. By the way, I speak a little conversational French if you think it'll help."

"Great idea," I said. "Remember, though, I don't want to upset him." Borrowing my entry technique from Goggles, I tapped lightly, entered, and called out. I didn't expect him to answer, and he didn't. Everything was much the same as it had been yesterday and just as I'd done then, I now checked the professor's reaction to my raising the window shade.

He was sitting upright, a limp pillow behind him pushing his neck into an uncomfortable-looking angle. Though he was in pajamas, his hair was neatly combed and his hands folded in his lap like he was waiting for a visitor. On the opposite side of the bed, his breakfast sat untouched on a wheeled tray.

"Hello again, Professor Dubois," I said. "I've brought a friend with me today. I thought you might enjoy speaking a little French."

Viktor stepped up, *"Bonjour, Professeur Dubois,"* he said and continued for a few sentences, none of which elicited a reply in any language. After a few more attempts, he gave me a shrug and settled himself in one of the comfy blue plastic and chrome folding chairs in the corner.

Time for a different tactic. Hiking my skirt so I could sit on the edge of Dubois's bed, I braced one heel on the side rail and crossed my legs. I scootched my butt lightly against Dubois's boney little knees. Slowly, I lifted one leg, admiring the ankle-ties on my peep-toe hemp wedge, and hummed a little tune. In the corner, Viktor's eyes grew large while Dubois's eyes moved ever so slightly in my direction. Then I went for the heavy-duty ammunition.

I took the pint of ice cream and plastic spoon from my tote. After helping myself to a spoonful, I gave it an exaggerated lick, then said, "May I offer you some Cherry Garcia, Professor Coester?"

The old German's jaw dropped open, and I took the opportunity to place a little of the soft ice cream gently on his tongue. He closed his lips around the sweet, icy treat. His eyes rolled back in his head. For a moment I thought he'd fainted, but then he blinked and, like a baby bird, opened his mouth for more.

"Good, huh?" I said, taking another spoonful for myself. "Was this always your favorite, or was it Wolfgang's?"

Without a moment's hesitation — and in an unwavering voice heavy with French accent and minus any guttural inflection whatsoever — the man I'd originally come to think of as Gerhard Coester said, "It was mine. Wolfgang loved plain old peach. Always did, God rest him."

No Sergeant Schultz here then; this man sounded more like Maurice Chevalier. I'd had a feeling the captain of *U-498* would be gone. The professor had an aura of loneliness about him that went beyond the isolation of old age. Relying on the mental image I'd conjured up that day Lucy described the two men in the yard planting the crepe myrtle tree and they way he said Wolfgang's name, I went way out on a limb: "He was the love of your life."

"Yes," Coester said, nodding in confirmation, a small smile played across his lip. "But in all these years that we loved each other, no one ever knew. Wolfgang moved two doors down, and we made sure we were never seen together at night unless we were out of state. How did *you* know?"

Giving him a gentle pat on the knee, I said, "I suspect more people than you thought were aware of your relationship, but it was a different time back then. Those things weren't spoken of, especially if the people in question were held in high regard."

"But how do you know my name? Wolfgang's name?" he asked incredulously.

I told him all about Lucy, how I met her looking for information on *U-498,* about the article that had put it all together for me, and how I'd come to acquire it from Hunter's computer.

"I remember Lucy well," he said, "though

I had no idea she — or anyone — saw us that night. It's amazing, the turn of events in time. Wolfgang and I were sent out to secure the map to the hiding place of one of this greatest of all art treasures, and on the way, a young girl sees us. If anyone would have believed her, the Amber Room would be back in its rightful place, but no one did and so the mystery continues . . ."

"To this day," said Viktor. "Which brings us to why we're here. It's time now to end the mystery."

"I believe you're right, my boy," Coester said, gently folding his hands in his lap.

Viktor and I waited, but he didn't say anything else. I looked at Viktor, and he looked back at me. Then we both looked at Coester, who had suddenly gone vacant. Had he withdrawn to the private world he retreated to when convincing the likes of Goggles of his senility? Viktor gave me a horrified look.

Frantically, I scraped the bottom of the pint of ice cream. We were out! Close to panic, I tried to think of something to do short of shaking the old gent when I considered that he could have fallen silent simply because he didn't want our visit to end. I motioned for Viktor to pull up his chair, and I grabbed one and did the same.

We sat by his bed like children waiting for a story. Eventually I asked casually, as if we'd never stopped conversing, "So about that night, you mentioned rowing in, but you didn't say why. Were you put to sea according to a plan, or was the sub attacked?"

"Attacked! And sinking!" he said, snapping back as if he'd never been mentally absent. "And fast too. I had always been prepared to leave. Wolfgang was supposed to put me over off the coast of New York. We went through the drill of releasing the lifeboat from the sub many times. I had American dollars, a French passport, and all the paperwork I needed to rent a safe deposit box at the Bank of New York to safeguard the cylinder until the war was over."

"New York?" Viktor said. "You missed New York by a long shot."

"Yes," Coester nodded sagely. "But you see, by the time we got that far, Wolfgang and I were in love. And you have to realize, neither Wolfgang nor I were members of the Nazi party. We were just two German men swept up in a course of events that even a blind man could see would be the destruction of us all. I was trying to escape the purge of the university that had been going on since 1933, and Wolfgang never wanted to be in Hitler's Kriegesmarine. For us to have said no, however, would have meant death by firing squad . . ." Coester's words drifted off and he paused again.

As we waited patiently, not wanting to hurry him, it occurred to me that he was hardly senile. In fact, his withdrawal, in such a place as this, might have been more accurately diagnosed as self-defense — maybe even survival. After a few minutes, I decided a prompt might be necessary after all.

"Did anyone else on the boat know about your mission?"

"No," he stated clearly. "We were the only ones, and we decided to keep it that way. Our plan was to tell the crew our destination was Uruguay. We intended to abandon the sub and the crew once there and hide in the mountains until the war was over."

"But that didn't happen because you were hit, right?"

"We were running on the surface when suddenly, without any warning from the radar, a plane was on us, dropping bombs. One was a direct hit. Wolfgang and I just made it to the lifeboat . . . but we were the only ones. The sub sank in just a few minutes. All hands were lost. After we got over the shock of what had happened, we realized fate had wanted us to be together.

So we rowed ashore and started a new life together. I had my passport and plenty of money, so I was able to purchase a fake one later for Wolfgang. I taught him French, and we changed his name on his new passport to Eudon Colbert. That's because he so loved Claudette Colbert."

My head was spinning. All this, and Claudette Colbert too. "I still don't understand the purpose of making a map and hiding it in another country when the artifact was in Germany?"

"Who said it was in Germany?" He sighed heavily. "Even I didn't know where it was. It was in twenty-seven enormous crates, so it wasn't like a painting or something that could be easily moved." He cleared his throat and smacked his lips. I dug out a fresh Evian from my tote — I keep everything in there — and handed it to him.

He took a swig. "Thank you, my dear." Then, sensing our confusion, he went on. "You see, only Koch knew the exact physical whereabouts of the crates. That was pretty easy to accomplish since so many crates containing so much looted art were being shuffled around. Who knew what was in what crate? Hitler ordered him to create a map to the crates to stand as . . . well, tender."

He took another sip, eyeing Viktor and me as we struggled to understand the plans of a madman. "Hitler already had plans in place for his escape to South America. The map to the crates was meant as payment to allow him admittance into one of the countries there. I was to await his orders, then retrieve the cylinder and bring it to him . . . wherever he ended up. Of course, as it turned out, Hitler was killed and Koch captured, so there was no one to call for the cylinder."

"Did you take it to New York according to your orders, just to be on the safe side?" asked Viktor. "I mean, after you settled in North Carolina?"

"No. What would have been the purpose? Besides, I didn't have it."

"What do you mean, you didn't have it?" I asked, stunned.

"Oh my God," Viktor said. "It *is* still on the sub, isn't it?"

"Of course. I told you, what was left of *U-498* went down so fast that if Wolfgang and I hadn't drilled beforehand, we'd have gone down with it too."

"But, but," I stammered. "Hunter said it wasn't there."

"Hunter?" Coester was confused, and I didn't blame him.

"I told you about him, remember?" I

asked. "He worked for the man who found the sub. He explored its remains with a remotely operated robot and reported the cylinder wasn't there. I only have limited information here, and it's second hand. But the gist was no cylinder, not even in the forward compartments."

He smiled, "Ah. This I can explain. Several hours before we were hit by the American bombs, we were running submerged, trying to get some relief from the pounding we were taking during a storm. One of the crewmen realized there was no torpedo in the top starboard tube. *U-498* had the usual configuration of four tubes, two up and two down. Not knowing the top starboard had been designated to hold the cylinder as *well* as some document boxes, he tried to load a torpedo in the tube, but of course, it wouldn't go all the way in. Document boxes and the heavily wrapped cylinder were in the way. When the crewman tried to pull the torpedo back out, he couldn't. It was stuck. I remember the day so well," Coester said, shaking his head.

"Wolfgang didn't want to risk an undersea explosion, so we surfaced. He had all nonessential crewmen move topside and stand at the stern while two crewmen disarmed the torpedo. I don't know if you're aware, but these bombs are very large. It takes two men to load one. Once they completely disarmed it, we tossed it overboard, and Wolfgang ordered the men back inside. Most went to their quarters. We were the last to climb down the hatch. That's where we were when we were bombed, and I suspect it's the reason we survived. We were the closest to the only means of escape. My knapsack was already with the inflatable. I loaned Wolfgang some of my clothes when we got ashore."

I looked at Viktor. He looked at me, then at the elderly man who'd just finished telling us this extraordinary story. "In all these years, you never said anything to anyone about the Amber Room? Didn't you feel some responsibility?"

"Of course we did. From the beginning, neither Wolfgang nor I had any intention of turning the room back over to Hitler. It was our plan to turn the map to the treasure over to the proper authorities once we got to a stable government and let them return it to its rightful owners. But that task was taken from us when the sub went down in over two thousand feet of water. It might well have been on the moon! And remember, we lived under constant fear of being revealed, not just as Germans, but as homosexuals."

Just then, a commotion arose in the hall right outside the room. Goggles was confronting a large man in a ball cap wearing uniform-style work clothes, starched and pressed, his shirt out over his trousers. "Didn't you hear me?" she demanded. "You need to come back and check in at the reception area before visiting a guest."

It was then I recognized him. "Well, well, Miz Cooper," said Davy Duchamp, pushing past the indignant nurse as he and his sons strode into the room. "We meet again."

Viktor and I rose from our chairs so fast his fell over. Momentarily at a loss for words, I could only gape as Goggles, close on Duchamp's heels, poked him in his beefy ribs. "I said you need to —"

"Get lost!" Duchamp snarled.

"Well, we'll just see what security has to say about this." She sniffed and stomped out without apparently noticing that Viktor and I were in breach of the rules as well.

"Davy. What are you doing here?" Viktor asked.

"Following you and her. We need to talk."

"I declined your *invitation* last night. Apparently you didn't get my drift," I said with way more authority than I was feeling.

"Well, you're not declining again." He

stepped aggressively up to me.

"Now just a minute," Viktor pushed between us only to get the stiff arm from Davy.

"Back off, Kozlov," Duchamp ordered. "I'm going to make this short and sweet. *She* is coming with me. I'm going to put her where she won't be in my way, and she's going to stay there until I get what belongs to me and my boys. After all, we're the ones that found the treasure." Then back to me: "You should have taken the hint to steer clear when Hunter caught you trying to read the internal log on the ROV and roughed you up pretty good. But you didn't —"

Realizing at last what had prompted the attack from Hunter in the first place, I started to protest the misunderstanding — I can't imagine why — when the question of how he'd managed to jump to that conclusion came to mind. I opened my mouth to ask, but about that time the twins jumped in the fray.

"Dad!" they cried in unison.

"You just kept on," Duchamp continued. "You hacked into Hunter's computer, learned way more than you needed to know. You're just like that stupid Eskimo, trying to take something that's not yours. I might remind you that what happened to him could happen to you."

What did that mean? "Are you threatening me?"

"I'm saying that until we get the cylinder and I settle my deal with the Chinese, you're going to be out of my hair."

"I can't believe what I'm hearing," Viktor said in disbelief. "Are you insane? She's not going anywhere!"

"Look here," Duchamp said, "it's time for you to pick a side —"

"Pick a side?"

"He already has," I said firmly, taking Viktor's arm and wondering two things: One, why I hadn't realized until this second that Hunter's body washed up on a Thursday, yet if my memory served me correctly (and I was pretty sure it did), Viktor had told me Voyager called him on Wednesday? So Duchamp must have known — from the twins? — that Hunter wasn't just missing, he was dead. And two, how would we make it safely past Duchamp and his sons?

"Viktor's with me, and we're leaving." I didn't get a chance to try, however because just then more visitors stepped into Gerhard Coester's room.

Twenty-Three

"What the hell are you doing here?" I squawked to Detectives Pierce and Myers.

"I've been following you, of course. Myers had his doubts, but I knew eventually you'd lead me to a person of interest, and so you have. Actually, they were following you, too, but that's beside the point."

"Wait!" I said. "I'm confused. You were following them, following me . . ."

"No," Myers said. "We were tailing you. Then those guys — two of whom we've already interviewed — fell in behind you, too, so all we had to do was follow the crazy train here, stand outside the door, and listen."

"Yeah," Pierce said, turning to the twins, "I must say, it was very interesting. Apparently we need to have another chat. This time we'll include your dad and find out what you three might know regarding a dead crewman and a certain *cylinder.*"

"Damn straight," Myers said. "You guys had me doubting my partner, which leaves me a little embarrassed, so what say we all go back to Morehead where we can take some statements?"

My mind was flying everywhere at once. For one thing, I'd just had another brilliant insight. The ROV team wore orange jumpsuits — the same bright orange as a particular little scrap of material Pierce and I had found stuck in Hunter's watchband. And all along I'd thought it was from Bud's lucky shirt. Now I was embarrassed . . . again. It wasn't enough that I'd stupidly thought an internal log was one kept by the tech team not the ROV itself.

But overriding all my thoughts was the driving need to complete what had became a treasure hunt for me the moment all the pieces of the puzzle started to fall into place and I'd realized I could go down in history as the person who found the Amber Room. In short, everything else paled when compared to the possibility that I could still pull this off. The gambler in me strained to go for broke. Now, I realize this is a bad character flaw in myself and that I should have been happy to tell the police everything I knew about this whole mess. See that truth and justice prevailed and all that. And, I would . . . maybe. Just not right now.

After all, Viktor and I were still the only ones with all the pieces. With a little luck, we could be the first to the cylinder. We just needed to convince the cops that we were not involved with anything Davy Duchamp and his boys might have been up to. Then we could skedaddle back to the *Magellan,* where we'd somehow manage to fish the cylinder up from the sub. I hadn't concocted a way to do that undetected yet, but I had some ideas.

However, I didn't have to give my dilemma any further consideration, because just then Duchamp pulled a handgun from his belt where it'd been hidden under his shirt.

"My boys and I aren't going anywhere," he said.

"Dad!" Dean shouted. "Stop. This whole thing is —"

"— getting way out of control!" Tim cried.

See, I should have realized this. I should have totally cottoned on to the fact that with a treasure as vast as the Amber Room, for Christ's sakes, a person would go to any extremes to acquire it, including taking on the law using a gun — a practice frowned upon by federal, state, and local authorities, to say the least. I was trying to think of something that would defuse the situation when our bedridden host — who, unbeknownst to us, had crept to the foot of the bed — did something that, just like in the movies, changed real time into slow motion. He launched himself off the bed straight at Duchamp, trying, I suppose, to swipe the gun from his hand!

And, just like in the movies, Viktor and I shouted, "Noooo!" simultaneously and lunged for him, as did Goggles and an enormous black orderly in a white uniform, the pair of whom had just arrived in the room. But, like I said, it was as if we were all moving in slow motion. Duchamp, eyes bulging in disbelief, was backpedaling so hard he lost his balance and careened into the rollaway food tray, the back of his head striking it first with a loud *thwack*! This was followed by another loud bang, much louder, as the handgun went off. Then, like a marionette with its strings cut, Duchamp, weapon still in hand, crumpled slowly to the floor.

Then real time resumed and total pandemonium broke out.

It's funny the things you notice in such a situation, but you know what stood out during the chaos that ensued? How tender and protective Goggles was toward Coester as she and the orderly gathered him up and placed him, unharmed, back in bed. You'd have thought he was her granddad or something. Go figure. Anyway, it seemed like forever before all the cops, EMTs (there must have been four that responded to the scene), and other government types who felt their presence was a total necessity in circumstances involving a firearm (regardless of the fact that no one was hit) did what they do and left.

Viktor and I had moved our chairs to the hallway to be out of the way. Pierce had ordered us not to leave. With no real privacy, we hadn't had a chance to speak alone since the shooting and just when I thought we would, Pierce and Myers approached us.

"We've just got word from Raleigh PD that Duchamp has regained consciousness," he said. "This is their jurisdiction, so we have to wait until they make their charges before we can take him into custody. Right now, though, he's still in the emergency room, so Myers and I are headed over there. His sons are waiting for us. But first, I've just got a couple of questions for you."

"Uh, sure," I said not without trepidation.

"Why were you two here? What's your connection to Mr. Dubois?"

"Don't ask me," Viktor said. "I'm just here

with Ms. Cooper."

Pierce directed his gaze to me. "Well?"

I struggled to remember what I'd told helpful Mr. Devereaux, over at Women's College.

"You gonna tell us *today*?" Myers said.

"Well, uh, neither Viktor nor I needed to be back on the *Magellan* until this afternoon so, since we had some time this morning and since Mr. Dubois used to be my aunt's French professor and I try to stop by when I'm in the area to say hello for her, I figured today would be a good time."

Pierce's eyes drifted sideways as he considered this. Then he said, "And you were in the area because . . ."

"Well, you may remember my friend here," I said, indicating Viktor. Pierce and Myers shook their heads in the negative. I introduced him as a Voyager crewman who was also working on his dissertation in economic petrology, then explained, "He and I were going to stop at the Archdale Building — it's practically across the street, you know."

I got blank stares. "The Archdale Building houses academic geologic papers as well as those produced by the North Carolina Geologic Survey."

Myers made a rolling motion with his hand.

"So, after I'd completed my social obligation," I told him, hurriedly, "we planned to do a little research on some of the latest papers on . . . siliciclastic sequence stratigraphy and . . ."

"Unstable progradational shelf margins," Viktor chimed in.

"Whatever," Pierce snapped. "So you're saying you were just making a social call, then going to do a little work-related research. Last question for now: those guys were following you because . . ."

When I didn't finish his sentence, Pierce raised his eyebrows.

I really didn't want to say this in front of Viktor so I pulled Pierce aside, lowered my voice, and said, "Maybe they think I remember what happened the night of the attack and it might tend to implicate them. The thing is, I'd rather discuss this with you in private."

"Tomorrow then," Pierce said. He called to his partner, "Okay Myers, let's make like a baby and head out."

It was almost three o'clock when Viktor and I headed back to Morehead. He was driving and not saying much.

"What do you think of our chances of getting the ROV and finding the cylinder?" I asked.

Viktor looked at me briefly, then said as if he'd already been thinking about it, "I'm pretty sure I can get the ROV without too many questions asked. What I'm worried about is how long it'll take to find the sub. We need to be able to go straight to it, not waste time looking, bumbling around, hoping the obstacle-avoidance sonar alerts us to something or we just happen to see it. The lights only project out about twenty-five feet down there."

"I think I can help with that," I said, grabbing my purse from the backseat. "It just so happens I have a copy of the seismic data that Global used to make the site survey."

"That's what's been bothering me!" Viktor smacked his palm on the wheel. "In this country there are strict guidelines on how close to a shipwreck a wellhole can be placed. Davy must have altered the seismic survey before he gave it to Global. I can't believe I didn't think of that before. All we need is an older survey."

"Don't feel bad, the thought occurred to me a little late in the game too," I said as I struggled to spread the map in my lap. "And you're right about an older survey; we could use it to pinpoint the exact location of the sub by comparing the contours and seeing exactly where Davy changed the offsets. But . . ."

"We don't have one?" Viktor asked.

"No. This isn't the Gulf, where everything's been mapped and surveyed many times over. Anyway, I seriously doubt another company has surveyed this area, because if they had, they would have found the sub. Besides, anything done by another seismic survey company would be proprietary, not available to the public."

"So what good is this altered survey going to do us?"

"Well, just hold your horses," I said, staring at the area in question on the survey. "Let me take a look here." After what felt like an hour of looking down at a zillion squiggly lines, I began to feel carsick. "I think I need to look at this again at the house." I laid my head back on the headrest.

"You look green," Viktor said.

"I'll be okay," I said, trying to hide my disappointment. I'd been so sure I'd be able to see some evidence of tampering.

"Chin up. We still have plan B: hope the lights and the obstacle-avoidance sonar alert us to something. Speaking of which, let's go over what we're going to do when we get back aboard the *Magellan.*"

"Okay, tell me what you're thinking and what I can do to assist."

"First," said Viktor, "you'll need to explain to the captain what I'm doing back on the ship out of rotation. Then, we'll go down to the lab, see if the ROV's down. If it is, we wait until right before their break time, then I go in and give Ray and the boys my story about wanting to go through some maneuvers that I had trouble with last rotation and ask if I can work with Scooter while they're on break. You watch from somewhere close by. When break time comes and they leave without me, you'll know I've got the ROV. Come on in and we'll see what we can find."

"And if Scooter's not in the water?"

"We just check the schedule. With things about to wrap up on the well, they'll have plenty to do down below."

"You think Ray will let you *practice* with the ROV?"

"I think so. I mean, they're only on break for thirty minutes, they'll still be responsible for surfacing and docking it. I don't know Ray very well, but he seems to be an agreeable fellow."

We reached the house and Viktor went to his hotel to pack a bag. I did the same, and while I waited for him to return, I looked at the seismic again. This time, however, I took a different tack and pinned it up on the wall in my office. Standing back from it about 5 feet, I squinted my eyes like I was looking at one of those trick optical illusions that hide a 3D drawing. I squinted and squinted, tilting my head this way and that, keeping in mind that I was looking at the underside of the seafloor, at indentions instead of raised areas, and just as I was about to give up in frustration: bingo.

There it was, not 300 feet from the wellhead. Of course, in the pitch blackness of the seafloor at almost 2,200 feet below the surface, it could have been a mere 50 feet away and the ROV lights wouldn't illuminate it.

Everywhere an offset line had been removed and replaced with one indicating a flat surface with no shipwreck, a tiny blank space was left, leaving a ghost of what had previously been there. In effect, instead of a dark shadow, as the sub would have appeared to Duchamp, I saw a very faint white outline. The shape was what I would expect of a wrecked sub: an oval about 200 feet long.

The more I looked, the more I saw it. I could even detect the outlines of scattered shapes indicating a debris field. Some shapes were large, indicating that a massive explosion had sent the sub quickly to its final resting place. I was still studying the survey when I heard Viktor slam the back door.

I called him upstairs to see if he could pick out the wreck. He was much faster at seeing it than I had been. We were so elated, we could have just about flown out to the *Magellan* by ourselves. But we chose, instead, to hitch a ride on the helicopter that was just loading the chief accounting officer, Patrick Donovan, when we reached the airport.

Once back aboard, I filled Powell in on why Viktor had returned with me, explaining that, as a fellow petroleum geologist, he wanted to be aboard while we plumbed the depths of a reservoir so similar to the ones described in his dissertation. As we talked, I couldn't help but notice that attention was again being focused on SunCo's *Able Leader.*

"What's going on?" I asked Powell.

"Looks like there might be a delay of some sort over there. Best we can tell, they have some type of riser problem in one of the wells. It's serious enough that they've shut down progress on the other well too, to concentrate all hands on the problem."

"Are they in danger?" Viktor asked.

"No. But they've definitely disconnected from the riser for some reason, so we're keeping watch. Meanwhile, things are going smoothly here for a change. We've completed the turn for the new angle and cut down another four hundred feet. We're only about two hundred feet from your target. We should be there in less than twelve hours." He paused. "Did I see Patrick come in with you?"

"Yes," I said. "Phil's still here, isn't he?"

"Yup," Powell put the binoculars back up to his eyes. "The gang is gathering. Hope you can produce one of those rabbits you said you had up your sleeve."

Grimacing inwardly, I closed the helm door behind us. It was actually two rabbits, he just didn't know it. "Bad news for SunCo is good for us; something else to divert attention from what we're doing," I reminded Viktor.

At the ROV area, we caught another lucky break: the warning sign was posted, which meant Scooter was in the water.

"Keep your eyes peeled," Viktor said under his breath as he headed for the van door. I kept walking, continuing along the deck to the logging lab.

A look of relief flooded Elton's face upon my arrival. "Thank heavens you're here," he said. "I could use some help since things are really starting to pop around here."

Not wanting to explain my delay as being due to a shootout at an old folks' home, I smiled, gave him a pat on the shoulder, and said, "That's what we've been waiting for. What's the latest gas reading?"

"Well over a hundred units, but I'm fighting just to keep up with the number of samples called for in the contract" — Elton stopped to suck in a breath — "and Grant keeps making my job harder by raising the bit and mixing up the samples at the annulus."

"Calm down, you're about to blow a valve yourself. Try cutting your sample rate to less than six an hour. About the mixing, have you talked to Grant?"

"No."

"What have I told you about communication? Let's go find him," I said, eager to get back on deck and be within sight of the ROV van. I made little progress, though. Just as I stepped out with Elton on my heels, I nearly collided with David Grant. "Ah, just the man you're looking for, Elton," I said. "Explain your concerns." I stepped back from the two of them to where I could see the door to the ROV van. Pulling out my iPhone, I pretended to check for messages. Lo and behold, there was one. A text from Pierce:

HEADS UP. DUCHAMP AND SONS OUT OF CUSTODY.

Great. A crazy guy and his two almost-as-crazy sons were back on the loose gunning for me. With an eye trained on the van, I hit redial for Pierce. He answered on the first ring.

"What do you mean 'out of custody'? Did he get a lawyer?" I asked.

"Well, technically he wasn't in our custody yet. Remember, Raleigh PD had jurisdiction. I had to wait until they charged him with the firearms violation before I could —"

Was he being intentionally obtuse? "Well, what? Didn't they charge him? I thought it was against the law to draw a firearm on a policeman in a public place, especially after said firearm accidentally discharges. Might I remind you it was only by the grace of God that none of us were hit."

Pierce made a little exasperated sound, then snapped, "I mean, he's out of custody because he was never in. He . . . escaped first."

Good Lord. "How?"

"That's not important."

"You posted a guard at his door, didn't you?"

"I imagine Raleigh PD would have," Pierce said. "Turns out he wasn't as incapacitated as we thought, so he never made it from ICU to his room where the guard was."

"Where do you think he went?"

"I don't think, I *know,*" Pierce barked.

"Okay, let's hear it."

"Knowing how all you oil people fly everywhere in helicopters, Myers and I checked at RDU and, sure enough, he hopped one to Morehead. We also found out through Fish and Wildlife that he recently applied for registration for a new boat, a very fancy Fountain. Turns out he keeps it in Morehead, too, so our guess is he'll try to use it to vamoose to Louisiana and territory he's more familiar with, where he thinks he can hide from us."

"You don't think he'd come out here?"

"Look, I already know he's taken the boat and gone. It's only a forty-minute chopper ride to Morehead from Raleigh, and the marina owner says his boat's been gone about an hour. Left with three men aboard. Don't worry, Ms. Cooper. We've called in the Coast Guard. We'll find him, and when we do, I'm going to get to the bottom of all this."

"I hope so, because — as I'm sure you're aware, you being on top of this and all — the ROV team wears bright orange jump-suits and —"

Just then, the ROV team trooped out of the van on their break. I looked back to Grant and Elton. They motioned that they were headed to the DC. I signaled back that I'd be right along.

"And . . ." Pierce wanted to know.

"You figure it out. Gotta go." I hung up my iPhone and made a beeline for Viktor and the ROV van. On the way, I tried to come to grips with the thought that one or both of the handsome Duchamp twins could actually have tossed Hunter over-board. Why? Was it, as their dad had said, that he'd gotten too pushy? Was it they who'd returned my limp, unconscious body to my room, knowing it'd be easy enough to frame me for his death?

Viktor was already at Scooter's controls as it prowled 2,200 feet below us. "Oh my God!" he exclaimed. "It *is* right here. Practi-cally right under us."

"Where?" I said, joining him in front of the monitor.

"Look how compressed it is from the pressure at this depth, and the damage," he breathed. "God, looks like a direct hit on the port side. It literally blew part of the bow off."

The ghostly images unfolding before me as Scooter cruised over *U-498* were far different from the ones Henri and I had seen when we dove the wreck of *U-352.* Here, instead of the abundant marine life that had made a home in that sub, only fine barnacles, silt, and rustlicles — a type of bacteria that eats iron and creates a tube structure of rust — were present. Even knowing we only had about thirty minutes to find our treasure, the two of us stared in awe.

"Damn!" Viktor said. "The part of the bow that's missing is the part that contained the torpedo tube we're looking for. We have to find it to find the cylinder."

As the robot reached the forward end of the mangled vessel, I saw an eerie sight: a boot standing upright, all alone in the far reaches of the light field about 25 feet to starboard. Just then Viktor sucked in a short breath as the ROV caught a strong current and pitched down violently. "Shit!" Clouds of sediment billowed around the ROV then quickly blew forward in the torrential currents. "Okay, let's play follow-the-mud-cloud. Maybe the current will lead us to where the bow landed."

As the wrecked hull disappeared from the monitor, another shadow appeared. "Wait!" I said. "What's that off to port about twenty feet?"

"I see it." Viktor pushed the juice to the aft thrusters, and Scooter glided forward to illuminate a large side plate of twisted metal. Its rivets, though still in place, had been severed as cleanly as though they been made of putty.

"A little farther out," I said, picturing the site survey in my mind. Scooter swayed in the water column as Viktor maneuvered it through the relentless snow of a miniscule percentage of the trillions upon trillions of tiny plants and animals that live and die in the world's oceans. They sink to the seafloor every minute of every day and have since life began: fuel for another day, millions of years from now.

"I bet that's it," he said as another dark shape slowly became visible in the bright headlights.

"It is!" I practically shouted, recognizing the snub-nosed shape of the sub's bow, which lay keel down. Other than being blown away from the rest of the sub, the starboard side looked remarkably undamaged. As Viktor carefully sent the robot over the remains, the light exposed the openings of the once-lethal torpedo tubes. They resembled the air scoops on a '57 Buick, except these had square edges, not curved ones. At the severed end of the wreckage, unrecognizable debris was scattered everywhere. Once Viktor directed the lights into the opening, we could see the hatch doors to the four torpedo tubes.

Only one was open.

Twenty-Four

"The professor did say the cylinder was packed into the top starboard tube, didn't he?"

"Sure did," I said, surprised at the size of the tube. It was as big around as my body. I was practically salivating to somehow magically slide inside it and collect its contents.

"Only one way to tell," Viktor said, reversing Scooter's thrusters and backing it to a better position. "See any light coming out?" he asked.

I shook my head. "Nope."

"Wait," Viktor said. He flipped a switch on his control board, which turned off the starboard headlight. "What about now?"

We were squinting at the monitor when suddenly I thought to check Mickey on my wrist. Uh-oh.

"Holy crap! Twenty-eight minutes have already gone by. Ray and the boys will be back any second now! Pull away from the wreck!" I jumped up, scurried to the van door, and peeked out. They were nowhere in sight. I looked back at Viktor, saw the frustration on his face. "There's nothing to do but come back later. I'm headed to the DC. Text me or call me when you can get Scooter again."

Just before I left I said, "Oh, I almost forgot. I got a call from that detective that found us with Coester. He said apparently Duchamp's head wound and concussion weren't bad enough to slow him down much and that he and the twins had 'left' their custody before they could be further questioned."

"Left. You mean they escaped?"

"Well, technically, no one has been arrested. But, yes, they left before Pierce could take their statements. It was up to him to then arrest Duchamp if he felt the incident at the nursing home justified it."

Viktor turned back to the monitor. "Did he say where they went?"

Scanning the catwalk for the returning ROV team, I said, "He says he's sure they've gone back to Louisiana because their boat is gone. I hope he's right."

He shook his head and said, "It would be very unlike Davy to give up without a fight."

Then, hearing the voices of the team, I

told him, "Here they come. Gotta go!"

Figuring Elton had returned to the logging lab, I was heading that way when I heard the pitch of the drill increase and I knew a break — when the rate of penetration increases — was about to occur. We were entering our reservoir, though it would be a little while before the computer printouts showed it.

Once at the lab, I wasn't surprised to find Elton freaking out again. His eyes bulged behind his glasses, giving him the look of a lunatic. Jonathan, the mudlogger currently on duty, was watching the monitors like a coyote watching a ground squirrel. "I think we're fixing to get a break," he drawled.

"Uh-oh. I should recalculate lag time," Elton said. Jonathan rolled his eyes.

"So, go do it!" I said. "They'll be making a connection in the next few minutes."

"Right," Elton said and dashed off for the supply room down by the shakers.

"That boy is going to make a fair enough wellsite geologist when he learns to settle down a bit and just go with the flow," Jonathan commented.

"He's determined, I'll give him that," I said.

Just then, there was a knock at the door. Jonathan looked at me and raised his eyebrows. I opened the pressurized door, saw Viktor, and stepped out to him.

"There's good news and bad news," he said.

"Okay, good news first."

"In two hours, Ray and the boys have to go over some new procedures on capping off a well. He said I could continue to practice docking maneuvers while they're gone."

"Great," I said, checking my watch. "The bad news?"

"They'll only be gone for another thirty to forty minutes. Then they're going to put Scooter up because that's the end of their shift."

I swallowed hard. "We'll find it by then. I know we will."

Just then Elton appeared out of nowhere. "We're out of carbides!"

"How can you be out? You're in charge of supplies for the mudloggers!"

"I miscalculated?"

"Well, that's one way to learn," I sighed.

"What should I do? If I can't make accurate logs, we'll have to stop drilling until I can get some flown out here from Morehead."

Imagining all the bigwigs on board waiting for word on whether Global would survive or not, I quickly nixed that plan. "No. Don't do that," I said. "Go up to the galley. Ask cook to spare you a bag of rice. Put that down the well. It'll work just as well. Then call Wanda at shorebase. You've established a good working relationship with her, haven't you?" He nodded. "Good. She'll send some carbides on the next flight out that'll get you through until the supply boat gets here."

He scurried off, and I turned back to Viktor, "So text me when you get access to Scooter again. Until then, hang out either here or in the DC. Of course, it's a bit crowded in here and there's Elton to contend with. Tell him you'll help bag and label samples. That'll calm him down a bit."

"Where are you going to be?"

"I've got to go find Phil Gregson, the senior geologist."

I paused when I reached the landing at *Magellan*'s top level. Almost to the horizon, SunCo's *Able Leader* was visible, positively glowing in the orange light of the setting sun. I wondered if they'd resumed drilling. The sound of another helicopter approaching quickly brought me back to the tasks at hand.

"Phil," I said upon entering the conference room where most the well data was stored. "Data will be coming in during the next hour that'll show us in the reservoir."

Phil jumped up. "Great! I haven't been down yet. I've been working on other projects all day. How do you feel about it? Any readings yet on gas content?"

"They'll be starting to come in soon. Assuming the lag time's correct — and Elton's seeing to that right now — we'll have a good idea of where to take another side core for rock eval."

"Sounds good." He started to pace nervously.

I checked my watch, counting the minutes until I could rejoin Viktor and the ROV. I was thinking maybe around two hours.

"Today's going to be a great day for this company," Phil said.

Soon we were joined by Duncan Powell, Braxton Roberts, and other Global honchos who wanted to discuss a press conference. Later, when the discussions turned away from my area of expertise to creating the nonexisting infrastructure for delivering the gas to shore, I checked my watch. The two hours were almost up, so I excused myself. Just as I reached the door, Bud came through it.

"Where are you going?" he whispered as I slipped past him. "I need to talk to you."

I should have planned on Bud's being included in this discussion group, but with so much going on, I just hadn't thought that far ahead. As usual, I was running headlong, making adjustments when needed. But what kind of adjustment was needed when one's ex-husband and current lover were both on board the same ship, I wasn't sure.

"I can't right now," I said. "We've hit our target. The first cuttings have come up by now, and I need to be with the wellsite geologist."

He followed me outside the conference room. "What's the plan?"

"Well, first off, you stay up here out of the way . . ."

Bud squinted at me.

"With the investors, I mean, and I'll send word up when we get to the bottom of the reservoir. We have equipment on board that'll give reliable estimates for all the biggest questions; namely, is the gas dry and abundant enough to put Global in the black? After that, if everything looks good, they'll run logs for days to be certain about what we have."

"Text me when you can get free for dinner."

"Uh, okay. Later," I said. I waited until he'd closed the door behind him, then booked it for the ROV van.

Two roughnecks dodged aside to avoid colliding with me as I raced by them. Breathless as I reached the door, I thought twice about opening it. I didn't want to startle Viktor and cause him to crash the huge ROV into something delicate . . . like a friggin' torpedo. I briefly wondered if the other three tubes were still armed. I softly pushed the door open. Viktor was biting his bottom lip as he manipulated Scooter's controls.

"Cylinder's definitely in the tube," Viktor told me as I entered. "There was some other rotted debris like old wooden boxes in there too, but they were within easy reach and I pulled them out of the way. Cylinder is a bit farther up in the tube."

I gave a fleeting thought to the top-secret military documents those wooden boxes were thought to contain. Now disintegrated, the horrors they'd likely reveal and the lessons to humanity were lost to the sea forever. But then the reality of the enormous find within our grasp overcame me, and I was giddy with excitement.

"The trouble is, I can't reach it from either end," he said. "So I'm looking for a piece of railing that I saw in the debris field between the main part of the wreckage and the bow. I think it's long enough to use to push the cylinder out the exit end."

He navigated Scooter along the bottom, using the levers to illuminate first left, then right until he found the railing. Manipulating the stainless-steel pincers on the jointed arm, Viktor grasped the railing, spun Scooter around like a jouster with a javlin, and made a beeline for the torpedo tube again.

"Good job!" I said, my adrenaline pumping so hard I was panting.

"I hope it's long enough to reach," he said, inserting it in the tube.

"Wait!" I said.

He jumped. "What?"

"You don't think there could be any explosives in there, do you?"

"Like what? The torpedo is gone. This is just the tube."

"Well . . . I don't know anything about bombs and warheads and stuff like that. But the sub was pretty wrecked. Do you think there could be pieces of the other torpedoes in there or something?"

Viktor gave me the same look my older brother used to give me when I asked girly questions. "No," he said, "there couldn't be. If you'll just . . ."

"Yeah, yeah. I know," I said. "Trust you."

"Right," he said, and rammed the railing into the tube.

Tap, tap, tap. Viktor and I froze at the sound of someone tapping lightly on the door. We stared at each other. "Who could it be?"

"Not Ray and the boys," I said, standing. "They wouldn't knock." I opened the door and poked my head out.

Bud.

"What are you doing here?" I was accusatory. "I told you to stay upstairs."

"I know but —"

"No," I snapped. "Obviously, you don't know."

"Huh?"

"Can't you read?"

"Read what?"

"That," I said, pointing to the NO ADMITTANCE WHEN ROV IS OPERATING sign.

"How would I know if the ROV is operating?"

Pushing him back a few feet and pulling the door closed behind me, I said, "Do you see the ROV anywhere?"

Bud looked around, feigning serious observation. "No, I don't," he said.

"Then it must be down below, huh?"

"Makes sense." A big grin spread across his face. "Actually I came up here looking for you and . . . your friend."

"Friend?"

"A guy named Elton said you might be with your friend, an ROV pilot." His voice held curiosity. "Viktor, I believe he said was his name. Have I met your friend Viktor?" he asked pointedly.

My adrenalin rush doubled down. I stepped to the railing to steady myself. "Uh, no," I said. "No, you haven't. I was looking for him too, but he isn't in there." The wind, continuing to gain in strength, now whipped my ponytail about my face and I realized I didn't have my hard hat on.

I slapped my hand on top of my head. "Jeez, I've got to get my hat and you need to go." I looked below to see if anyone, like a safety inspector, had seen me. That's when I spotted Davy Duchamp.

He was talking to Braxton Roberts. Their conversation looked heated. This last surprise sent me into lightheaded land. Bud, following my line of sight, startled me even further by shouting down to them. "Braxton! Davy!"

Oh my god. "Bud! What are you doing? Do you know that man with Braxton?"

"Of course I do. Name's Davy Duchamp, from SeaTrek. He's an investor."

"Investor?"

"Yes. It's quite common for oil companies to take other companies in as investors," he explained impatiently. "Especially those with an ongoing stake in a project."

I looked down again for the two men, but they'd disappeared. Clumping sounds on the stairs to my right let me know where they were headed. I grabbed Bud's arm and turned him in their direction. "I hear your friends coming. You shouldn't be up here and neither should they. Why don't you go head them off, let them know the ROV's down. I need to go find my hat. Oh, and Bud?"

"Yes?"

"Don't mention me to them, okay?"

"Okay," he said, drawing the word out dubiously. "But what about dinner?"

"Maybe later," I called over my shoulder just before I descended the stairs at the opposite end of the catwalk. Halfway down, I stopped. I knew I'd be leaving Viktor in a vulnerable position, yet at the same time I desperately needed to talk with Bud . . . alone. I had to find out what he knew about Duchamp, who was obviously here looking for Viktor and me.

What if Duchamp looked in the van? What would he do? He'd already pulled a gun. I needed to think. I sat down on the stairs and tried to make out what the three men were saying. I couldn't. But when metallic clumping at the other end of the catwalk told me they were leaving, relief washed over me. I tiptoed back up the stairs and peeped over the railing to make sure the coast was clear before entering the van.

"Davy's here!" I told Viktor as I closed the door.

"I knew it," he said. "I knew he wouldn't give up so easily."

"How much time do you think we have left?"

"About fifteen minutes by my calculations, but I'll make it. I've already pushed out the packing that was jammed in the torpedo exit and I'm pulling it apart now, looking for the cylinder."

"Great!" I said, jumping back into my chair to watch him operate the hand-sized duplicate of Scooter's jointed manipulating arms. With the plastic arm resting against his thumb, he opened and closed the pinchers, shredding the rotted material. Then, in the flash of an eye, the cylinder rolled out of the murky cloud of mangled wadding and silt onto the sea floor, looking just as it had in the photo when Erich Koch handed it to young Gerhard Coester back in 1945.

Viktor and I gasped in unison.

"You know what has to be done now?" Viktor asked.

"Uh, bring it up and hide it until we can get it off the ship, of course."

"Of course. Problem is, in order to get the cylinder, we'd have to dock Scooter. That takes three strong people. Even if the two of us could manage, we might be seen. No, our best option is to hide it somewhere below the waterline on the *Magellan.*"

"Do what?"

"You heard me," he said, pushing the ROV at top speed back to its cage, spinning it around, then backing it in. "Ray and his crew are responsible for ascent and docking. Anything out of the ordinary would bring about an immediate inquiry. We don't want that."

All I could do was shake my head. We were so close! Viktor looked at me. "Don't worry. I've got the perfect place to hide it where we can easily collect it later. But we have to hurry. Bringing it up two thousand feet will take a few minutes."

I waited as he began the ROV's ascent, then asked, "So, where *are* we hiding it?"

"On one of the thrusters."

"On a thruster! Are you crazy? How do you expect to *collect* it as you say? They operate constantly."

"Correct. But if we go to the back side of the thruster, out of the propulsion stream, and avoid the intake stream, we'll be quite safe. There is a graduated space between an arm that projects from the rear of the thruster and the hull of the ship. It is part of the housing on the thruster and doesn't move with it. I'll just jam the cylinder between it and the hull. Then we come back tomorrow night and pick it up," Viktor said casually as he were talking about dropping by Pizza Hut for two large pies to go.

"How do you know this? There are several different models of thrusters used on drill-ships, and they're all slightly different."

"We did some observation right after I came aboard. Captain Powell wanted the starboard one checked for vibration, so I know exactly what they look like."

"Have you not noticed the security boat that patrols the perimeter here 24/7?"

"Yes, yes," Viktor said dismissively. "Tomorrow night we rent a fast fishing boat to get out here, then pretend we have steering problems that cause us to slowly cruise in a large arc beyond the patrol boat. You act like you're working on the problem, smile, and wave to the security boat. But, meanwhile, I go over the side. I pick up the cylinder, swim back to you. We pretend the problem is fixed, go back home with our prize."

I checked my watch. Ten minutes had gone by, so only about five were left. With a sinking feeling in the pit of my stomach, I watched the ROV change direction by 180 degrees and approach the rear of one of Magellan's gigantic thrusters. Then, just as Viktor had described it, Scooter's jointed arm extended and shoved the precious cylinder between the graduated arm and the hull until the fit was tight. Next, the robot backed away, executed a smart turn, and began the return trip to its cage.

I left my chair and went to the door. "I've got to get back to run pyrolsis on samples of the reservoir. I'd really like it if you could . . . um . . . go back ashore."

"What, without you? How will you deal with Duchamp?"

"Don't worry about that, I'm going to call Pierce right now, let him know Duchamp's out here. He won't try anything with so many people around. Besides," I said, "I'll be right behind you as soon as I square things up out here."

No sooner had I reached the deck below than I heard Ray and the crew clomping about above me, proving once again that life is a game of inches and seconds.

Twenty-Five

Buffeted by the wind, which had now picked up to a steady 20 knots out of the southeast, I ducked my head so I could use both hands to pull open the door to the logging lab. I squeezed into the tight space occupied by Elton and the ever-smiling Tom. Apparently there'd been a shift change, as Jonathan was nowhere in sight.

"Listen, Elton," I said. "We need to come up with an estimate for size of the reservoir. The execs on board will need it when they conference with Houston. We know it's just an estimate, but we want it as reliable as possible. Got that? I need to step outside right now and make a call, but I'll be right back."

Detective Pierce's cell went right to his voicemail. I left the following message: "Cleo Cooper here. Your theory about Duchamp was wrong, buddy. He's on board the *Magellan,* where I am. I don't know about his sons. If I were you, I'd send your friends from the Coast Guard out here for him. Oh, and just a suggestion, but the orange jumpsuit material in Hunter's watchband would seem to me to indicate that the twins might know something about what happened to him."

Time to get back to my other treasure hunt: natural gas.

It was exactly like Christmas morning when I handed out the preliminary reports on the size of the second reservoir and the quality of the gas it contained. Elton and I had gone over the numbers one more time before we printed the report. Immediately upon entering the room, I'd scanned the men assembled there for Davy Duchamp. As an investor, I wondered if he'd be included. He was no where to be seen.

There were collective gasps as the numbers were read. Braxton Roberts was practically crowing. "By God, this discovery is the largest domestic find since Prudhoe Bay!" That he had so recently wanted to pull out and start another well somewhere else was long forgotten.

Bud sat next to me, patting me on the back from time to time like a proud parent. I hated to dampen their high spirits, but since it was my job as an outside consultant to bring objectivity into the picture I stood, tapped on the table for attention, and said, "If I could just remind everyone: we have some waiting still to do and some numbers to be crunched."

"But we aren't expecting any big changes to our projections," Roberts declared firmly. "And what about SunCo? We will still beat them to the punch, won't we?" They all looked at me since I was still standing.

Quickly sitting, I pointed to Duncan Powell, who stood and said, "We've kept up our observations of SunCo's activity and it's clear that after reconnecting to their riser, they're drilling again. More than that, we don't know. We don't even know if they've made a strike." He paused. "However, there's no way they could catch us even if they had."

There was more cheering. You can't blame a bunch of guys who are about to make a whole lot of money for getting excited.

Fine for them. And good for me. I was a winner here, too, after all. But it was nice also that they were distracted. At this moment my mind was on treasure number two and my need to catch up with Viktor and make plans to retrieve it.

A quick stop at the radio operator's office

let me know that a Sikorsky would be arriving in about thirty minutes. Arrangements were made for me to hitch a ride back to Beaufort. Then realizing I hadn't eaten since I'd shared ice cream this morning with Coester, I headed for a drink machine in a quiet area up near the bow.

Icy cold and spicy, the soda tickled my nose and gave me the sugar rush I needed. But I had to get off the ship and away from any danger Duchamp might pose. Suddenly I realized the wind that had been so strong earlier today had dropped out altogether. I stepped to the rail and looked to the horizon.

A waning gibbous moon reflected a streak of hammered silver over the black, gently heaving swells that belied the massive currents just under the surface. I watched their progression until they boiled and roiled against the hull. Standing there, it seemed odd to have realized such a goal — the gas deposit — and yet feel nothing. I told myself the enormity of my good fortune just hadn't sunk in yet.

Another swallow of soda slipped cool and sweet down my throat. I thought I heard voices. Taking a step back into the shadows under some stairs leading up to a pair of lifeboats, I listened.

"I'm telling you, Davy, get the fuck off this ship now. The radio operator told me he just received word that the Coast Guard is making arrangements to pick you up. We don't need this kind of publicity. I don't know why you came out here in the first place. We agreed —"

"Calm down, Braxton." Duchamp's voice held menace. "We agreed to nothing. I know what I'm doing, and we can still accomplish our goal here."

"No, we can't! You said it yourself. Your man couldn't find the cylinder. Give it up! We don't need it anymore. When you came to me with this harebrained scheme, I agreed to help you by putting your people onboard *only* because I figured if the well didn't come in, we still had the Russian treasure and your deal with the Chinese, which you agreed to share for a percentage of the company. Well, the well did come in, there's no Russian treasure, and a man is dead!"

"Now just a damn minute —"

"No! Stop right there, Duchamp. I don't know how to make it any clearer: I was only going along with you to save the company. That's not necessary any longer. I don't want to hear another word about it, and I especially don't want the Coast Guard back out here picking you up, making things public and jeopardizing the entire operation —"

"Shut up! Keep your voice down. I've already taken care of everything. There *is* a treasure, and you'll get your share. And for your information, a chopper's already on the way to pick me up."

I didn't hear Braxton Roberts's reply, but I could tell by his footsteps that he was heading my way. Remembering the reflector bands on my hard hat, I jerked it off and squished myself farther underneath the stairs. He was within 10 feet of me when he turned back and said, "And for God's sake, don't call me or contact me in any way." Then he was gone, and I slumped with relief.

That little conversation certainly explained a lot, but what did Duchamp's "taken care of everything" mean?

With my hard hat still in my hands, I eased over to the edge of the stairs trying to figure out Duchamp's next move. Problem was, I didn't hear anything so I tiptoed behind some barrels and listened again. That's when Davy Duchamp seemed to materialize out of thin air, grabbing me by the throat and jerking me off my feet.

"You stupid witch! I knew I'd find your

dumb ass alone if I waited long enough."

"Hey, knock it off, moron!" I answered with a false bravado as my hard hat hit the deck. Struggling to regain my footing — an impossibility, as my feet were barely touching the deck — I landed a few ineffectual punches on my captor's brawny arms. He responded by shoving me hard into the bow rail.

"Moron? You're calling me a moron?" he repeated contemptuously. "Do you have any idea how much trouble you've caused me? How much you almost cost me and my people? Not to mention bringing the police down on me and my boys! Questioning *us* about a death we had nothing to do with!"

"Er, you didn't?" I gasped, trying with both hands to prize his steel fingers from my neck.

"No! But not to worry, 'cause you're the only person standing between us and what's rightfully ours. And now I can use you."

"What?"

"For the first time in our brief but miserable acquaintance, you are exactly what I need: a diversion. Goodnight, Ms. Cooper!" And just like that, Davy Duchamp tossed me overboard like so much garbage.

Remarkably, as I plummeted to the warm Atlantic 22 feet below, my brain was still in analytical mode *and* I was thinking of someone other than myself. Shouldn't I get points for that? What had Davy meant when he said I was the only person standing in his way? Had he found Viktor before he left the ship? Had he killed him too? For that matter, was I really going to die?

Then I hit the inky black water.

I suspect the impact would have been much the same had I hit a concrete sidewalk, but maybe not, since I was pretty sure I was still in one piece as I kicked and fought my way back up. Thank God for safety training. I'd hit the water feet first with relaxed joints, but I still couldn't feel my legs. As though in a dream, I heard myself gasping for air when I surfaced. Alarms were blaring, the water had turned from black to ice blue, and any second now, the *Magellan,* outlined in a blaze of lights, was about to plow me over. Technically I was being pushed into it by the ripping currents brought about by a tide change in full swing, but this wasn't the time for semantics.

I barely got my arms up over my head before I collided with the hull and was sucked under with a force far greater than I'd ever have imagined. Leaving the lighted water behind, I was dragged, rolling and tumbling, down, down, down 40 feet until I reached the bottom of *Magellan's* hull. It all happened in a few seconds, yet they were the longest ones I'd ever experienced.

I had one thought and one thought only, which was to get out of the flow of water being pulled into the thrusters! I'd seen diagrams of how they worked — videos complete with arrows showing the flow of water through the gigantic 12-foot circles of steel enclosing five spinning propeller blades — and knew whatever went into those blades would come out on the other side with quite a different molecular arrangement. There wouldn't be enough left of me to make a decent sausage patty.

Since I had been standing slightly to starboard of the point of the bow, apparently I missed being pulled into the first of the three thrusters. Briefly, the possibility of survival crossed my mind. Just then, the propulsion stream of that first thruster hit me and I was tossed about like a T-shirt in a washer. Water churned by 7,000-horsepower motors practically washed my eyeballs from their sockets. I don't know how many times I bounced off the hull, hearing crunching noises each time I hit. I tried to relax my body to lessen the impact of the blows, but I was utterly helpless to shift my direction out of the stream of water toward one of the side mounted thrusters.

Being enveloped in total darkness, not even knowing which way is up as you're hurtling toward the ultimate meat grinder was a horror so intense it was paralyzing. My lungs burned. The desire to breath, to suck in anything, was overpowering. I could feel my life slipping away. I just hoped to die before I was sucked into a thruster. Even as a few brain cells valiantly kept firing, trying to keep me conscious, I simply gave up, rolled into the fetal position, and waited for the inevitable.

Then something warm and comforting enveloped me; it felt like someone cradling my balled-up body in their arms. Instantly my brain fired up to wide-damn-open and I groped for the source of my hope. Opening my stinging eyes, I saw a face mask. It was attached to the person jamming a respirator into my mouth.

Viktor! Hungrily, I sucked in several deep breaths and felt the life flow back into my limbs. The desire to live returned with a vengeance and I fought to help him as he doggedly pulled me from the propulsion stream, out from under *Magellan*'s hull, and we began our ascent.

After a few powerful kicks of his strong

legs and fins, Viktor stopped. We fought the current while I took another buddy-breath. Then he took the respirator back, grabbed my hips with both hands, and, kicking hard, propelled me straight up until I could see the emergency lights on the surface above me. Only at that moment did he let me go.

I wasn't even surprised. Call it sudden insight arising from a near-death experience, call it whatever you want — but for a few seconds, everything came crystal clear. Just before I resumed my struggle to the surface, I looked back down. The headlight from Viktor's mask grew faint, then blinked out.

This time when I surfaced, I was on the port side of the *Magellan* and the current was carrying me diagonally away from and down the length of the ship. I needed to get someone's attention before I was swept out of the lighted area. Fortunately, the alarm had been cut off. I let out a howl like I was facing down a band of al-Qaeda.

All the men on the rail who'd been looking past me instantly turned my way. Several life rings hit the sparkling blue water about 10 feet from me . . . up current. That's when I realized my arms weren't working right, there was blood in the water and I was fast becoming too weak to stay afloat. Even adrenalin has its limits.

I was giving it my all, but with every feeble stroke I was losing ground and sinking into unconsciousness. Then I saw a familiar figure running along the rail ahead of me. Without a pause, he dove off the edge, life ring in one hand, life vest in the other. Bud! The only man I know who can save your life and give you choices while doing so.

TWENTY-SIX

Next thing I knew I was being loaded into a friggin' helicopter. Great. I was really safe now. My eyes were stinging and burning. I closed them and let darkness overtake me.

When I opened them again, everything was blurry, but I was pretty sure I was in a hospital. Blinking, trying to bring my surroundings into focus, one thing was certain: every part of my body hurt. I tried to raise one arm. It was in a temporary cast. My head pounded. Good grief. I shut my eyes again and let sleep overtake me.

The next time I felt like opening them, I thought better of it. I mean, what would I find this time? Would my legs be in casts, too? After a few minutes of listening to hospital sounds, wondering what was making that damn beeping noise, curiosity got the better of me. At least this time the room came into focus and so did the person sitting on the edge of my bed looking at me, his face etched in sorrow.

"Bud," I croaked.

Tears sprang to his eyes and ran down his cheeks. He bit his lip and sniffed. And right then I knew. I knew with the clarity only a cerebral lightning strike can bring, that I'd played this scene before.

I stared at him and he stared back at me, tenderly cradling my hand in his, just like he had that night on the ship. Then he let out a shaky sigh, stood, and, being careful not to disturb the IV needle in my arm — the source of the obnoxious beeping no doubt — laid my hand on the bed.

"I'll go get a doctor or nurse . . . or somebody," he muttered and left, wiping his face with the palms of his hands.

Warmth from where he had been sitting radiated through my hand, the IV beeped, and my mind flew back to the night I'd been attacked on the *Magellan.* The first time. I remembered how I'd awoken in my bunk with Bud leaning over me, crying. He'd rescued me from a fate worse than death — maybe from death itself, too. Bad memories and bad questions made me squirm, bringing on a fresh jolt of pain. I resolved to lay still . . . but I couldn't stop thinking: Didn't that mean I was back to my original fear that Bud was Hunter's killer?

I supposed someone else could have come along after I fainted, smashed in the back of Hunter's head, pushed him overboard, and left me lying where Bud found me later. Maybe one or both of the twins, since orange material similar to their jumpsuits was found twisted into Hunter's watchband, and since their dad believed Hunter had been trying to steal the treasure out from under him. He'd implied as much at the nursing home. Then it dawned on me: it had been four in the morning. Why would the twins be in their work clothes? That was a definite plausibility gap.

Back to Bud as the killer, then. If he'd done the deed and then pretended to have come looking for me and found me knocked out cold as a cod on the ROV pad, obviously the victim of an attack, wouldn't it have made his story more believable if he'd caused an uproar? Demanded justice for me? Of course it would. And if he did just happen along and found me unconscious, Hunter already overboard, wouldn't he still have been furious and insisted on finding the culprit? Of course he would. Wouldn't he?

My headed pounded with all my deliberations, but I couldn't stop my brain. It was like Tulip when she picked up a scent. What about the cylinder — the reason I was lying in this miserable place in this sorry state in the first place — what happened to it?

And where was Viktor? Thinking of him made my blood boil, but not with lust anymore. I might have been pulverized to within an inch of losing my life, but I knew betrayal when I experienced it and I wondered: how long had it taken him to decide to steal the cylinder and leave me with nothing? Was it immediately upon my confiding in him that night in my driveway when he'd saved me from the twins, or had it taken a few days for him to succumb to greed? Okay, so he'd also repeatedly saved my life, but apparently that came with the territory if you were spending time with me.

I'd thought his saving me meant he'd switched his loyalty to me, that I could trust him, that we'd sort of become partners. The more I pondered my last hours on — and under — the *Magellan,* the more convinced I was that he'd never been loyal to me. Common sense told me Duchamp had had more to offer.

My thoughts were interrupted when Bud bustled back into the room with a wizened little doctor who somewhat resembled the gnawed end of a pencil. He explained my injuries: contusions, abrasions, lacerations

— a few requiring stitches — a broken arm, two sprained ankles, and a concussion. Then he hustled out like he was late for something. Next came a nurse who went over my medications: painkillers, antibiotics to prevent infections, and more meds to prevent blood clots from the deep bruising. Before leaving, she disconnected the IV and asked a few stupid questions. "Would you like to watch television?" Hell no. "Would you like to up your pain medication?" Hell yes.

Bud rose stiffly from a corner recliner and returned to my bedside. "There's a police detective named Pierce in the hall waiting to see you."

Despite the pain killers, I perked up. "How long's he been here?" I asked. "For that matter, how long have *I* been here and where, in fact, is here?"

"Here is Carteret General. Amazingly, your injuries weren't life-threatening, so I managed to convince everyone who wanted to have you flown to Duke that I knew you best and you wouldn't want ridiculous measures taken when all that was needed was some serious bandages and lots of bed rest. Now, with the emergency stuff done, I'll take care of the bed rest. I've made arrangements to take you home soon as they discharge you later this afternoon."

"This afternoon? Last time I looked, it was night."

"We got you here around nine last night. It's now a little after four . . . p.m. The detective guy has been prowling around out there like an hungry cheetah. He's very insistent about talking to you. You want to see him?"

"Damn right. Precious time is wasting," I said, trying to push myself up straighter in bed. "Ouch! Ouch!"

"Here, let me help," Bud said, reaching for me.

"No! Go get Pierce! Oh, and Bud, what about the kids?"

"I've called them —"

"Finally, Ms. Cooper, you're awake." Here came Pierce. "Hope you don't mind my barging in, but I heard voices and —"

"Listen, I've got a lot to tell you. Bud, you need to hear this too. The man who pushed me overboard and his buddies have a thirteen-hour jump on you —"

"Pushed you overboard!" Bud's face twisted in anger. "I thought you fell!"

"Bud, please. Have I ever just fallen off a boat?"

"Well, no, but —"

"If you'll just be patient, I'll tell you what

happened."

Despite the fact that from time to time my brain would fog up — apparently banging one's head repeatedly on the steel hull of a ship doesn't do good things for it — soon the two of them knew everything about my saga of almost finding the Amber Room, starting with meeting young Viktor Kozlov three weeks and a lifetime ago. (Well, I did leave out the part about my unwitting fall from grace into Viktor's bed. But seriously, who wouldn't?)

I looked at Bud and my gut squeezed. His expression was stony, but his eyes told a different story. Suddenly I realized how much I must have hurt him by confiding in Viktor instead of him. Pierce's expression stayed steady on furious.

He said, "Remember our interview just this last weekend? You said you didn't know of anything of great value hidden in a cylinder on the ship. Something Hunter might've been looking for. That was a boldfaced lie, huh?"

"No, it wasn't," I shot back. "You said on the *Magellan.* At the time, the cylinder was on *U-498,* two thousand feet below it."

"You might think you can split hairs with me, Ms. Cooper, but I'd like to point out that if you had voiced your suspicions regarding Mr. Duchamp sooner, it would have saved you from being keel-hauled the way you were."

"The hell!" I fumed. "You're the one who screwed up and let him get away — *after* he pulled a gun on you, I might add. If anyone is to blame for my nearly ending up as chum, it's —"

"Knock it off, you two," ordered Bud. "What's done is done. Cleo, you should count your lucky stars that . . . friend of yours, Viktor, did double-cross you and was under the ship stealing the booty at the precise moment you needed him and that Duchamp used the alarm as a distraction so he could leave the ship unnoticed."

Pierce now jumped in. "How do you think Viktor got under the ship? And do you think he knew Duchamp was intending to get rid of you?"

I heaved a sigh and blinked away the heavy cloak of exhaustion that was threatening to drape over my brain again and said, "Here's how I think things went down. Viktor knew Duchamp had 'left' your custody because I told him not long after you told me. At that point, we all but had the cylinder. Soon as I left the ROV van to go back to the logging lab, I think he called Duchamp, told him he'd found the cylinder and that he'd need diving equipment — a small twenty-minute tank of air, a mask, and some fins — to retrieve it. Duchamp probably brought it with him in a small duffel in the chopper and stashed it where Viktor told him. Likely near one of the personnel escape lines. They're stowed at various locations along the rail and can be lowered in seconds."

"Wouldn't someone have seen him going overboard?" Pierce wanted to know.

"Not if he chose carefully, probably somewhere near the bow. He could have easily found a blind spot behind some of the tons of equipment and supplies stacked there. Besides, it only takes a few minutes to throw the line over and hustle down. It is for emergencies, after all."

"But how did he get to shore with only what was left on a twenty-minute tank?" Bud asked.

"He didn't have to. Remember, from the time I told him his old boss and apparent benefactor had escaped, Viktor and the twins had over two hours to throw together a plan. Duchamp left the *Magellan,* flew somewhere, and waited for them. You thought he'd picked up his boat in Morehead and taken it to Louisiana, right?"

"Yeah, the Coast Guard did stop the boat. There were three guys on it. Duchamp had hired them to take it to his home in Louisiana."

"So, they didn't have a boat," Bud said, playing devil's advocate. "Plus, it takes over four hours to reach the *Magellan* by boat."

"If you leave from Morehead or Beaufort it does, but it's only forty-five miles to the ship from Oregon Inlet. Departing from there, depending on wind and tides, it would only take a little over an hour with an offshore excursion boat. You can rent them from several places up there and they can easily run forty to fifty miles an hour. The twins waited, lights off, at agreed-upon coordinates outside the area the drillship's patrol boat covers. He swam to them, they picked him up, went ashore, and met up with Duchamp. The big question: Where did they go from there?"

Pierce said, "I see what you mean. It wouldn't take a rocket scientist to put that together —"

"Mom!" Henri and Will gasped in unison upon busting into my room. "Oh my God, Mom, your face!" Henri wailed.

My face?

"Henri!" Bud cautioned. "What did I tell you?"

"Oh," she sobbed, both hands over her mouth.

"Somebody get me a mirror, right now!" I demanded.

"I'm outta here," Pierce said, pulling the door back open. Then, he stopped, turned to me, and said, "I forgot to tell you that I looked into matching the material we found twisted in the vic's watchband with the jumpsuits worn by Voyager's crew."

"Yeah?" I said, now less interested in all the recent skullduggery and more concerned about my face.

"Yeah, and it wasn't a match. Not even close. But I shouldn't have bothered."

"Huh?" I said. "Why not?"

"Because it was four in the morning. Why would the twins be wearing their work duds? ROV crews only work during the day."

I didn't say a word about this already occurring to me. "Then why did Duchamp threaten me saying if I wasn't careful I could end up just like Hunter? He had to have known Hunter was dead because he replaced him with Viktor *before* the body washed up on shore," I said. Henri was still staring at me, stupefied. "Mirror!" I shouted. She gulped and nodded.

"The fact that he got someone replaced on a job just means he obviously had connections at Voyager. Doesn't necessarily prove he knew the guy was dead, only that he could get a friend a job pretty damn quick."

I held out my hand to Henri.

"Right," Pierce said, picking up on the hint and taking one step closer to the hall. "Keep in mind, we're still going to pick up Duchamp in the matter of drawing a gun on me and pushing you overboard. But there were no witnesses to that; we only have your statement. You *are* going to press charges this time, right?"

Henri handed me a compact. I heard Pierce say, "Uh, we'll talk later." Taking a deep breath, I opened the compact, held it up, and stifled a scream.

I looked like Frankenstein. See-through steri-strips covered large blue stitches holding together a 4-inch gash running along my hairline from my widow's peak to my right temple. My hair was caked in dried blood, the first 3 inches of it being spiked up like a punk rocker while the rest hung in limp strands. Purple circles were forming under my eyes even as I stared in abject horror at myself. Quietly, I closed the compact, handed it back to Henri, and turned my face to the wall.

"Mom," Will said. "I don't understand. What did he mean about pressing charges 'this time'? Were you attacked *before* this? You've been attacked more than once in a couple of weeks?"

"Not now," Bud said. "Mom needs her rest."

"Come on," Henri said glumly. "We'll wait for them at Seahaven. Oh, and before we go, Mom's friend left this at her house."

I turned back over to face them. "What? What friend? Left what?"

"Your . . . friend. You know? Viktor. I went straight to the house after Dad called and told me to pack some of your clothes and to wait there until you were ready to see us. I called Will and —"

"When did you see Viktor?" I interrupted her, noticing Bud over her shoulder as he quietly slipped from the room.

"Let's see," Henri said, handing me a small white envelope. "I guess it was around eleven o'clock last night. He seemed in a hurry. Just gave me that, said to give it to you when you got home, and left."

Inside was a note from Viktor.

I know you think I have forsaken you. I have. That does not mean I did not care for you. Trust me, the only way to put the Amber Room back where it belongs in the Ekaterina Palace is to go along with Davy and the plan he has for it. Time is short. We'll meet again.

The note was signed Afanasy Viktor Kozlov.

Epilogue

Clackity-clack rumbled my carry-on as I exited the skybridge into the terminal in Prudhoe Bay, Alaska, and headed for the ladies room. Since my brush with death a little over six weeks earlier, I'd spent over a week recuperating at Seahaven. Bud had hired a nurse for me, as he wasn't there. I'd only stayed as long as I did in hopes that he'd come back so we could talk and I could explain that I never meant to hurt him; that I'd wanted to tell him all about the sub and the treasure that day on the *Magellan,* but then he'd showed up with her and well, things just went from there.

Finally I gave up waiting and moved back to Morehead with Will and Henri where I finished my recovery and did a few light consulting jobs. Global had capped off the well awaiting production, and the *Magellan* had steamed away to other adventures on another exploration site.

I'd heard Elton's next job had him down in the Gulf on one of the ultra-deep wells. I smiled, knowing he'd be just fine. Strangely, I'd heard very little from Detective Pierce except to say that he was stymied in his investigation of Hunter's death and my being thrown overboard because Duchamp and the twins had left the country. He seemed to have lost some of his determination, but it was hard to tell for sure.

Seeing the ladies room up ahead, I headed toward it but got a call on my iPhone just as I stepped inside. My contractor at the house in Raleigh. He had completed his renovations. We made arrangements to do a walk through. After using the facilities, I dabbed a touch more concealer at my hairline. I had been assured that the bright purple, ultra-thin scar revision — plastic surgeon speak for turning a horrific scar into a less horrific one — would fade over time. Satisfied, I adjusted the girls and took off for the car rental kiosk.

The stifling heat of late August in North Carolina had me looking forward to the cooler temperatures afforded by a two-day consulting job for a small independent energy company on the Alaska North Slope. Trudging along on my way to the parking lot, I caught sight of the general aviation building and a magnificent Bombardier Learjet 35, the ultimate daydream aircraft for me. That's why I knew the custom paint job on this one was called Phantom Grey Metallic. To me, this beauty was more than just a bad-to-the-bone rich man's toy, it was a work of art.

The area wasn't fenced off, so I sauntered over for a closer look. Several service vehicles were parked nearby. Heat still radiated from the engines, but since no one seemed to be around, I reached up to feel the craftsmanship of the almost invisible door seam. That's when the center seam popped open, the top half of the door rose, and a large man with dark curly hair, Slavic features, and a poorly fitting suit lowered the stairs.

"Pleased not to touch plane, Miss," he said in an accent I was familiar with.

Totally embarrassed, I backed up as another large and muscled man, this one bald, angled himself out of the jet and stood by. Then Viktor Kozlov stepped into the doorway.

Though I heard my case clatter to the concrete — I'd unconsciously let go of the handle when my fingers curled into fists at my sides — I wasn't really surprised and knew instantly that he'd arranged this "chance" meeting. After all, hadn't his note said we'd meet again? I'd wondered at the time if he was just blowing smoke or if he really meant it. Apparently he had, and from the looks of it, he'd meant to do so in fine style.

But how had he known where to find me? My eyes narrowed as he slowly walked up and stood just out of my reach.

"Your plane?" I asked icily.

"In a manner of speaking," he replied nonchalantly as though nothing serious — such as his absconding with a priceless treasure and leaving me empty-handed — had happened between us.

"Nice ride."

"Yes," he agreed. Curly and his sidekick eased over to stand behind him, but he motioned them away. The jet's turbines ticked as they cooled and I studied the subtle differences six weeks had made. His hair was shorter and slicked back. He was wearing a black silk casual shirt and charcoal Armani slacks. His python loafers were Ferragamos. But more than his appearance, his demeanor had shifted slightly from easygoing, fun-loving student to a cooler, more sophisticated person.

"I suppose you are very angry at me," Viktor said.

"Ya think?" I said. "*I* flew out here in that nasty commuter over there jammed in beside a very large woman who needed two seats but only paid for one. But never mind that, why are you here?"

"I must speak to you on an urgent matter and time is limited."

"Well, that makes two of us, because I've got an urgent question for you."

"Okay, but quickly."

"Why'd you do it, Viktor? Why'd you double-cross me?"

"For the same reason you went after Manteo One. For my country."

I looked at him. "Cut the crap."

"No!" he said firmly. "You of all people know it's true! I am sure you went after the gas first for your country, second for your own personal gains. Yet, when I take back what belongs to Russia, somehow I'm the bad guy. Why is that?"

"You don't know me at all," I said, shaking my head. "I went after the gas first for myself, second for my country. It's always been my motto to take care of myself so others won't have to."

"Yes," he said, nodding his head like an old sage. I was seething as he continued, "That may be so. I won't argue that point. But you *do* take care of others. After all, you put the old professor in a nicer retirement home in Florida."

"How the hell do you know that? No one else but my lawyer does! For that matter, how did you know I'd be here?"

"Doesn't matter."

"It does to me."

Viktor ignored my questions. "And for the record, it is you, who doesn't know me at all."

"Clearly."

"For instance, you don't know that my parents were murdered when I was a toddler. That up until the time I was eleven, I was raised by a band of street urchins. That a kindly bureaucrat took me in and raised me after I was caught in one of the many street roundups and sent to a labor camp."

"Oh, boohoo. So you came up hard. Lots of people do. That doesn't give you the right to turn into a lowdown, self-serving polecat. And, personally, I don't give a rat's ass about any of that." I knew I should dial it back, that I was getting way too fired up, but I couldn't help myself.

Viktor's face flushed, but he remained calm. "Who I am has everything to do with turning into a 'lowdown polecat,' as you put it, and placing my country and family first."

"I thought you said your family was murdered?"

"There are all kinds of families," he shot back, then looked around to see if the two goons were listening to us. They weren't.

"Besides," I said, aiming for a calmer tone, "how did you know *I* wasn't going to give the Amber Room back to Russia? Yeah, maybe I was thinking of extracting a small finder's fee, enjoying the fame that comes with uncovering one of the world's greatest treasures, maybe even writing a book . . . but what did I get? Nothing. Not even the satisfaction of seeing the stinking map."

Viktor looked as if he were deliberating over something. "It was written in German and in code. You and I alone could have done nothing with it. A team of German and Russian experts had a hard enough time. Then the diplomats got involved . . ."

Diplomats?

A hint of a smile pulled at one corner of Viktor's mouth. "I must say though," he continued, "the hiding spot old Koch chose was very clever. No one would have ever thought to look in that particular German salt mine because it wasn't abandoned at the time he hid the crates there. He disguised them as containing explosives, shoved them to the back of a supply room, and marked them WATER DAMAGED — DON'T USE. Years later, by the time the mine closed, all kinds of junk had been abandoned there, including the spoiled explosives."

"Yeah, yeah," I said sarcastically. "Koch was a real Einstein. So where is the Amber Room now? How come there's been no great fanfare coming out of Russia about the big discovery? Oh, wait. Could it be because your note to me was all a lie? You fell right in with Davy Duchamp and slipped those crates out of Germany, didn't you? And there's no news of the Amber Room being returned to Russia because it's in China!"

Viktor bit his lip, counted a few beats, and said, "The China deal was, shall we say, cancelled. Davy was compensated with full immunity from prosecution of any crimes he may have committed in your country and awarded a very lucrative contract with Russia's largest state-owned oil company. His sons quit Voyager and are back working with him. They are running seismic data off the coast of North Africa now."

Duchamp was compensated? How? By who? Is that what the diplomats were for? And for that matter, how did Viktor possess such a wealth of information about me —

about everything, actually — including my current geographic location? Suddenly it dawned on me. I'd been a world-class chump. There existed a dark and slimy world, a viper pit, really, of international industrial espionage. And I, literally a babe in the woods, had been squashed by it without even knowing what did the squashing.

I pointed my finger at Viktor. "You're an agent of some kind, aren't you? Russian Intelligence planted you with Duchamp to make friends after they somehow learned, probably from hacking his private email, that he might have found the Amber Room." I shook my head at my failure to see what had been right under my nose and looked in his eyes. As you may remember, I'm pretty good at reading poker faces and though I'm sure Russian Intelligence trains their agents well in the art of stoic expressions, I had enough personal experience with this man to know I'd hit on some version of the truth. "Wow," I said. "Imagine his surprise when you double-crossed him too. Thing I can't understand is, what happened? Where is the Amber Room now?"

"I'm afraid you're not going to have the answers you seek. And what I'm requesting you do — for both of our sakes — is to forget this extremely exciting but ultimately very dangerous episode we shared."

That was a nonstarter. I was quite sure I'd never see Viktor again after this day, so if I was going to get answers, now was the time. "But, I'm confused about so much," I said. "Are you or aren't you a geologist? Are you really a doctoral candidate at Duke?"

"Yes to your first question," he said, patiently. "Of course I'm a geologist. As to Duke . . . well, that part has been changed. I'll be conducting my dissertation work somewhere else." He started to leave.

My brain was still working frantically to process everything. "Just please tell me this one last thing, did you somehow kill Hunter? I mean, your people?"

"No," He shook his head — sadly, I like to think — and moved to take his leave again.

"Wait! This is important to me," I said, my tone pleading now. "I've thought so much about all that's happened. I never told you this, but the first night I was onboard *Magellan,* the night Hunter died, he attacked me and I've come to believe he did it because he thought I was looking for the ROV's internal log. Maybe he saw me — who showed up out of nowhere to *consult* — and thought I was checking on the discrepancy between it and the time he'd logged for the ship's billing records. So he decided to kill me. Only someone killed him first and because I fainted, I *still* don't know who it was. Was one of your people aboard? Did they use the incident with me to disguise his murder because he was causing trouble? Tell me! Please, I have to know!"

Just then a man in a captain's hat stepped to the door of jet, looked down at us, and pointed to his watch.

Viktor nodded, turned to me, and said, "I have to go now. Please, tell me you'll take my words to heart."

"Okay," I said. "You don't have to worry about me anymore. Just please, tell me who —"

Viktor lifted my palm to his lips, kissed it, held it against his heart, and for a brief moment, I was again with my carefree young Russian friend. "Listen carefully, as I have one final piece of advice: stay close to your ex-husband. He takes very good care of you." Then he did a strange thing. With his other hand, he reached into his pant's pocket, removed something, and placed my recently kissed palm over it before I could see what it was. Slowly, I clinched my fingers around it and withdrew my hand. He smiled wistfully, then turned on his heel and left. Without even looking, I rammed the object in my jeans pocket, retrieved my carry-on, and booked it for the parking lot.

The balmy Alaskan summer day now had a chill to it. At least that was my excuse when, with shaking hands, I fumbled and dropped the key fob upon reaching my rental car. When I finally bleeped the door open, I heard my text tune but didn't read it. Locking the door, I retrieved the object Viktor had stealthily slipped me, and knew two things instantly: I was holding a piece of history in my hand and, more than likely, only I would ever be able to enjoy it. Shaking my head sadly, I turned the palm-sized medallion of carved amber in my fingers.

Of course I could never be positive, unless the Amber Room was restored to its rightful place during my lifetime and I could visit as a tourist, but I was reasonably sure this medallion had once been part of the intricate wainscoting I'd seen in historical photos of the room. Raising the lovely translucent artifact to the light of the car window, I smiled at two little ants caught in the smooth center of a carved flower. Quite naturally, they appeared to be swimming as they would have been — for a few seconds anyway — after dropping into a big glob of sap millions of years ago.

In strange irony, the little drama had left the pair positioned as if they were holding hands, one dragging the other along, now forever frozen in time. Very apropos. I wondered if the medallion had accidentally broken off one of the thousands of pieces that made up the room or if it been helped along by Viktor. Clearly, he'd actually been in the presence of the crates that held the room. Did he, perhaps, dig through broken pieces to find just the right one for me? I'd like to think he did.

As I placed the medallion carefully in my bag, I was reminded of another object: the little pressure valve I'd found under the ROV. The one that had set into motion one of the most exciting chapters of my life. I'd probably put the medallion together with it in a satin pocket made into the liner of my jewelry box. Who knew, maybe someday when I was old and gray, I'd pull the objects out and tell their story to Will's and Henri's children.

Small consolation and definitely not what I had in mind, but maybe I was looking at this whole thing the wrong way. Maybe the tale itself was the treasure. After all, aren't our life experiences the only things we can take with us when we leave this mortal coil? I blew out a frustrated breath and smacked my fist against the steering wheel.

"Ouch! Dammit!" I said aloud, rubbing my hand. Well, hell, at least I was trying to think positive. That's about all there was left for me in this deal. I started the car, then I remembered my text alert. It was from Bud:

BURGERS ON THE BEACH WHEN YOU GET BACK?

As it turned out, the beach burger dinner wasn't Bud's idea. Will and Henri had engineered it, and he, still nursing his hurt feelings — and I imagined happily in love with the tantalizing young Amanda — had gone along to get along. From a comfortable spot under Seahaven's gazebo, I stirred my bloody mary with a crisp stalk of celery and watched as Henri and Will tried to teach Tulip to ride a skim board. The few quiet days in Alaska and the long plane ride home had given me lots of time to think about my reunion with Viktor.

He'd pulled down a veil over the time we'd spent together, but it wasn't enough to switch off my curiosity altogether. I wondered, for instance, who in Russia commanded wealth and power so vast that they could take possession of a state treasure like the Amber Room without so much as a word leaking to the press. One of the Yeltsin oligarchs who managed to survive the Kremlin purges to carry on in the Putin era, perhaps? Maybe a political heavyweight. Maybe even Putin, himself . . .

A clatter at the sliding glass door let me know Bud needed help. I hurried over to open it, and he whisked through carrying a tray loaded down with condiments, dip, and a bag of chips.

"Just leave it open," he said. "I've got to get the burgers." Then, with pointed politeness, he added, "By the way, when is your Morehead lease up?"

"End of the month," I answered just as politely. "Tulip and I need to start packing for Raleigh tomorrow, so I can't make a late night of it." I didn't add that I was also planning to fly up to Canada in a few days. A friend had put me onto the possibility of a long-term, lucrative gig consulting for a gold mining company there. Frankly, it was at the bottom of a list of possibilities, and I hadn't given them a definite answer yet. I needed to check things out in person first, but now seemed like a good time for a change of scenery.

"Don't worry," was his clipped retort, though he did squeeze out a thin smile before disappearing into the house. It seemed Mr. Nice Guy was more upset with me than I'd realized. While I understood his anger, I couldn't help feeling a pang of loss for the new relationship I thought we'd finally reached after six years of divorce.

I sighed and I went back to my thoughts regarding my recent visit with Viktor. No matter how much I wanted to know who killed Hunter, I had to remind myself that, in the end, he was a victim of his own bad deeds. I could almost buy into the notion that the material in his watchband could have come from anywhere, maybe snagged on something while he worked. Operative word: *almost.*

Truth was, no matter how hard I tried, I was failing to offload the burden of uncertainty. Odd to think that I, who'd always scoffed at the talk-show notion of "closure," now knew what it felt like to have none.

"Here, let me have that," I said, taking the burgers from Bud, who'd returned. I deposited them on the picnic table, which had been set with a colorful cloth and matching napkins from back in the days when the children were little. I smiled. Henri and Will. They never stopped.

"Thanks," he said. "That bloody mary looks good. Be right back."

Airline food being what it is, I was starving so I decided to fire up the grill myself and hurry dinner along. Besides, I still had a long drive back to Morehead.

When I opened it, I saw a good cleaning was in order and grabbed the scraping tool hanging along the side and proceeded to get to work. Obsessively, I turned the scraper sideways and started to run it along the edges of the grate. Then it got stuck at the top corner. What the heck? Annoyed, I gave it a sharp tug and it popped free, carrying with it a scrap of something.

I knocked it against the rim of the trash can, but the smidgeon of whatever it was refused to drop off. Delicately picking it off with an index finger and thumb, I realized it wasn't a food remnant.

On closer inspection, I found it to be a burned scrap of silky, bright orange and white material — all that was left of Bud's lucky shirt, the one he'd had on the very first day we had visited the *Magellan.* My breath caught in my throat, and I knew right then and there that if I could compare it to the tiny piece of orange material from Hunter's watchband, it would be a perfect match.

Hearing the glass door slide again in its tracks, I shoved the scrap in my pocket and went back to the grill just as Bud, drink in hand, headed my way.

"You look a little pale. You okay?" he asked.

"Yeah, I'm fine," I said, rubbing my head. "Just a little jet lag."

"How about your arm?" he inquired. "Still sore without the cast to support it?"

"A little," I said, draining my bloody mary.

Bud raised his eyebrows.

"Say, Bud . . ." I began, but then I couldn't think how to frame my question. I mean, what's the best way to ask your ex-husband if he committed murder on your behalf?

"Yes?" he said, drawing out the word. When I didn't respond because I was still at a loss, he made a diagnosis. Declaring, "I can see another bloody mary is called for," he headed back into the house.

My heart was pounding and I felt a little shaky. I flopped down in a chair and pulled out the scrap again to inspect it. Yep. No doubt about it. It had once been part of Bud's lucky shirt. I put it back in my pocket. There was only one reasonable explanation for his burning it: He wanted to get rid of it in such a way as to leave no trace. Why?

Funny how in the time it takes to scrape a charcoal grill, the earth can shift under your feet and you're not standing where you thought you were. I thought I was standing on the deck of the home of a man I had known and lived with longer than I had lived with my parents. A man I knew like I know myself.

Apparently I wasn't. Apparently there was a lot about Franklin Donovan Cooper IV that I didn't know.

Was he capable of killing another human being? For that matter, what kind of man kills another man because he finds him trying to rape his unconscious ex-wife? Answer: a good one. And, if Bud did send Hunter to his just reward, did I really want to know? Answer: probably not.

Bud came back and handed me another drink. I removed the celery, took a big slug, then stuck it back in the glass and swirled the contents.

"So," Bud said, "did that help loosen your tongue?" As I gazed at him, I realized my perception of him had shifted dramatically. "Remember? You were trying to say something," he prompted, then waited a beat before adding impatiently, "I guess not."

The tongue loosener apparently was having an effect on me because I blurted out, "I did try to talk to you, you know."

Bud gave me a confused look. "When? Just now? I didn't hear you."

“No, that day on the *Magellan* when you brought Amanda out for PR photos. I wanted to tell you then all about finding the sub and the map to the Amber Room, but it was obvious you and she were . . . together . . . and that you had moved on with your life. I didn’t want to interfere . . .”

“Interfere?” Bud interjected so abruptly I backed up a step. “Have I ever treated you like an interference?” He glared at me, seeming to grow angrier by the second. I was trying to think of something to say to calm him down when suddenly he banged his glass on the picnic table, sloshing the thick cocktail over his fingers. He snatched up one of Henri’s folded napkins and wiping them said, “And by the way, your dumping our marriage doesn’t mean I’m supposed to take a vow of abstinence and join a monastery. And since when did a little recreational sex become proof I want to move on to a life without you?” He smacked the napkin down on the table with a crack.

Forgetting my plan to diffuse the situation, I snapped back, “A *little* recreational sex! You were exhausted every time I saw you! Hell, you had to hide at my house to catch a breather!”

“Oh, like *you* weren’t trying to set new endurance records with the Russian stud muffin, who, if you'll recall, double-crossed you in a world-class way."

"Stop right there," I demanded. "First, I don't need to be reminded of that, and second, we are not — I repeat *not* — discussing our sexual exploits."

"Well, good to know, 'cause I don't have the week it'd take to hear about yours!"

An angry silence spread between us. We stared out at the ocean. After a while, I dared to look at him. That tendon thing in his jaw was still jerking furiously, but I didn't care. Besides being stunned by his behavior, I was confused — not my favorite state of mind.

I asked pointedly, "So do you or don't you have a relationship with Amanda?"

"No! How could I? Someone has to be on call 24/7 to save your fancy ass."

The anger that instantly rushed over me quickly dissipated. Don't ask me why, because generally a remark like that would elicit a tirade from me on how just the opposite was true, to be followed quickly by a litany of how overprotective he'd always been. Where was my steadfast insistence that I needed no one, least of all him? Probably not far from where it had always lived in me. Just right now, it was in the way of my figuring out who the guy standing in front of me was and where Bud Cooper had gone.

Bud's face screwed up in an impressive scowl as he backed me into the corner of the deck, placing an arm on either side of me, his body pressed so tightly against mine I had to lean over backwards. "*Please,* tell me you don't have the gall to say your ass didn't need saving when you got tossed off the *Magellan.*"

"Well . . . it is fancy."

One corner of Bud's mouth turned up — slightly — and he pulled back a little. I could feel the tension lessen in his arms and abdomen. Then, he pushed away from me and I straightened up. We fell into our familiar Mexican standoff. I smiled and batted my eyelashes. He raked his front teeth with his tongue, stepped to the railing, and looked back to the ocean again.

"Woo-hoo!" shouted Will and Henri from the beach as Tulip, barking ecstatically, skimmed the glassy ripples on the thin, round board. They would be coming in soon.

We resumed sipping our drinks. Sea oats stirred in the evening breeze making whispery noises as the darkness descended around us. While I watched him, Bud lifted the grill's grate, tipped in the charcoal, spritzed it with lighter fluid, and applied a match.

"You know," I said, mentally ditching the Canada job. "It'll be a while before Manteo One starts to pay returns on my investment so, to keep the wolf from the door, I've been thinking about getting involved with some of the fracking opportunities over around Sanford. I've had several interesting consulting offers to work in that area and honestly, it'd be nice to be close enough to Raleigh to sleep in my own bed for a change. Maybe it's something you should look into as well."

"Depends," Bud said.

"On what?"

"On whether you'll reconsider doing something as foolhardy as driving back to Morehead tonight after three cocktails."

"Well, that depends too."

"Oh what?"

"On whether we're having dessert or not," I said firmly. I mean, I had to take a stand on something.

After thoughtful consideration, Bud said, "Maybe."

AUTHOR'S NOTE

To me, the best mysteries are those infused with the truth. To that end, I liberally wove historic and scientific facts into *Trusting Viktor.* Here are some examples.

There really was an Amber Room in the Catherine Palace in Russia, and Hitler really did place Erich Koch in charge of dismantling and hiding it. The Graveyard of the Atlantic Museum does exist in Hatteras, North Carolina. And most of the facts concerning the German U-boat attacks of North Carolina during 1942 are true, including those concerning *U-352,* now a popular dive site. *U-498* as I described it, however, is totally fictional.

The Manteo Exploration Unit, or Manteo Prospect — the mega deposit of natural gas off North Carolina's coast — is most certainly real. I did my best, within the context of the story, to describe its geologic history and characteristics accurately. Also, just as

Cleo described, the outer continental shelf of the United States is divided into blocks for leasing purposes, each one about 9 square miles in size. The Atlantic Ocean is divided into three regions, and all of this is controlled by the federal government. The Manteo Exploration Unit is made up of twenty-one of these blocks and lies within the mid-Atlantic region. Though some of these blocks do have a history of attempted exploration, none of them have ever been drilled. Today, there are no active leases in the mid-Atlantic region.

Since facts and figures about off-shore exploration can be a snooze to some readers, I left them out wherever possible. It is interesting to note, however, that each year the United States uses about 24 trillion cubic feet of gas. The Manteo Prospect may contain as much as 5 trillion cubic feet of natural gas. For those interested, here's a quick rundown of what would happen in real life if Cleo and Bud actually invested in a wildcat well like Manteo One:

First, because such an operation could cost upwards of $70 million, they would have to partner with one of the major oil companies. Since the Manteo Prospect lies in water 2,100 feet deep, a drillship like the *Magellan* would be used. After arriving at the site, it would use its global positioning propellers or thrusters to hold itself over the site, where they'd "spud in," or force about 400 feet of 36-inch metal casing into the seafloor to provide support for the well.

Then a bit would be lowered into the well at the end of a drill string to cut another 2,000 to 3,000 feet. Synthetic mud would be forced down the well to carry rock chips to the surface for people like Cleo to analyze. The mud also cools and lubricates the bit and controls the pressure in the well. Next, a 22-inch casing would be run down through the original casing and set with cement. A blowout preventer (BOP) and marine riser would then be added on top of the well. The BOP stops dangerous gas bubbles from reaching the surface and causing explosions, and the marine riser is a large-diameter pipe that runs from the seafloor to the ship and serves as a conduit for the pipe and mud.

The remainder of the well would be drilled until the wellsite geologists were sure they'd reached the good stuff. Logging equipment would then be run down the well and tests run to determine if the well had producible hydrocarbons. In this story, Manteo One is a dry natural gas well, not an oil well. (Remember, *gasoline* is actually a liquid; Cleo and crew are searching for a true gas.)

Also, while many of the locations in my story are real, the ships, companies, and people are entirely creations of my imagination.

ACKNOWLEDGMENTS

Several folks were essential in creating *Trusting Viktor* and deserve a grateful nod from me. First, big thanks go to my editor and friend, Michele Slung, who never shies from herding cats. Everyone at Llewellyn Worldwide/Midnight Ink, especially my editors there, Terri Bischoff and Nicole Nugent, deserve loads of credit, as does my agent, Kimberley Cameron.

For this book, a good deal of on-site research was needed. Thankfully, J. W. and Barbara Grand introduced me to Marcel and Susie Duchamp, who graciously loaned me their fish camp in southern Louisiana and took me out into the Gulf to the offshore oil rigs. Ione L. Taylor, PhD, Associate Director, U.S. Geological Survey — besides answering endless questions about reservoirs — was an inspiration from the beginning. Stan Lewis, retired Senior geological advisor at Anadarko; and Richard

Ingram, retired engineer from Schlumberger, were also fonts of information as well as early readers. Randy Adams, owner and president of Sea Support in Cut Off, Louisiana, also merits a nod for educating me in the role of support boats.

For all issues of a criminal nature, I went to my friend Mardy Benson, retired captain, Johnston County Sheriff's office. For taking time to share his knowledge in oil-well investments, Charlie Rushton of Hardrock Oil has my gratitude too. My husband, Allen, gets the red badge of courage for patiently answering my questions about boats, cars, trucks, and anything else with an engine. Thanks also to Bob Murray for his patience and attention to detail in preparing a map that reflects the story. And lastly, to early readers Boo Carver, Helen Ellerbe, and Bet Barbour: thanks for your encouragement.

ABOUT THE AUTHOR

Lee Mims holds bachelor's and master's degrees in Geology from the University of North Carolina–Chapel Hill, and she once worked as a field geologist. Lee is a member of Mystery Writers of America and Sisters in Crime. *Trusting Viktor* is her second novel. Currently a popular wildlife artist, Lee lives in Clayton, North Carolina. Visit her online at LeeMims.com.

The employees of Thorndike Press hope you have enjoyed this Large Print book. All our Thorndike, Wheeler, and Kennebec Large Print titles are designed for easy reading, and all our books are made to last. Other Thorndike Press Large Print books are available at your library, through selected bookstores, or directly from us.

For information about titles, please call:
(800) 223-1244

or visit our Web site at:
http://gale.cengage.com/thorndike

To share your comments, please write:
Publisher
Thorndike Press
10 Water St., Suite 310
Waterville, ME 04901